A Part of Me
Karin Aharon

To my mother, Cathy, who gave me life, twice.
To Gabi, who changed both our lives.
I love and miss you.

Producer & International Distributor
eBookPro Publishing
www.ebook-pro.com

A Part of Me
Karin Aharon

Contact: karinaharon8@gmail.com

ISBN: 9781086098457

A Part of Me

KARIN AHARON

My mom had cancer, but she passed away from what you have." That was the last thing the technician said to me before leaving the room. The examination started and the device began spinning quickly. I was surprised that only five minutes after getting my lab results, they had already taken me to get a CT scan. Now I know why. I was in real danger.

I took deep, long breaths and tried to relax. I felt heat spread from my belly towards my feet and realized it was probably the ink they injected. At least I hoped that's what it was. I looked up at the exam room's boring ceiling. I was disappointed they didn't have a TV with some soothing, pastoral view. I needed something to soothe me. The room was painted in a bright color, that might have been white, and was empty except for a medical cart. The examination ended somewhat quickly and the technician came in and helped me get dressed. I was so cold that I was willing to endure the pain of getting dressed just so I could keep warm.

The technician held the door open and before I left, she asked me: "if you knew this was going to happen, would you have done it all over again?"

"Of course," I smiled as I walked into the emergency room. When Michael saw me approaching, he gave up his seat for me. I was surprised that even at 3 A.M. this terrible place was so busy and noisy that we could hardly find any free seats.

I could see the doctor approaching with my medical file. But I knew, regardless of what he might say, I had already saved myself.

CHAPTER 1

All I wanted was to see my mother. I cared about nothing else. Not home. Not work. Nothing. Only for my mom to land and come over. I paced around my office impatiently. I felt like a little girl waiting to be picked up by her mom from an awful daycare.

She and Tommy arrived in the evening. I was nervous Adam might not remember her, but the minute she walked in he was happy to see her. She gave him a small, plushy koala and one of his favorite red Teletubbies. He jumped excitedly from one sofa to another and even hugged her voluntarily. After fifteen minutes, mom left for grandpa's home and Tommy stayed behind. It was understandable, seeing she had been on a two-day journey from Sydney. They came for a two-week visit and decided to split up – my little brother stayed at my place, and my parents at grandpa's. Jonathan, my second brother, who was in the army when my parents left for Australia, stayed at my place for a couple of months. He moved out of his room for Tom's sake and moved into our uncle Jonny's apartment, which had become the perfect bachelor pad. After having lived with him for a while, I couldn't even imagine what was going on there.

I was happy to have Tommy over because I had barely seen him this year. We saw each other a couple of months ago when we visited them in Sydney with Adam. Flying to Australia with a 16-month old baby was challenging as well as getting a month's leave off work. But the holidays made things easier, and I would have flown to the moon if it meant spending time with my mom. It was hard living so far away.

The time differences made it difficult for us to talk over the phone. Every day without speaking to her was hard for me. When she lived here, we would talk several times a day. Michael didn't understand what we could possibly have so much to talk about. He could talk to his parents once a week at Friday night dinners and that was more than enough for him. I never understood it.

**

The next day I left for work as usual, but couldn't wait for the evening to see my mom and spend some time with her. Right after she booked her flight ticket to Israel, she gave me a list of healthcare professionals she wanted to make appointments with - dental hygienist, dentist, and cosmetician. That day, she took Tommy with her while running her errands.

Her friend, Julie, scheduled an appointment for her with a gynecologist. I was annoyed the appointment was scheduled for the afternoon because that was the only time I could see her. But I hoped she would finish quickly and come back early enough for us to have dinner together. Mom finished her appointment at the dental hygienist and called me from the road, "how are you honey?" I could tell from her voice that she wasn't alone. "How are you feeling?" Ever since I told her I was pregnant, she started every conversation by asking about my medical condition.

"As usual. Who's with you? Tom?" before I shared anything, I had to find out who was listening.

"Yes. After my doctor's appointment, I'll drop him off at your place."

"Good. I want to spend some time with you. I didn't see you at all yesterday."

"Of course, sweetie, of course. I'll call you when I'm done."

It was too cold to take Adam to the park, so I had to play the Teletubbies CD for the umpteenth time. I hoped it would buy me some quiet time since the pregnancy made me more tired than usual.

"Mm… mm… mm…" Adam shouted and ran towards me.

I sat him in his highchair and he insisted on eating on his own. While I waited for him to finish smearing soup on his hair, I skimmed through the new case I had gotten today. As a young lawyer I didn't have much say so about the cases I got, but I had specifically asked for this one. When I heard we were representing ALUT (the Israeli Society for Children and Adults with Autism) I approached the senior partner, Nathan, and asked to take it. I was glad we had a case that had more to it than just the pursuit of money. I think Nathan was so surprised I took the initiative and asked to take the case that he simply gave me the statement of claim without saying a word.

The phone rang and it was mom.

"Hey mom, are you here?" I was happy thinking someone might give me a hand with Adam's shower. Michael was usually in the office at this time, so any help was more than welcome.

"No." I could hear from her short answer that something was wrong.

"What happened?" Adam squirmed in his chair and tried climbing out. The papers I brought home from the office were stained with soup.

"The doctor sent me for an urgent test at a special clinic. She saw something weird with the shape of my ovary and said that I have liquid in the abdomen. Tommy is coming with me. We'll talk later." I took Adam out of the chair and he began running around the small kitchen table.

"Ok, keep me posted. We'll talk later." I didn't know what to do with that information. I stood there for a few seconds with the phone in my hand, and my thoughts wandered off to bad places. What could it be? Why was it so urgent to send her for a test at 7 P.M.? It has to be something terrible. But maybe it's just because she's going back to Sydney soon and they need to quickly figure things out? Maybe that was why the doctor was so anxious.

Adam started climbing the table and put a stop to my hysterical thoughts. After the usual struggle, he got into the bathtub. I looked at him playing with his colorful rubber duckies. He threw them back and out again, and laughed every time the water splashed at him, and me, of course. But I couldn't bring myself to smile. Michael always tells me that I immediately think negative thoughts, of the worst kind. But I don't think that's true. Something was really wrong, and this time it wasn't just me exaggerating, otherwise, why would the doctor send her urgently. I didn't know the reason, but I had a strong urge to justify my anxiety.

I checked the phone again. When I saw there wasn't any news, I sent her a text. "Any news?" She replied "still waiting."

By the end of Adam's bath, I was soaking wet. But surprisingly, he cooperated and was ready for bed within minutes, wearing his cute pajamas, the one with the small cartoon cars. We were sitting in the living room, and he was about to finish his evening bottle when the phone rang again.

"What's up, mom?" I tried sounding relaxed but couldn't help myself.

"They said the same thing," she was almost whispering.

"Ok, so now you should call Dr. Gidron and find out what's the next step. But call him now, mom."

"I'll be at your place in fifteen minutes, but I'm dropping Tommy off and going back to grandpa's. I'm too tired to come up."

"Ok." That hysterical doctor cost me a day with my mom. There are only ten days left before she goes back to Sydney.

***

Dr. Gidron was our family gynecologist. I trusted him, though I didn't have much of a choice in the small town I grew up in. We were one of the first 120 families who moved to Maccabim, which was then considered at the edge of the world. One day, after living in a tall apartment building in a bustling city, I found myself in the middle of nowhere. The only thing I could see from my window was the neighbors sitting in their living room by candlelight because there was no electricity. Later, they built a grocery store, a medical center and a swimming pool. That was basically it, that's all we had in the beginning. Dr. Gidron was the only gynecologist in Maccabim, and we kept going to him after we moved by force of habit.

I was pacing back and forth in the living room as Adam was lying on the sofa with his milk bottle, looking like a drunkard. I felt the blood coursing through my body, and then took two slow breaths. Even though I was hoping that it would all turn out to be a mistake, I could tell something was wrong. Something was really wrong. I decided to do some research once Adam went to bed.

When Tommy came, I was busy putting Adam to sleep (good night, teddy, good night, dolly). I meant to question him about what exactly they told mom, but when I stepped into the guest room, I saw that he had fallen asleep. I looked at him sleeping, and for a moment, he looked like the sweet boy from way back when. Tommy was a rather easygoing baby, unlike Adam. He was a bit bossy, so we would call him Napoleon. But other than that, he was really good. It was nice that some of that childlike sweetness was still there even when he started looking (and smelling) like a teenager.

"Tom, what happened with mom?" I moved him gently.

"I don't know." He turned to other side.

"Did you hear what the doctor told her?" I sat next to him but he kept his back to me.

"No."

"Did you hear anything?"

"No. We left the doctor's and mom didn't say anything. She just started crying in the middle of the street and then she called dad. That's it."

"Ok, go to sleep. Good night." I left the room and turned off the light.

I turned to my research. I went into the bedroom and turned my computer on. I typed into Dr. Google everything mom had told me, and then I saw it. Ovarian cancer. All the symptoms mom told me about were there – abdominal liquid and swelling, ovary mutation. When we visited her in Sydney, she told me that she gained weight and felt bloated. We blamed it on the fatty Australian food and didn't think even for a second about anything else.

I laid in the dark and tried organizing my thoughts. It couldn't be cancer. No one in our close circle had cancer. It doesn't make sense. It happens in other families, but not ours. Tomorrow things will clear out. All my mother's friends, who passed away from cancer, came to mind. Bold, bloated and sad. I remembered their children and my mother's stories of their suffering and the pain in my mother's eyes as she spoke about them. But now it was she who was on the line and it was inconceivable. Something so terrible can't happen to my mother. It's just unfair. It has to be something else. It seemed that because of the pregnancy's exhaustion, I was tired enough to fall asleep, despite the frightening thoughts running through my mind.

CHAPTER 2

I woke up early as usual and left while everyone was still asleep, Michael too. I didn't even hear him coming back home. On my way to the office, I tried thinking when would be a good time to call mom, and what would I even say. I didn't want to wake her up, but I had a feeling she wasn't sleeping.

I had my first meeting at 9A.M. with Nathan and Samuel. Samuel was one of those annoying clients who thought they deserved everything just because they were rich. That must also be the reason he allowed himself to grow such an impressive potbelly. We were always expected to be available when he walked into the office unannounced, and listen to his endless stories about his new yacht. All the partners fawned over him, waited for him to bring in more cases so that they could bill him hundreds of dollars per hour, VAT not included, of course.

I looked at Nathan's face so that I didn't fall asleep in front of them. It was amusing to see how he pretended to be fascinated by everything Samuel said. Nathan was more or less my age, but looked much older than me. His bald head didn't help either. He's a brilliant lawyer but was an avid workaholic, who was also convinced that everyone should work like he did. Children were important to him, as long as someone else raised them. That someone, preferably, shouldn't work in his office. Whenever I wanted to let Ida, Adam's nanny, leave early while there was still some daylight, he would blurt his cliché sentence, "taking the day off?"

I would usually smile and keep walking, but when I could, I would take a detour when leaving the office so that I wouldn't walk by his room, sparing myself from his regular jokes. When he found out I was pregnant again, he moved me to a smaller office so he could give the bigger one to a different lawyer. He didn't like the concept of pregnancies, let alone a second one.

When I started working here, I didn't think I would last long. Two months later and already I wanted to quit. The vibe wasn't good for me. Obviously, I woke up every morning as usual, but couldn't wait to get pregnant again, so that I could have a maternity leave to look forward to.

The phone vibrated in my hand. Mom. I excused myself and left the room. Nathan was so concentrated in Samuel's fascinating stories about his travel itinerary, that he didn't even respond when I left.

"Hey Mom, what did Dr. Gidron say?" I stood as far as I could from Nathan's room but kept eye contact in case I was needed.

"He brought an expert and they both examined me. I'll be hospitalized tomorrow at Tel Hashomer hospital."

"But why? What did they see?"

"They don't know exactly. Something is wrong and they need more tests to make a diagnosis." It seemed she was crying and I was really holding myself not to cry with her.

"We have our first prenatal screening tomorrow in Haifa, and then we'll come to the hospital." I took advantage of my day off to be with her, even if it was at the hospital.

"Thanks sweetie, we'll talk."

Our meeting with Samuel ended without any new insights. He got the attention he wanted and gave us a small case to take care of; someone who didn't pay the rent. He would probably pay us more in retainer than what we'll get for him, if at all.

I went back to my small office and called to see if Tommy woke up.

He didn't answer. I decided it was time to talk with Jonathan and see if he knew what was going on, but he didn't answer either.

"Shirley," I heard Nathan call me, "step into my office please so we can work on the ALUT case. We have to make some progress." He sounded nice and he used the word "please." Someone must be in the room with him.

I gathered the papers I brought from home and hoped I had read enough to know what the lawsuit was about. "This is our best lawyer; she'll be taking care of your case." Nathan stood at the entrance and introduced me even before I could see who was there. On the chair sat a young man with a knitted kippah and a warm smile. He introduced himself as Joel from ALUT. I was wondering whether I should shake his hand, but he stayed in his seat so I sat down too and smiled politely. If Nathan would have bothered telling me the meeting was today, I would have at least tried to finish reading the papers.

"Come share your thoughts with us about the neighbour's claim." Nathan sat back behind his desk and leaned backwards, his hands folded behind his bald head.

"From what I read, I think there's a good chance the lawsuit will be rejected," I said, and chose to ignore Nathan's dissatisfied expression. "I would be happy to visit the hostel and see what's going on there. I find it hard to believe that it bothers the neighbours so much that it should be shut down."

"You're more than welcome to visit. My family and I live there, so I'm there all the time," Joel smiled and it seemed like he really meant what he said. I've encountered so many hypocrites in my profession that I didn't know who I could believe anymore. "What do you need from me to move forward?"

"I'll send you an email with a list of the information I need for the case and we'll stay in touch."

Joel gave me his business card. I planned on creeping back quietly into my office, but Nathan couldn't help himself and said to Joel, "You'll have the list tomorrow, by the end of the day tomorrow."

"I'm not working tomorrow, remember?" I tried to keep smiling.

"No, what's tomorrow?" Nathan asked sheepishly, as if I hadn't reminded him a million times and wrote it down in the office schedule.

"I have tests, and I already let you know I was taking the day off." I didn't understand why I had to explain myself in front of the client.

"No problem, she'll send you the list later on today." Nathan stood up, signaling the meeting was over. Or rather that his patience ran out, and that this was a pro bono client so he didn't want to waste more time than necessary.

I smiled and quickly left the room, before I was assigned anymore urgent tasks for today. On the way to my office I got a text from mom: "Dad is taking Tommy to his friends in Maccabim." At least I don't need to take care of a teenager for the next few days. It was strange that she used the word "dad." She usually called him "Gabi" when she spoke to me because he wasn't 'officially' my dad.

I had known Gabi since I was four, and although he was my dad in every aspect, I still called him "Gabi." Once, I even apologized to him that his own kids called him Gabi and not dad. But since I left home, his name changed to "dad."

I tried to read the lawsuit in my small office. It was so boring that I had to reread every sentence just to understand it. The neighbors' main claim against the hostel was the noise. The autists were screaming and it bothered them. They actually used the terrible word 'shrieking.' That's how our society is. NIMBY was written all over the claim - Not in My Back Yard. Everyone is pro integrate people with special needs, until it comes to their neighbours. I wrote an email with a list of questions for Joel and asked our intern to look for any precedents.

I ate my takeout lunch in front of my computer, as usual, and at 3 P.M. I decided to send the email since I really had to leave. I CCed

Nathan of course, so that he knew it was done and wouldn't call me. Or at least I hoped he wouldn't.

On my way out, he tried to talk to me, but I took advantage of the elevator arriving and said: "I really have to go. I'll see you on Sunday." I hoped he would get the message. One of the things I hated most about working with him was him calling me when I was on my way home. I'm home, let me be. But no. He had to call me and share his every thought on every case we had. He would also dictate documents and give me assignments. Impulse control wasn't one of his strengths.

The elevator door closed in his face and I felt as if I had just escaped from some max-security facility. The pressure of that terrible place followed me everywhere, even when I wasn't there. I would sometimes wake up in the middle of the night, anxious about things I forgot to do.

I came back home and immediately changed into comfortable clothes. When Adam fell asleep, Michael was still at his law firm and I couldn't wait for him any longer. Although I had planned to talk to mom, I fell asleep five minutes after Adam did.

CHAPTER 3

In the morning we waited for Ida and then left early for Haifa. I saw that Jonathan had called me after I had fallen asleep, but there was no point in trying to call him back in the morning. It was also the first time since mom had arrived that I had time to talk with Michael about everything that was going on.

"Anyways, I think they suspect she has ovarian cancer, but in the meantime, no one is really saying it," I summarized in a sentence.

"OK."

"What's OK?" I raised my voice without meaning to. "It's not OK at all. It's a deadly type of cancer, Michael. The deadliest of all types of women cancers. It's something that almost no one recovers from, especially at this stage. Do you know what that means?" Although I still had some hope, deep down I found it hard to believe it was something else. Dr. Google was right from time to time.

"I realize that it's problematic, but what do you want me to say? Wait for a diagnosis before you start killing off people."

"I'm not killing off anyone, but it's scary." The rain grew stronger and we could barely hear one another, so I kept silent. Michael had no chance of calming me down.

Last time we went to this doctor was when I was pregnant with Adam. We went especially to him after they found a problem in the first scan we received from an expert in Tel Aviv. Everyone recommended we get a second opinion from the legendary Dr.

Cooperman in Haifa. We gave into our family's pressure and drove there. Of all the doctors who had examined me throughout my pregnancy with Adam, and there were quite a few, his results were closest to the truth. Which is why I trusted only him.

For this pregnancy, I scheduled an appointment with him the moment I found out I was pregnant. It was exactly a week after we came back from Australia. But this time, on our way to Haifa, I was more concerned about what was going on with mom in Tel HaShomer.

I called mom and she didn't pick up. The further we drove north, the stronger it rained. The ride was noisy and exhausting. I couldn't believe the weather was so nice in Tel Aviv but so wintery in Haifa. When we arrived at the clinic, I tried calling mom again, but she didn't answer. I tried calling Gabi.

"Hey Shirley," I heard muffled P.A. sounds.

"Anything new? Did they say anything?" I was next and didn't have time to waste on small talk.

"We're still waiting for the doctor to go over the results. How about you?"

"We're next. I'm coming from Haifa straight to Tel HaShomer. What ward are you in?"

"Gynecologic Oncology. It's at the end of the gynecology ward. But call us before you come, because we keep going in and out of tests."

"Ok. Tell mom I said hi."

Conversations with Gabi were always short. He wasn't a great talker. That is, he liked lecturing about things he cared about, but phone calls weren't his thing. He would quickly lose patience. Gabi was the ideal partner for practical conversations.

It was our turn and we stepped into the familiar room. Dr. Cooperman didn't remember us of course, but was nice and pleasant throughout the test.

"To sum it up, the test is completely fine and you have a girl. You can get dressed." At first, I couldn't believe everything was really OK. I was so excited that I couldn't keep myself from crying. I immediately thought about the moment I would tell mom it's a girl, and became even more excited. We got the CD and papers and left the room in a bit of a shock. The last pregnancy test took about an hour and always ended with a recommendation for further tests. This time, it was fifteen minutes later, and we were out.

Michael got off on the way and took a taxi to work while I headed to the hospital. When I entered the gynecology ward and saw the sign "Gynecologic Oncology", I shivered. I couldn't believe I was here. I couldn't believe my mother was here. I walked in silence on the brown-purple tiles, which seemed to have been there ever since the hospital was built. I passed a few pregnant women who were waiting in line to see a doctor. Other women, who until yesterday were probably still pregnant, walked slowly down the halls with their partners, who held bags with baby stuff, and seemed extremely tired as if they have had the baby themselves. They were pregnant like I was, but it wasn't the same. They were there for a happy occasion. It was astonishing how different mom's circumstances were compared to all the other things happening in this building.

I walked through a large double door, and when I entered, I was surprised to see that the ward had only a few rooms and a nurse's station at its center. A beautiful slender woman stood by the station. A white handkerchief covered her bald head and her left hand held onto the metal pole where her I.V. hung. She seemed thin and weak, but spoke with the nurses and laughed. I couldn't imagine there was anything funny about this place.

It seems the rooms hadn't been renovated because they looked just as they did when I came to visit mom after she had Jonathan. The same old beds covered with instruction stickers. The same broken night-stands with sticky drawers that could barely open. There was a strong hospital smell, and a weird silence. The phone at the nurse's station wouldn't stop ringing. Three nurses walked in and out of the rooms with carts full of medicine. I noticed there was a laptop on the cart. At least something was new here. The blue stripe on the white curtains seemed worn-out and sad. Every room had three beds, and in one of them I saw mom laying in the middle bed, which was usually given to the patient who arrived last.

I hugged her and was so excited that I nearly fell on top of her.

"Careful, my tummy really hurts," she said quietly, not wanting to disturb her neighbours.

"Oops, sorry." I stood up and hugged Gabi too. I hadn't really seen him since they came to visit. I was so preoccupied with mom's issues, and he was probably busy with his errands. He hadn't changed in the last few months since we last visited them, yet, something was different. He was standing even though there was a chair right next to him, and he swayed nervously from side to side. Gabi had always been my rock when I was in trouble. But at this very moment, at the hospital, he seemed fragile and lost.

When I joined the army, he laughed when he heard I listed his name as an emergency contact. "Didn't I get rid of you, already?"

"Mom would just panic, so it's better they call you. Anyways, you'll never get rid of me. You're doomed."

"It's a shame I didn't know that when I met your mother. I would have reconsidered," he smiled, pleased. When Gabi annoyed me, I would joke and tell him that we had already replaced one husband and if he gave us any trouble, we'd replace him too. Mom frowned but he would smile. We had our inside jokes. We could say things to each other without being offended. Apart from Michael, there was no one else I could talk to about anything. His very presence calmed me down.

The patient next to the window sighed in her sleep. She was very pale and looked so different from mom, that it seemed like mom was in the wrong place.

"What did the doctor say?" mom asked and tried sitting up. I could tell by the look on her face that she was in pain. Her brown straight hair was combed and pulled back. She looked beautiful even when wearing the ugly hospital robe.

"I have a healthy daughter," I said quietly, and the smile that spread on my face didn't quite suit the atmosphere.

"That's great, sweetie. Did he check the heart and everything else?"

"Yes, mom. Don't worry, she's completely healthy."

When I was pregnant with Adam, mom came with me to see Dr. Cooperman. She knew Haifa from her days at the Technion and offered to drive Michael and I to the test. I was happy she was there because I was afraid I wouldn't be able to comprehend everything he said. I wanted her with me in case there was any more bad news. We came because of a kidney issue, so he checked that first. He confirmed that the kidney was not in its usual location, but it was functioning. It was a great relief. He continued the scan and when he reached the heart, he fell silent. I looked at mom and Michael and realized something was wrong. For the next 20 minutes, he examined me in complete silence. When he finished, he simply said: "Come, get dressed and we'll talk".

Dr. Cooperman explained his findings and referred us to a pediatric cardiologist to make sure we could continue the pregnancy. I spent the next few weeks going through different tests to make sure that the pregnancy wouldn't be terminated. It was the first time I was facing such a medical problem and it was a terrible, stressful period. I was anxious throughout the entire pregnancy. This pregnancy was a healing experience. It was normal and simple. But my anxiety was back, only this time it was directed elsewhere.

"I have to go to the bathroom. Gabi, come help me." Mom tried lifting herself up using the bed handle, but couldn't. Gabi helped her get up and took her to the bathroom.

I smiled at mom, but when the door closed behind her, I whispered to Gabi, "What's going on? Two days ago she was walking and driving. What happened?"

"Things took a turn for the worse. She can't move because of the pain and abdominal liquids." I could see in his eyes that he didn't know what to do with everything that was going on. "She'll probably stay here for a couple of days, so I'm going to get her some things from grandpa's house. Are you staying here?"

"Of course."

"They'll soon come to give her another test, so keep me updated."

"Sure, I'm with her. Don't worry."

"Ok." Gabi let mom know he was going, and then placed his hand on my shoulder and gave me a look that I couldn't figure out. Maybe he was trying to cheer me up. Maybe he was trying to cheer himself up.

It took mom several minutes to get out of the bathroom and I escorted her back to the bed.

"With everything going on, I forgot to tell you – Adam really loved the presents you got him. He's even sleeping with the Koala bear." I sat as close to her as possible.

"That's great," she held my hand firmly and smiled, "and are you feeling well?"

When she smiled, she looked as always; beautiful and noble. She always looked younger than her age, and would boast about not needing to dye her hair. I hoped I at least got that from her, as I didn't get her height or beauty.

"Yes, everything is really great."

"That's good." Mom laid back and sighed with pain.

Just when I was wondering if I should go ask for some medication to ease her pain, a doctor came in. He looked somewhat young, but I assumed he was a senior doctor because there were several doctors running after him, as though they were in "doctors' summer camp."

"This is Catherine and we need to take a sample of her abdominal liquids and send it in for a biopsy," the doctor stood by my mother's bed and spoke to the doctors who wrote every word in their tiny notebooks. On a second thought, he didn't look like a typical doctor. He was short, his eyes smiled and he spoke quietly.

"You can call me Cathy," mom said as she tried sitting up again but it seemed like an impossible task. "And this is my daughter Shirley, she has a girl in her belly." I had a feeling she would tell that to anyone who came into the room from now on. Mom smiled and pulled her hair behind her ears, as if that's what mattered most.

"Nice to meet you, I'm Dr. Carmi. Congratulations." He shook my hand gently. There was something very humble about his behavior. He asked for mom's permission and then gently checked her belly. He didn't act like he owned the place.

The entourage moved on to the next bed in the room and I returned to my post next to mom. Although Dr. Carmi spoke quietly, we could hear him explaining to the pale patient about the chemotherapy she was about to receive. I kept talking to mom about Adam and anything I could think of that would distract her from what was going on and the place we were in. I tried making her feel like we were meeting at a coffee house. We were only missing an apple strudel.

One of the doctors who followed Dr. Carmi, came back into the room. When he was setting his things on the table by the bed, I saw a large and frightening syringe that reminded me of the amniocentesis and it made me sick. I smiled an encouraging smile at mom so that she wouldn't feel my anxiety. "You can stand next to her, but on the other side," he said as he shut the drapes. He didn't even introduce himself.

I moved to the other side and held mom's hand. Every time he touched her belly she was in pain, which made me hold her hand even tighter as if I was in pain. The doctor sterilized the area and stabbed mom. The needle went out and then in again, this time in a different place. Then again and again. A tear poured down mom's face. She didn't say a word. I felt I was shrinking. I held my breath in from the stress and forced myself to breathe out. I nodded at my mom, who looked at me in such a terrified look that I don't think I will ever forget.

"I can't get the liquid out. I'll call an expert to do the test," the young doctor gathered his equipment, moved the curtain aside and left the room. I stroked mom's face and wiped the tears away.

Gabi came in quickly just a few seconds after the discouraged doctor left. He approached mom and just by looking at her, understood what had happened. He leaned over and hugged her. Mom started crying. I was sure he would stand back up, but he stayed hunched above her. And then something happened that I had never seen before – Gabi cried with her. I was shocked and scared and felt I needed a break to get my thoughts straight. I shut the drapes around them and left the room to give them some privacy.

I decided this was a good time to go to the bathroom. A scrawny nurse saw I was going into the bathroom next to mom's room and stopped me. "It's better that you don't use the bathroom here. The women are going through chemotherapy and it's not good for your pregnancy. You should go to the gynecology ward. Also, at home, you shouldn't use the same bathroom as she does."

I didn't really understand what she wanted, but I nodded and left the ward. The nurse must have confused my mom with the patient laying next to her, but I was too tired to argue. My bladder signaled that I had to hurry up.

I passed by a baby store and looked through the big window. I saw a lot of pink dresses on the hangers and tried imagining what would it feel like buying all these pink clothes. Last time, before I gave birth, I went shopping with mom and we bought clothes for Adam in all shades of blue.

When I left the bathroom, I called Jonathan to let him know what was going on.

"You won't believe it, but dad just cried." I had to share this absurd event with him.

"Are you serious?" I could hear the fuss of the mass hall he was at.

"Yes. I can't remember ever seeing him cry. Even when grandma Leah passed away, he didn't cry like that. It means things are really bad." I tried justifying my hysteria. "When are you returning home?"

"Tomorrow morning. I'll be home until Sunday."

"OK, so let's try to meet, all three of us. Tommy is in Maccabim with his friend, but he'll probably come back tomorrow. We all need to meet."

"OK, I have to go. Keep me posted."

"Of course."

I went back to the room and moved the curtain that was still hiding mom's bed. "Gabi went to grab something to eat," she He really does seem nice."

"Yes. He was here and told me that an amniotic fluid specialist will come to do the test."

"Wonderful. We probably need someone with experience."

"You know," she said quietly, "Rose, the woman in the bed next to the bathroom, they just took her to a CT scan to check whether the cancer spread. She also had a swollen belly when she was diagnosed," she placed her hand on her belly and squinted with pain. "She had a tumor in her ovary."

"But you don't have a tumor, right? So, that's a good sign," I tried to encourage her hesitantly.

"The one next to the window didn't have one either, and they still found ovarian cancer. I guess it's different for everyone."

"Well, they still haven't told you anything, so it might be something else."

"Perhaps," mom said, and didn't look as optimistic as usual. I could always tell what she was thinking. For better or worse, she always wore her heart on her sleeve. She couldn't hide anything. I found something that I did get from her.

When Gabi came back, I kissed them both goodbye and left. Only when I got into the car and was alone for the first time that day, I allowed myself to cry. I couldn't believe it was happening to me. To my mom. Nothing made sense, like in a bad dream. I thought about Tom, who at the age of fifteen had to face such issues. I hoped that my mom would call and tell me it was all one big mistake and everything was actually alright. "Never mind," I would tell her, "as long as you're healthy." And she would tell me that it's such a shame they had wasted her vacation in Israel. But mom didn't call. I cried all the way home.

CHAPTER 4

On Friday afternoon, we met for a family dinner. Or at least the closest thing to a dinner that I could arrange. Michael didn't have time to cook and things were bad enough without having to subject Jonathan and Tommy to my cooking. I decided to order some Italian food for everyone, and we met mom at the hospital. The ward was almost empty. This was not where people wanted to have their Friday dinner.

Jonathan and Tommy came, and we sat with mom to catch up. Jonathan told us about his military course and Tommy brought us up to date about news from Maccabim. Mom sat in her bed and smiled. It's been several months since we were all together with mom on the same continent. She even wore lipstick for the occasion. Unlike me, she would always try to wear makeup and look her best. I, on Fridays, would walk around in my high school sweatpants that still fitted me despite the pregnancy.

Mom wasn't well enough to get out of bed and we weren't comfortable with having a feast in her room. So, I left her pasta and took the boys outside to eat. We sat on a bench in the dark hall in front of the ward.

"Just like old times, having dinner on Fridays at mom's," I said and handed them cutlery.

"Totally. It's a shame dad isn't here." Tommy said.

"True. But he needs some time off from this depressing place. You realize hard times are coming, right?"

They didn't answer and kept eating. It was mind-boggling how much food teenage boys could consume.

"Mom will probably need some treatments and perhaps also a surgery. She has blood clots in her legs, which means she can't fly. In any case, we're going to have a lot on our plate." Tommy and Jonathan nodded and kept eating. I couldn't comprehend if they were repressing the truth or just didn't have anything to say.

The building was quiet and somewhat abandoned. Every now and then people crossed through the hallway and looked at us. It was probably getting dark outside, but it's easy losing track of time in hospitals. Hospital time seems to stand still.

We finished eating and cleaned up. We went back to mom's room and saw that she had gotten her hospital meal, however she didn't take a bite, nor from the food I brought her. Tommy and Jonathan left to go out with their friends while I stayed with mom a little longer.

"You didn't eat anything. Do you want me to bring you something else?"

"No, sweetie. Gabi will come soon with some food from Ruth and Eric." Ruth, who was married to Gabi's brother, was a great cook, her food was worth waiting for. "Maybe you should go home and rest?"

"Soon. I'll stay until Gabi comes. When do you think they'll discharge you from here?" I had to go to the bathroom and was too tired to walk all the way to the other ward, so I decided to hold it in for a while.

"Perhaps on Sunday. We'll get the test results, and then see," her smile disappeared. "I'm fed up with being here. I came for a vacation and winded up in the hospital."

"Yes, it really is annoying. But it'll work out; you'll see it'll all be fine." I held her hand and tried cheering her up. Perhaps, myself, too.

"That one," mom whispered and pointed at the bed by the window, "she was told she has ovarian cancer that metastasized to her stomach."

"Don't freak yourself out. Everyone is different," I whispered back. We sat quietly and mom caressed my belly and smiled.

"Cathy," we heard a familiar Hungarian accent. "There you are. I could barely find this ward. What kind of dump did they put you in?" Julie walked in and hugged mom gently, then me. "You have a wonderful belly. You look great." Under her purple hair, I could see a faint shade of her natural blond.

"Thanks, I'm seventeen weeks pregnant. Soon I will be much bigger." I stood up so Julie could sit next to mom. "Ok, mom, now that Julie's here, I'll head home. Maybe I'll see Adam before he goes to bed."

"OK, sweetie. Go rest a bit. Say hi to Michael and Adam." Mom held my hand and I leaned over and kissed her. "Good night, my sweet. Drive safely," she told me. "Don't take your eyes off the road."

I hadn't left the room and they were already talking in Hungarian. They could gossip as much as they wanted and no one understood. They've been friends forever, as close as sisters. Julie was like an aunt to us.

I looked at them and was happy to see mom almost back to her usual self; lively and smiling. I reminded myself on the way home that there was still a chance she wasn't sick. Until they prove it was cancer, it might be something else. But I knew I was lying to myself.

At the parking lot, before I got out of the car, I looked at myself in the mirror. I could see my eyes, red and puffy from crying. I didn't want Adam to see me like this, even though he was too young to understand.

When I walked in, Michael was waiting quietly outside Adam's room. We stood together in the dark hallway, hugged each other and heard Adam mumbling words we partially understood. My tears smeared all over Michael's shirt and left small stains scattered all over his chest. He knew better than to talk. There was nothing to say. I heard my phone buzzing, so I went to the living room and left Michael standing at his post.

"I'm staying at a friend's," Tommy wrote. I was happy that I wouldn't have to cook tomorrow the endless amount of food he consumes. Perhaps we would have enough food from what Ida cooked for Adam. A small comfort in a sea of worries that could drown me at any given moment.

CHAPTER 5

It took another week for the doctors to officially announce that mom had ovarian cancer. My worst nightmare came true, despite all my fantasies about some doctor's mistake. Chemotherapy started a few days later, and after the first round she was discharged and went home, actually to Grandpa's place.

Mom's vacation in Israel was about to end and decisions had to be made.

"I'm not flying back to Australia and Tommy is staying here, with me," mom told me over the phone. I was really happy to hear that, because her moving to the land down under was hard for me. "It's too dangerous for me to fly because of the blood clots. I'll stay here and Gabi will go back to Australia to work, at least until we see what's going on. I told Gabi I want to be with you."

I always missed her when she was far away from me. Once, when I was 10, I mustered the courage to leave for scouts' camp. I was fine during the day, but when night fell, I started missing her. I told the instructor that I wasn't feeling well and asked could I call home. Mom was awake, as if she had been waiting for my call. When she answered, I tried my best not to cry. I asked them to come and pick me up. Gabi was already on the way. He didn't complain during the drive, but he kept reminding me years later about the time he had saved me from camp. The truth was that in many ways he had saved me many times, not just then.

I tried not to be too happy about her returning to Israel, because things were far from being ideal, so I remained practical. "Where will you stay?" For all I cared she could stay with me for as long as needed, but I had a feeling she didn't want to.

"I don't know. We need to look for an apartment."

"Good, so come live near me."

"We'll see. In the meantime, I'll move in with Julie. She has a spare room for me. Can Tommy stay with you for now?"

"Yes, as long as you need," I said and knew Michael would agree too. After having Jonathan for six months, Michael was already used to it, even though this time was different. Jonathan would come only on weekends and could take care of himself. This time we would get a teenager who actually needed to be taken care of.

I was already imagining mom moving next to me and we meeting all the time, when mom started crying.

"It's going to be OK, mom. Really, you'll get better." She didn't respond. "I read there's a 25% recovery rate from this cancer."

"Why would you say that to me?! I can't hear these things!" She was really yelling and then hung up. I was shocked. I was only trying to cheer her up. I didn't understand why it offended her so much. It was the last thing I wanted to do. I felt so guilty for making her cry. I felt I should call her back but didn't know what to say.

I laid on the sofa. Adam kept building exceptionally symmetrical buildings with his blocks, as if nothing was happening in the world. At least he was sitting still and letting me rest. My eyes shut on their own will. I didn't really know how to cope with mom's anger. It wasn't something I was familiar with in our relationship, and I hoped that by tomorrow she would calm down.

I was always close to my mom, and ever since I became a mom myself, we became even closer. You could say I was usually nice to her, except for when I was a teenager.

The first time I had really annoyed her was during summer vacation. I was sixteen and all I wanted was to go to the music festival with my friends. Tommy was going through surgery, and mom and Gabi were with him 24/7. I disappeared and was completely preoccupied with myself, like a typical teenager. When I came back, mom gave me a look I had never seen before. It wasn't anger. It was real disappointment. That moment, I promised myself I wouldn't do anything that would make her give me that look again.

Ever since I could remember, my mom was the most important person to me. There were times when it was just the two of us against the world. When I was sick and there was no one to stay home with me, she would take me to the architecture firm she worked at and I would help her color the blueprints. Even when I accidently painted the cement wall in the color meant for demolition, she wasn't mad at me. I wonder if there really is a building in Tel Aviv that's missing a wall.

Although it took them a few years to get married, I accepted Gabi from the start. He was always there for me as a reliable and dependable figure. Mom always seemed fragile and gentle compared to him. In a sense, I felt we were taking care of her together.

I dragged myself from the sofa. Exhaustion from the pregnancy was killing me. That, plus worrying about mom, prevented me from working even when I was at the office. Adam was still busy, so I opened the ALUT drat folder I brought home with me from work. I hoped this case would take my mind off all of my family's mess.

From what I had learned from Joel, the hostel had replaced its windows' isolation to reduce the noise. We addressed a specialist who wrote a detailed recommendation about the severe repercussions these changes have on children. It was strange referring to them as children, seeing as they were in their twenties and thirties. But they would always be referred to as children, the specialist had explained.

We were supposed to meet Joel the next day, and I had to finish reading this document. I couldn't stand anymore of Nathan's complaints about the time I was putting in the office, or rather not putting in the office. After Adam fell asleep, I went over the document again and again until I felt confident I understood everything the specialist had written.

"I wonder what they'll do with their apartment in Sydney," I contemplated out loud while lying in bed and reading the claim once again. Michael gave me a look that meant something between "I don't know" to "that's not as interesting."

Michael came to bed and a minute later I could already hear his snores growing louder. I tried to finish writing all the questions I had for Joel but I guess at some point I fell asleep.

In the middle of the night I woke up and found all the papers scattered on the bed and that the pen had stained the sheets with blue ink. Luckily it was next to the pillow. I thought it could hide it. I turned off the light and went back to sleep.

CHAPTER 6

On Friday evening, as usual, we went to dinner at Michael's family. I really didn't feel like seeing them, or anyone else for that matter, but I didn't have much of a choice. We sat around the table, with plenty of food I disliked, and Adam sat next to us in his stroller with his bottle.

Everything went by as if nothing had happened. As if my mom wasn't sick with cancer and wasn't going through chemotherapy. It was absurd that the world kept revolving and didn't collapse into itself. I acted like a talentless actress playing at a less than mediocre theater; I came to the office, played the part of the lawyer I was expected to be, went through the day with great difficulty and then went back home. I didn't want to talk to anyone and was cooped up in my room with a cup of tea and cookies. Lots of cookies. It was weird seeing Michael's family so close together, while my family was scattered all over; Gabi was in Australia, mom at Julie's, Tommy at my place and Jonathan at Jonny's. Even though I tried not to, I couldn't help myself from comparing, which made me even angrier.

My sisters-in-law were unsuccessful at trying to make Adam laugh, and I just kept looking at the clock again and again. I wasn't sure if Michael had even told them. I certainly wasn't going to talk about it on Friday dinner.

I met Michael at law school when I was twenty years old, a fresh-out-of-the-army geeky soldier who just had to start school right away. Within a few months we had already moved in together and knew we were going to get married. What we didn't know back then, was how hard it would be having two lawyers in the same house. Truth be told, if he hadn't encouraged me to finish my BA, I would have probably dropped out during the first semester.

Although we had known each other for almost ten years, his mother still didn't like me. It wasn't that she said or did anything. She just wouldn't talk to me, except for when she wanted to confirm we've returned the food containers we took the week before. As far as she was concerned, Michael hadn't married well. Not only did I work all day, but I never cooked for her poor son, either. To her, having me for wife was indeed a failure.

I found some plain rice and took a piece of chicken. I saw Michael's dad smiling at me. At least someone noticed me. He did talk to me much (although at the beginning he would call me Sharon), and would mostly check I was eating. It was the most important thing for him.

"Dad, pass me the plate," Michael said when everyone stood up and started cleaning up the table.

It reminded me I still hadn't told my dad about mom being sick. I had to have this conversation one way or another, and it also seemed like a wonderful excuse for being locked up in a room rather than cleaning up the table. I whispered to Michael that I have to make a call, and excused myself from the table. Adam's look followed me to the hallway, and then I disappeared.

My dad and I were never close. Gabi was always the dad I had called when anything happened, good or bad. Gabi was the one who would come to Parents' Day and school activities. Even when I had to go to my dad for the weekend as part of his visitation rights, I had a hard time and just wanted to go back to mom's as soon as possible. I missed her, and being away from her was unbearable. The nice part about visiting him was spending time with my cousins, who I hardly saw.

However, with time I visited him less and less, and we became even more distant. During my pregnancy with Adam I saw him only a couple of times, and there were long periods of time when I didn't even know where he lived. It always bothered me and I always hoped it would change. Although Gabi successfully filled his shoes, there was a small part of me that hoped he would want to know me and be a part of my life. But it never really happened.

Despite it all, I knew that he had always loved mom and she was very important to him. And there was no way around it; I had to let him know what was going on. I went into the small room that used to be Michael's and closed the door. I dialed his number and just before I had given up, he answered.

"Hey, dad. Shabbat Shalom."

"Shabbat Shalom," he replied quietly. I could hear the TV newscasters in the background.

"I need to tell you something about mom." I paced in circles around the room and tried starting the conversation somehow.

"How is she?"

"Do you remember mom came over to visit? So, she wasn't feeling well. She was hospitalized to have some tests done and they found out she has cancer. Ovarian cancer." He fell silent. I waited a bit longer, but he kept quiet. "She's staying here for her treatment and also needs to go through surgery."

"She'll recover," he said, which was exactly what I was telling myself.

"I really hope so. She has to recover."

"I told her she should get checked. I kept telling her." The conversation made me sweat so, I stopped pacing around and stood next to the window. I needed some air.

"She was tested before they left for Australia. They didn't find it."

"She shouldn't have moved to Australia. The doctors aren't any good there." Talking to him was always challenging, because I had a feeling he wasn't really listening to me. This time I didn't have any patience for his nonsense. It was clear he was trying to blame it on her moving to Australia.

"Ok, it doesn't matter right now. She's staying here."

"What hospital is she in?"

"They discharged her. She's at Julie's place until she finds an apartment."

"If they discharged her, it's probably not that bad." I had to take a deep breath in order to continue the conversation.

"Dad, it's cancer. A brutal one. She goes back to the hospital for her chemotherapy but she doesn't need to be hospitalized. It doesn't mean that things are OK." His way of ignoring the facts was impressive, but at that moment, it didn't work for me. "I have to go because I'm at Michael's parents, having dinner. We'll talk next week. Bye dad."

I didn't wait for an answer and ended the conversation. I sat on the chair that Michael had probably sat on when studying for his SATs. I cried uncontrollably. Every time I told someone it became more and more real, also making it harder for me to repress. My mom had a deadly cancer and we were fighting for her life. I tried thinking of what would happen if we lost. Rachel, Michael's mom, who couldn't stand me, would be my children's only grandma. I would stay with my two fathers who could barely be in the same room together, and that wasn't going to change. Adam might not even remember her.

I gently caressed my tummy and tried promising myself and the baby girl inside, that she would get to know her grandma. There are six months until I'm due, and I wouldn't have it any other way. Grandma will be with us in the delivery room, I promised her, and the tears kept pouring down my eyes and on my belly.

I stayed in the room until Michael called me and told me we were going home. Since we had Adam we could leave earlier. Who said there weren't any advantages to having a kid with a short attention span?

CHAPTER 7

"How are you? Where's Tom?" Michael asked when he walked into the bedroom after having yet another long day.

"He went to a scouts' gathering and still hasn't come back. He's out at night again." I turned down the TV.

"Isn't it late?" Michael sat on the bed and took off his shoes.

I looked at the clock, it was quarter to eleven. "I asked him to come back home earlier, but that brat said he wasn't a baby and he could come back whenever he wanted."

Michael smiled.

"That's how teenage boys are. What did you expect? He's actually not so bad, doesn't give us much trouble. I was way worse. I kept fighting with my sisters."

"Whenever mom asks about him, I tell her everything is fine. But he keeps going out every night with his new friends and when he's home he sits in front of a screen. He barely talks to me, just asks for money for his private tutors and that's it."

"As least he has friends; it's not easy starting over again at a new place at his age."

"Yes, but what do we even know about them? He doesn't bring them home. It's impossible knowing who he's hanging out with."

"He's probably hanging out with the geeks from his high-school film major. What could they possibly do? Watch movies together?" Michael amused himself.

"I'll ask Jonathan to talk to him. Maybe he can get to him." They were both boys and they didn't have much of an age difference, so I hoped Jonathan would understand Tommy better.

I got into bed and tried finding a comfortable position to fall asleep in. Even though a few hours had passed, the house still smelled of the cauliflower latkes Ida had made for Adam. I have always hated cauliflower and the smell made me nauseous again. Like that time when my parents went abroad and I stayed with grandma and grandpa, Gabi's parents. I didn't need a babysitter, but Tommy and Jonathan were still young.

I was having a busy school week and had four terrible exams. And that was the easy part of that week. The day before mom and Gabi returned, I came back from school and the house reeked of cauliflower. I found grandma Leah in the kitchen over a pot that could feed an entire village. She smiled proudly and said she had made my favorite soup especially for me.

I don't remember how long it went on, but when I told her that I hated cauliflower, she was so mad at me she didn't speak to me until mom and Gabi came back.

I drove with grandpa to pick them up from the airport. It gave me an opportunity to get away from grandma Leah's disappointment. On the way back, I sat in the backseat with mom and she hugged me almost all the way home.

"Next time you leave, I'll babysit Tommy and Jonathan, ok?"

"OK, sweetie, I'm sorry it was hard for you. She'll calm down and forgive you, don't worry."

We kept hugging each other until the car stopped and we had to get out. Although it had been more than a day, I could still smell the cauliflower.

When my parents went away again, I was actually left in charge, it was better this way.

That moment, when I was laying in bed trying to fall asleep, I felt as if my parents were gone again and I was babysitting Tom.

After visiting the bathroom twenty times, I finally fell asleep. I woke up when I heard the door open and Tommy came in. I was praying that Adam wouldn't wake up, but I heard him whining and Michael went to him. You could say my motivation for finding mom an apartment, grew every time Tommy woke Adam up during the night. I would find myself at 2 A.M. saying goodnight again to teddy and dolly, so that Adam would go back to sleep. I would sometimes struggle going back to sleep myself, having so many thoughts going through my mind. By now, they had nothing to do with my work cases.

Michael came back from Adam's room and brought in with him scents from the kitchen. I was nauseous again. Didn't I already mention how much I hated cauliflower?

CHAPTER 8

Every afternoon, I would sneak out of the office (taking the long route, of course), and try completing others tasks, all while looking for an apartment for mom. I would drag Adam along, from one apartment to the next, until I found a place that was just a five-minute-walk from mine.

I knew mom's surgery was approaching. The moment I got the date, I tried planning on how to ask Nathan for a day off. I knew he wouldn't be too happy about it, but I assumed he would understand the importance of the matter at hand. It is, after all, my mom.

The next day, I walked into his large office with a big polite smile.

"Hey, I finished Samuel's deposition. Would you like to go over it?"

"Leave it here, I'll go over it later," he didn't even look at me; the smile I tried so hard to keep was unnecessary.

"I wanted to ask you something," I waited for a reaction, but when it failed to come, I went on, "My mom is having surgery on Sunday and I would like to take the day off." I took a deep breath and hoped the hard part was behind me. Nathan logged into his itinerary and I waited patiently.

"Samuel is coming in to sign the deposition on Sunday. I'm not familiar with the details, so you have to be there. You can leave once the meeting is over."

"But it's a really hard and complicated surgery," I couldn't believe he didn't authorize it.

"You're not the one operating on her, right?" he lifted his eyes to me, as if he was waiting for an answer. "The doctors will do just fine without you, don't worry," he said and looked back at his screen.

"But it's important that I be there. It's my mom," I held the tears and tried not to whine, but struggled.

"But it's important to **me** that you'll be here. You're barely at the office as it is, and it's unacceptable." He turned to face me and leaned forward with a sense of formality.

"You know we've been going through some rough times. Her disease, and the fact that they don't have a home and my brother living at my place."

"I understand, but everybody has rough times and it can't compromise the professionalism of this office. If you're taking care of a client you need to be present at his meetings, especially when you're the one who prepared the deposition. That's the meaning of being a lawyer, and it's very sad that I should have to explain it." He raised his voice and Mayra, his personal assistant, stood up and closed the door.

"Can't we move the meeting with Samuel to a different day?"

"The meeting can't be moved because Samuel is flying to Spain the day after. You should have known that, seeing as you're the lawyer attending to his cases." Nathan yelled angrily, "If you want to work here, you need to adjust to the office requirements."

I didn't know what to do. I wanted to curse him (and his mother) but I didn't utter a word. I just stood there and kept myself from crying in front of him.

"I'll call you after I go over what you've written. I hope there's not much to correct, like the other deposition you gave me."

I opened the door and left the room in shock.

Mayra approached me with a glass of water and took me to my room. "Are you OK?"

"Yes," I replied, but still didn't know if it was true. I was shaking and felt that I would faint any moment.

"I'm shocked he didn't authorize it." I sat on my chair and drank the water. At that moment, I wanted to throw all of Samuel's dossiers out of the window, take my things and never come back. I didn't know how I could ever look at Nathan again.

When I called mom, I cried on the phone and she tried calming me down. "In any case, it's not good for you to spend so much time at the hospital. There are so many germs and diseases, it's bad for your pregnancy."

"But what he's doing is awful. He's taking advantage of the fact that I need this job and don't have any other choice, no one's going to hire a pregnant woman. If he could, he would have fired me, for sure."

"It doesn't matter right now, please, calm down. All this stress, it's unhealthy for you."

She was right, but I was still shaking with anger.

CHAPTER 9

On the day of mom's surgery, I came into the office angry, more than usual. I walked into the conference room, slightly late, and sat next to Samuel. Nathan was already deep in conversation with him and didn't even respond when I came in. Samuel, on the other hand, stood up and warmly shook my hand. I made an honest attempt at smiling, but was so mad that I just couldn't.

"Is everything fine?" Samuel asked while I placed in front of him a copy of his deposition.

"Everything's perfect, thanks," I said nervously.

Samuel was browsing through his laptop, while Nathan played with his phone. I was starting to get annoyed by this useless waste of time, so I decided to speed things up.

"I understand that you're leaving tomorrow, so how about we start working on the deposition?" I looked up only to realize that no one but me had bothered to open the document I handed out.

"Come, see how I renovated my yacht." Samuel turned the computer screen to Nathan, who was kind enough to take his eyes off his phone.

"Wonderful!" Nathan said with excitement he had reserved only for his high paying customers. Then Samuel turned the screen to me.

"Congratulations, it really is beautiful," I said and Samuel kept scrolling through the pictures, adjusting the screen so that Nathan could also see the new shower he installed. I checked my phone but there weren't any new messages since the one Gabi sent me at 7 A.M., telling me mom was taken into the surgery room.

"And that's from the trip we took across the east coast during the holidays. I took all my family on a whale watching cruise, it was crazy good." Samuel kept scrolling through the pictures on his laptop and Nathan kept acting enthused. I was starting to get hot, so I took my jacket off. It felt like Nathan was taking his time on purpose. But why should he care, considering he charges by the minute? I checked my phone again, still nothing.

"That's us at the White House," Samuel continued, as he scrolled through more photos of his family standing in front of the White House. I was slowly losing my patience.

"What a beautiful family!" Nathan said, and all I wanted was to smash Samuel's computer on his head. My leg tapped nervously, as if it had a life of its own, and I was sitting at the edge of my sit.

"Are you in a hurry?" Nathan asked with an innocent expression, while Samuel scrolled to a picture of him and his wife wearing thin rain coats at Niagara Falls.

"Actually, yes," I said, and Samuel stopped and looked at me. "My mom is having surgery at the moment and I would love to finish going over the deposition, so Samuel would sign it and I can leave for the hospital."

Nathan's expression was extremely furious, but before he could say anything Samuel said, "no problem, I can sign the document you prepared." Samuel took a pen and started flipping to the last page of the deposition.

"We can't just do that. You need to read everything and make sure that it's right," I said when Nathan stood up and looked at me with anger.

"No need. Did you put in what I told you?" he asked, and I nodded. "So, I trust you." Samuel scribbled his signature on his copy and took Nathan's too. "How many copies do you need?"

Nathan paced back and forth by the table, "Samuel, there's no pressure. You can read quietly and Shirley can wait." He looked at me, as if wanting me to agree with him, but I kept silent.

"It's all good, Nathan. You have three signed copies. Do you need anything else?"

"No, thank you, Samuel," I said and slipped all signed copies back into the folder.

I stood up and shook Samuel's hand. "Have a great flight, and enjoy yourselves. When you come back, we'll talk." I'm sure Nathan would love to see pictures from this trip too, I wanted to say, but kept silent.

CHAPTER 10

Mom still had three rounds of treatment left. But only a week after her surgery, she was back at her old workplace and they were happy to have her back. Mom got used to her wig, and despite her having a different skin color and swollen face, she looked like herself again. Although she complained about looking terrible, to me she still looked wonderful. Whenever someone would say I reminded them of her, I felt it was the best compliment I could possibly get.

I kept working as much as I could, but as my due date approached, my motivation ran lower. I couldn't wait for my maternity leave. I took as many sick days as I could and used them to rest. When I did work, I would sit with Sarah and brief her about my cases, preparing her for when I would take my maternity leave and she takes over.

Sarah was one of those single women who lived life to its fullest. She loved sitting at trendy restaurants and traveled as much as possible, especially thanks to her previous job at El Al. Marriage, especially children, seemed unnecessary to her at this point in her life. Despite us being in different places in our lives, Sarah was my only friend at the office. She was honest, not fake like many other lawyers who worked here. I also knew that she was on my side.

"I'm literally counting the days until my due date. I can't believe I have three months left," I told her at lunch, while eating our usual order from our favorite restaurant.

"How can you not like sushi, I don't get it." Sarah dipped her sushi in the sauce and swallowed it whole.

"You know that in any case, I can't have sushi during pregnancy, right?" The things she said would surprise me sometimes.

"Of course I know." She smiled and had a piece of seaweed stuck between her teeth. Sarah was one of those women who could eat whatever they wanted. She would probably look gorgeous even if she were pregnant with twins.

"There are so many things that I don't like. Not just sushi. I'm really fed up with that idiot, Nathan. He keeps commenting about my hours and giving me the stink-eye. He's probably waiting for me to come back from my maternity leave and then he'll fire me first chance he gets. If I could afford it, I wouldn't even come back." I signaled her to clean her teeth.

"Time will fly, don't worry." Everything was simple for Sarah. "You're a wonderful lawyer, the clients love you, he won't fire you so easily."

"I hope you're right." I took a bite and felt my phone vibrating in my pocket.

Mom called to tell me she had a checkup at the hospital.

"What did they say?" I signaled Sarah that we would sit together later, and I walked quickly to my room. I closed the door behind me. If I needed to cry, it's better having the door closed.

"I took a genetic test, because they say that this type of cancer is mostly genetic."

"But no one in our family had ovarian cancer."

"True, but that gene also has to do with breast cancer, and my cousin has the gene and she had breast cancer." I remembered her telling me that her cousin had breast cancer and was a carrier of the breast cancer gene. At the time, mom was nervous and asked her regular physician what she should do. He said it wasn't carried on from the father's side which is why she shouldn't worry. However, mom made sure to get checked on a regular basis. She never skipped her annual mammography and made sure that all the women she knew got checked.

"So, they took a blood sample and we're waiting for the results," she continued, because I didn't reply.

"OK." I didn't know what to say. I immediately thought about myself and the baby girl I was carrying. What does that mean for us?

"If it's positive you need to take the test too," she said, as if she knew what I was thinking about.

"OK, I'll talk to you later, I need to finish some things if I want to get home on time." I left the door closed and leaned on it. How did this happen? Did I pass on cancer genes to our daughter? I remembered hearing it could be genetic, but no one had said anything until now. I assumed it had nothing to do with us.

The tears started pouring, and I felt that my room, which was small as it is, was closing in on me. I took a deep breath and dialed Michael's number.

"Hey, do you have a minute?" I asked quietly.

"Five minutes and then I'm off to a hearing. What's going on?"

"Listen, I don't know what to do." I stopped for a second, took another breath, and for the first time understood what it meant to be chocked up with tears. I could barely speak. "Mom was at the hospital today, she had a checkup. They told her that ovarian cancer could sometimes be genetic."

"Is hers genetic?"

"They don't know yet, they took the sample today," I said with a whisper. I felt my body was deflated like a balloon. I wanted to go home, get into bed and hide from the world.

"When will she have the results?"

"I don't know."

"So we'll wait and hope for the best. There's a chance it's negative, right?"

"I don't know," I mumbled, "but if she has it, I'm sure I have it too."

I'm sure I'll have cancer." I felt how the universe was slowly marking my forehead with a small red circle, actually, marking my ovaries.

"Aren't you going too far? You don't know if she even has it."

Michael wasn't usually an optimist. He would repress. One of those people who never thought of trouble until it came, and even then, they would face it heroically, without pitying themselves. You could say our approaches were slightly different. I never thought of myself as a pessimist, but rather a realist. But to me, the moment they thought it was genetic, all possible and scary scenarios ran through my mind. I could see myself bald and hooked up to an IV.

"I don't need to wait for results. It's surely genetic and I'm sure I have it."

"Let's wait a bit, Shirley. You know that no matter what happens, we'll handle it and everything will be fine."

"I don't know what to do with myself."

"There's nothing you can do. We'll just have to wait."

"OK," I replied and blew my nose, but the tears wouldn't stop. I didn't know how I'd survive the wait. It was like waiting for a verdict, only this time, it wasn't about who was entitled for rent or owned the property, it was my life. And anyways, things were already bad, what else could go wrong?

I heard Nathan shouting outside. "Where's Shirley?"

As usual, he ignored the fact that he could call my line rather than shout in the hall.

"OK, we'll talk later. Nathan is shouting." I hung up without waiting for his response. In any case, there was nothing he could say that would cheer me up.

I wiped my face with some left-over tissues I found in my bag. It's a good thing I never wore makeup, otherwise I would have looked like a clown.

When I felt I ran out of choices, I went to Nathan's room. He was going over his emails. "We got a response on the ALUT case," he said without lifting his gaze, "go over it and write a reference. They're coming in tomorrow to go over it."

"Can't we postpone the meeting? We have at least two weeks. Why does it have to be tomorrow?" I took the big white envelope from his table, and took the depositions out. Why is everything so urgent? Why is everything last minute here? Since Adam started daycare, I didn't have Ida, so I had to leave the office on time.

"Do what you think is best. You're responsible for this case."

Some responsibility, I thought to myself. You even schedule my meetings for me, "I'll take care of it."

I was at the door when Nathan surprised me and asked, "How's your mother?"

"Relatively OK," I peeked in and he even looked at my direction. "She's suffering from the chemo's side effects. But she has three more rounds and that's it."

"Good, send her my regards."

"Sure, thanks." I smiled and walked away. I had already forgotten that he could be nice. He was actually pleasant during Adam's pregnancy. He even sent me flowers and a card after I gave birth. His attitude changed when I came back and couldn't work fourteen hours a day like I did before.

I came back home exhausted. Again. I took the papers with me and couldn't make much progress because I fell asleep a few minutes after Adam did. Again.

CHAPTER 11

Mom's treatments were over and we felt as if everything was behind us. Two weeks after her last treatment, I was admitted for the second time at the hospital delivery room. I came for a check up and wasn't even thinking I would go into labor. Since I didn't bring my hospital bag with me, I had to send mom to bring my things from home. She joined me at the delivery room and made it fifteen minutes before Ariel was born. Luckily, Gabi's flight back to Australia was that evening, so he got to see baby Ariel on his way to the airport.

The first days were intense as it usually is when a new baby arrives. This time, we were home after two days. It was a healing experience after Adam's birth.

When Adam was born, they immediately took him to the E.R. and he was in NICU for a week. We were anxious and my heart literally hurt when I returned home without him. I sent Michael back to the hospital to be with Adam and I stayed at home depressed and nervous. We didn't have the joy of having a newborn, only existential anxiety. Every morning we would drive to the hospital just to be with him at NICU until the evening. I lost all my pregnancy weight just from the stress, so there were some advantages to that situation.

Things were different with Ariel. She also didn't like to sleep much, but she was much easier to take care of. However, having the two of them together was too hard and I needed help during the afternoon. A lovely young babysitter named Natalie came over almost every afternoon and saved me from a definite meltdown.

When Sarah came over, I told her about the labor like a man would tell of his experiences from the battlefield. "The moment the anesthesiologist came in, I felt I was in labor. He didn't even give me the epidural and Ariel jumped out. It was insanely scary and hurt like hell, but then it all ended. Michael's neck was all covered with scratches. Mom was so excited she kept filming the entire time; even things no one should see."

"It's unbelievable you had a natural birth." Ariel was laying in her crib in the living room and Sarah was caressing her hand.

"Trust me, if I had time I would have taken the epidural. But the anesthesiologist wouldn't give me anything at that point. Next time I'll ask for the epidural the moment I get into the delivery room, just to be on the safe side."

Sarah laughed and Ariel flinched. "What big eyes she has," Sarah said, as if this was the first baby she had ever seen.

"You sound like little red riding hood. That's how babies are, when they're born, they're cute and with time they grow out of it."

Ariel started crying and Adam (who suddenly seemed so big compared to her), covered his ears with his hands and walked away. Sarah picked up Ariel and tried calming her down.

"He's having a hard time with all this change," I whispered to Sarah, "he keeps complaining that her screaming hurts his ears."

"She really is a screamer." Sarah handed Ariel to me. "He'll get used to her in no time. When my sister was born I almost threw her out the window. Good thing my parents were there." Sarah spread on the sofa and sighed, "I'm completely exhausted."

"Don't go there," I told her when Ariel finally latched on. "I think Adam would have been happy if we took her back to the hospital. She's a nuisance to him."

Sarah napped lazily on the sofa and I looked at her with envy. Not only because she was able to fall asleep in any situation, but also because she had an inner calmness that I could only dream of.

CHAPTER 12

When mom would come over to help, it was usually straight after work. The first thing she would do was take off her wig. She was OK during the winter but in the summer, she got really hot. On the other hand, she still didn't feel comfortable going to work without it. I think she hid behind it, since it saved her from a lot of questions.

Adam loved mom and when she came over, he wanted to be only with her. They had a special bond. He even made his first steps at 10 months when he was with her. He practically ran to her.

One evening, when Ariel was still latched on and Adam was silently drinking his bottle, mom sat next to me and gently caressed Ariel's head.

"She's so sweet this one," she said, and then looked at me somewhat concerned. "I wonder who she will look like when she grows up."

"Right." I looked at Ariel, who was focused on breastfeeding.

"I wonder if I'll be here to see her," she mumbled, as if to herself. "We can't tell."

I didn't know how to respond. Her words pierced through my heart. The chemotherapy side effects were still visible on her face; it was still puffy and yellow. Every checkup we were praying and crossing our fingers, we didn't know what to expect. Our lives had changed in a heartbeat and we didn't know yet the results of the genetic tests. Although it was clear that ovarian cancer was lethal without having any genetic background, I was still anxious for mom, but also for myself and Ariel.

"You'll be fine," I said and hoped for all of our sakes that I was right. "I can also see that your hair is growing back." I tried changing the conversation to a more certain topic.

"Yes," mom caressed the fuzz growing on her bald head, "but it'll take some time." She yawned and got up to leave. I could see she was tired. "I think I'll be going."

She kissed me and Ariel, Adam ran to hug her with his free arm, as she kissed him goodbye. When she opened the door Adam started shouting "Cathy, Cathy, hat" (she didn't want to be called grandma just yet, she thought she was too young for that title). Mom turned around and Adam threw his bottle and ran to the dining table. He grabbed the wig and ran to her.

"Thank you sweetie." She leaned over and kissed him.

When she closed the door behind her, Adam still stood there hoping she might come back.

CHAPTER 13

I was trying to get some sleep so I turned my phone off. When I gave up on my attempts at falling asleep, I saw I had five missed calls from mom.

"What happened?" I asked the moment she picked up.

Mom lingered a bit, and then said, almost whispering. "The test results came in, and they're positive."

"Meaning you have that gene?"

"Yes, and now you need to take the test."

"I'll check with Dr. Gidron as to where I should take the test," I replied after a few moments of silence. "I'm supposed to see him this Monday. Ariel woke up, we'll talk later." I remembered Gidron telling me he was a member of the genetic tests committee. I never thought I would meet him there.

On my way to Ariel's room, I dialed Michael, but after two rings I reached his voice mail. He texted me that he can't talk. Ariel was screaming by the time I reached her bed. She received me with a smile and enthusiastic waves, but I had a hard time smiling back at her. I changed her diaper as if on autopilot. I tried taking in what mom had said, that it was my turn to be tested.

I can't run away from it any longer. I felt everything turning black, except for Ariel who was wiggling in my arms.

The phone rang and Michael sounded more tired than usual. "What's going on? I'm in the middle of a hearing and we only have a few minutes break." Ariel kept us up all night and Michael didn't have the privilege of napping during the day.

"Mom got her test results today, and like I told you, she's a carrier," I said and started to cry in despair. Ariel stopped moving and gave me a weird look, because crying was supposed to be her thing.

"It still doesn't mean anything about you. There's still a good chance that you aren't a carrier of the gene," Michael said, and it seemed the conversation woke him up a bit.

"Of course it does! If she has the gene, then so do I." Ariel really started going crazy in my arms so I sat with her on the bed.

"You don't know that."

"I'm sure that I got it from her. We're alike when it comes to these things, and don't start to telling me about statistics and numbers. I hate statistics! When I die you can tell everybody all about the statistics."

"I realize that you're stressed, but I have to get back to the courtroom. We'll talk about it at home in the evening." I heard a muffled sound of people growing louder.

"Bye," I replied and threw the phone on the bed, as if it was responsible for the bad news I got.

I took Ariel to the living room and breastfed her. My hands were shaking a lot and I felt hot, but I couldn't reach the AC remote control. I sat on the sofa crying and waited for her to finish breastfeeding. I sent Sarah a text not to come. I couldn't see anyone, especially hearing another person telling me, 'it's going to be fine.'

I placed Ariel on her colorful activity mat and she rolled from side to side, happy she was able to reach the toys that were scattered around her. What are the chances that I don't have this gene? Why should I be this lucky? Mom told me that when she was pregnant, a friend took her to a strange fortune-teller, who told her she would have a daughter and her daughter would have a good fortune in life. From the way things were going, it seemed she had it wrong, big time.

We spoke every now and then about why mom got sick. It was this need we had, to find who or what to blame. But we hadn't found anything yet. Mom thought it had to do with the pressure she was under these last few years. The test revealed the real cause. She was predestined for this fate. The target was marked around her from the moment she was born, actually, even before that.

What really infuriated me were all these thoughts running through my head about how we could have prevented it. I wanted to find the idiot doctor who had told her it wasn't genetic, and yell at him that it was all his fault. He was the person to blame because this fate could have been prevented. I was overwhelmed with anger. If she would have known she would have done something about it. I was mad that in one moment, without thinking, that doctor had condemned her.

Ariel's scream stopped me from writing my hypothetical complaint letter against that doctor in my head. I found her stuck under the table, after having reached the cool floor. It turns out she already knew how to roll over.

CHAPTER 14

By the time I was supposed to have my genetic consultation, it seemed that everything was back to normal. Gabi decided he was fed up with living alone in Australia, so he quit his job and returned to Israel. Adam was happy at Tammy's daycare, and Ariel was with Ida the nanny, which allowed me to stay at the office a little longer.

On the day of the consultation meeting, Natalie babysat Ariel and Adam and I drove straight from the office to the clinic. Dr. Gidron's presence calmed me down a little and I was thankful that he was the one who introduced my family history. After the geneticist neatly drew my family tree, she said that in any case I needed to take the test because mom was a carrier.

"Listen," I said to Jonathan as I stepped outside, and into the crowded street, "if the results are positive, they'll call to schedule a meeting, because they don't give them over the phone. They send a letter only if they're negative."

"Great," he replied, as if it had nothing to do with him.

"Mom's mutation is not as dangerous. But still, it increases chances for other types of cancer. Did you know that men can also get breast cancer?" I tried making him realize that he needs to be cautious about it. It wasn't something he could just brush aside.

"Are you implying that I'm fat? It's not breasts, it's all muscle." As usual, he was trying to joke around and avoid any form of serious conversation.

"Hardly muscles," I mocked him.

"I don't think I'll take the test for now, it doesn't seem that urgent."

"As you wish." I gave up. I didn't understand how he took this so lightly. I always had the need to know everything. "I'll talk to you later." I decided to leave Jonathan with mom. In any case, he would only listen to her, so if someone could convince him, it was only her.

***

The next day, I met Sarah in the small kitchen.

"You won't believe the guy I met yesterday, he was stunning." This explained her insanely large cup of coffee. "So, how was the test yesterday?" Sarah put the milk back in the fridge and leaned against the kitchen counter, while I was contemplating what tea I would have.

"They took some blood, and now we wait."

"Great. Fingers crossed that the results are negative." Sarah cupped her coffee mug and tried warming up. I really can't understand why these offices are always freezing. "But, what do you do if you have the gene?"

"Once you're done having children, you have an oophorectomy to remove your ovaries. There also these crazy women who remove their breasts so they don't get breast cancer."

"Wow, that's pretty extreme. Ok, let's hope yours are negative, and that's it."

"I don't think so. When it comes to me, anything that can go wrong – goes wrong."

"Don't think like that, sweetie. See what gorgeous kids you have. It's not all bad. Come on, I can hear Nathan coming. Let's pretend we're working, so that things don't get really ugly. Chinese today?" she yelled while heading to her office, and then disappeared.

I went back to my room, the same one I had after coming back from my maternity leave, and took comfort in knowing I could close the door and drink my tea in silence. At home I hadn't drunk hot tea in a long time.

CHAPTER 15

It was my twenty-ninth birthday. Michael came home early from the office and we took Adam and Ariel to a jungle gym at the mall, a typical outing for a young mom celebrating her birthday. We had already strapped the kids in their car seats, and had sat in the car when the phone rang. An unknown number was never a good sign. I answered and the call connected to the car speakerphone.

"Shirley Moshe?"

"Yes?"

"We're talking from the genetics clinic," I felt my pulse rise by the minute. "I'm calling to schedule an appointment for you with our team of health consultants."

"OK," I didn't get any letter in the mail, I thought. The results were positive. I felt my heart pulsing and I couldn't breathe.

"Wednesday, two weeks from now at five thirty, does that work for you?"

"OK..." I looked at Michael like a sad puppy, I think he understood what my look meant. Adam started shouting "tele bubbies, tele bubbies", and Michael tried looking for the CD in the glove compartment box.

We didn't speak all the way. Michael probably didn't know what to say, and I was too shocked to speak. But there was one thing I did want to say – why me? Why was I dealt this screwed up hand? I woke up healthy on my birthday, and now I will end the day knowing that horrible disease is coming my way. However, I kept quiet since Adam was old enough to understand. I just wanted us to park, so I could get out of this cage.

When we arrived, I left Michael at the jungle gym and went to the bathroom. It was the only place I could have some privacy. On my way I looked at the other people, walking around without any worries. I just wanted to scream. I could barely hold the tears in, until I found an empty stall and closed the door behind me. Although I knew there was an actual chance it would happen, I couldn't believe the results were positive. Couldn't they have waited until tomorrow? They simply had to call on my birthday. They have my date of birth on file, for god's sake, how insensitive can they be?

I leaned against the door and cried quietly. I could hear behind the door a couple of women casually talking about different discounts and sales they just had to go to. At that moment, it sounded like they were having the silliest conversation in the world.

And then I thought about mom. How would I tell her? How could I break her heart like that? It was obvious she would blame herself. I decided that my birthday wasn't the right time to tell her that I too would probably have to face this terrible disease. I knew that mom would have a hard time hearing such a thing. Ariel was the next thought that crossed through my mind while standing in that reeking bathroom stall. What would I have done if I had known before? What do I do if the terrible gene has passed on to her too? How could I live with myself?

"Are you OK?" Michael sent me a text, bringing me back to reality. I didn't have a choice, I had to get out of my hiding place and go back to being a mom.

"No," I honestly replied, and tried pulling out some tissues from the annoying dispenser that would produce only one square at a time, "but I'm on my way."

***

"What does that mean, exactly?" Michael asked when the kids fell asleep and we could speak without being disturbed.

"It means that I have the gene. Just like I told you," I rubbed it in. In fact, this time, I wanted to be wrong. I threw my clothes into the washing machine and went to bed. What a screwed-up way to end my birthday.

"So, now what?" Michael laid on the bed and looked at me.

"Now we try not to die from cancer."

"Good idea," he said, "and how do we do that?"

"I actually don't have a clue, but I don't want to talk about it right now. I want to go to sleep and be done with this terrible day." I turned my back to Michael and turned off the light. He placed his arm around me and hugged me. We stayed like that until he fell asleep and then I gently rolled him on his side.

That's how my sleepless night began, only this time I couldn't stop crying. I felt as if I had been sentenced to death. That's it. My life was cut short. In a couple of years I'll get sick and then die. That's all I could think of, over and over. I thought about all the things I wouldn't get to do. I won't see my kids growing up, won't get to see them getting married, won't get to know my grandchildren. And if they have the gene, what would happen to them? Who's going to be there for them? There was nothing that Michael could say that would calm me down. It was obvious things could never go back to the way they used to be.

Now, what should I answer when someone asks: "do you have any health issues?" So far, I answered 'no.' But now? "No, but I have a high chance of getting cancer."

In the morning I woke up feeling like a different person, but definitely not a better one. I felt as if I could never smile again. I came to the office with even less enthusiasm than usual. I threw my purse on the chair in my office and went to the kitchen. I stared at the kettle and completely disproved the theory that a watched pot never boils. I didn't even feel like turning around when Sarah walked in, and by simply hearing her 'good morning' I could tell she had a better evening than mine.

"Morning," I replied in a tone indicating that the word 'good' would not come out of my mouth today.

"Well, did you have a party yesterday? Did you go out?" "No." She couldn't sense the tone.

"We were at the mall with the kids. But I wouldn't call it a party." I poured the boiling water into the mug, but mostly onto the counter. "Oh, crap."

"You're such old drags." Sarah elegantly pushed the capsule into the machine and leaned against the dry part of the counter. Her curls bounced happily from side to side. I took a rag and started wiping the puddle, but the water had already started dripping to the floor.

"The clinic called me yesterday to schedule an appointment," I said while on my knees, without looking up at her, "it means the results are positive."

"Why are you jumping to conclusions?"

I stood up and gave her the angriest look she had ever seen, "because they said that if it's negative, they send the results in the mail. So, it's not negative. What else can it be?"

"It still doesn't mean anything. When did they schedule your appointment?" Sarah whisked the milk for her latte and I finished mopping up the floor.

"In two weeks." I finally made some tea.

"OK, so wait for your appointment and listen to what they have to say. It doesn't always end badly."

"So far, your theory hasn't really proven itself. In any case, I'm tired. I'm going to start working so I can be done with this day." I didn't wait for her encouraging response, and took my tea, because there was nothing she could say that would help. She couldn't even begin to understand what I was going through.

I walked really slow holding my tea; I was too tired to mop other floors.

CHAPTER 16

I cried myself to sleep every night, and in the morning pretended to be a lawyer and dragged myself to the office. I wasn't actually working, more like trying to get through the day without doing any damage. My indifference to Nathan's comments was bordering on rude. I even lacked the patience to answer all his silly comments. Nathan kept blaming the children for my distraction and made a point to constantly mention that a lot of lawyers who are also mothers, in fact get their work done ("are they also about to die?" I wanted to ask, but kept quiet). Even Sarah couldn't cheer me up with her usual "everything will be fine", but at least she was now helping with some of my cases.

The only case I could somehow focus on was ALUT's. Joel was charming and patient, but he spent his days caring for people with special needs, so it seemed inappropriate to whine to him. After all, I'm completely healthy, how can I complain?

On the day of my appointment, Joel came over to look at the depositions we wanted to submit. "God willing, everything will be fine," he said at the end of the meeting.

"Amen."

"Don't forget you're welcome to visit us and see the hostel for yourself. I thought to arrange a meeting with the parents, because they have a lot of questions."

"Sure, I'll talk to Nathan and we'll put something together."

Joel left and I quickly grabbed my purse. Natalie wasn't available so I had to pick up Ariel from home and drive to the genetics clinic, at the afternoon rush hour. Adam had a playdate with a new friend from daycare and I was hoping that mom wouldn't call me during my appointment.

Michael met us by the clinic's front door and helped me carry the stroller to the second floor. In the waiting room, I sat quietly and didn't utter a word, which was very unlike me. Ariel was playing in her stroller and I stared at her thinking about what her future might hold. Or actually what her future held because of me.

We entered the room and Dr. Gidron smiled at us as if this were another pregnancy scan.

"How are you, Shirley?" The geneticist started speaking as soon as Michael closed the door.

I wanted to answer that I was feeling crappy and I hated everything about this world, but I held it in. "Well, since I'm here, it seems things could have been better."

"So, as you have probably realized by now, the test results came back positive and you're a carrier of the BRCA1 genetic mutant," she looked at the papers in front of her as if she needed them to give me the news. "Which means that you have an 85% chance of having breast cancer, depending on the research."

"OK," Ariel started whining in her stroller so I sat her on my lap. She pulled out her pacifier and started banging it on the table. Everyone turned their attention to Ariel's big eyes and smiled at her.

But there wasn't much of a choice and the geneticist continued. "Your chances of getting ovarian cancer are 50%, again, depending on the research. You can choose to have a preventative surgery. It won't eliminate your chances of getting sick but it will reduce them considerably. If you remove your ovaries, you could reduce your chances of getting breast cancer by 50%. We recommend having that surgery at the age of 40. Breast amputation is also an option you could consider."

"What does that mean exactly?" I really tried to focus, but felt that I couldn't.

"We remove the existing breast tissue and reconstruct the breasts at the same procedure. But you should also remember that it only reduces your chances, it doesn't eliminate them. You can choose whether or not to keep your nipples."

"I don't think I'll do that." I looked at Michael, who simply shrugged and kept silent.

"All right. I understand that you have two children. If you want more, I suggest you hurry up."

I looked at her with shock. "Wait, these are my only options? Removing everything?"

"Look, you'll have semi-annual checkups, and if something comes up, you'll be treated immediately." I looked at Michael and then at the doctor who kept talking as if reading from a grocery list. "Ovarian cancer isn't something we can detect early, so the only solution is removing the ovaries. It's all written down in this letter."

Dr. Gidron nodded in consent. I remembered that a friend from law school had told me about a girl who had a preventative breast removal surgery because her mom had breast cancer. I was shocked by the choice she made, but back then I didn't know what having this gene meant. I didn't even know it existed.

"At the moment, I'm not removing anything. I'll have regular checkups." I looked at Michael again, but he was too busy picking up the pacifier Ariel kept throwing on the floor. "All right," the doctor handed me my verdict letter, "wishing you good health."

"Wishing you good health" was the least appropriate thing she could have said. I won't have good health, I thought to myself. Perhaps she should have wished me good luck?

I smiled politely and left holding Ariel in my arms. A young woman held the door for Michael, who followed me with the stroller.

She entered the room and closed the door behind her. We waited for the elevator in silence. I didn't know what to say to him.

"You'll have checkups and everything will be fine," Michael told me as we left the building, but I think he was saying it more to himself.

"Were we at the same meeting? Because I don't think you understood what they were saying."

"I understood perfectly well. There is also a chance that you won't get sick, you know?"

"So far your statistics didn't really prove themselves. In a few years I'll get breast cancer and die. That's what's going to happen."

"You can't know for sure. There must be women who have the gene and didn't get sick. You'll have checkups as they recommended and everything will be fine."

"Stop telling me 'everything will be fine', Michael. Nothing is fine. You have to accept that. Besides, what do you care? You'll be a desirable widower and you'll find a new wife. Widowers are even hotter than divorcees."

"You might be right," Michael said teasingly and hugged me. "See, everything will be fine."

"Shut up," his hug finally helped me release the tears I had held in, "only I'm allowed to joke about it."

We stood there for a long time, hugging next to the green trash cans.

***

Ariel was surprisingly quiet, which allowed me to call mom on the way back home.

Mom felt guilty. As if it were her fault that I got this gene. I explained to her that it was completely the other way around. Thanks to her being sick I was able to find the gene early, take care of myself and get an early detection if something will go wrong. I told her the truth, that she had actually saved me, but at this moment I could hardly believe it myself.

We picked Adam up and went back home. We barely spoke. Michael was in charge of bath time and I made omelets.

At night, when everyone was quiet in their beds, Michael hugged me and said, "maybe they'll find a cure for it in a few years, something genetic that will fix the deficiency. You can never know. Science is constantly evolving."

"Maybe. But I am now entering the danger years. I don't have time to wait for a miracle. It might be relevant for Ariel, but not me."

"She might have not gotten it from you. Maybe she got my exquisite genes?"

"I wish. You can't say that I didn't try upgrading my Ashkenazi genes," Michael laughed.

"Nothing beats the Yemenites; great genes."

"I don't think I'll be able to fall asleep tonight," I said and laid on my back. I noticed the dust on the lamp. "There are too many things bothering me."

"So, what do you want to do? Do you want to watch a movie? We recorded some that we haven't seen yet." Michael looked for the remote control. We recorded the movies while I was pregnant with Ariel, and we still haven't found the time to watch them.

"Won't you be exhausted tomorrow?" Thursdays were always long days at the office, everybody pointlessly trying to finish as many things as possible before the weekend.

"Nonsense."

"I want to have another child," I surprised him.

"Me too, but not now. We said we'd wait longer this time, right?"

"Obviously not now. But I don't want to wait too long. We can't tell when I'll get sick."

"Can we wait another year?" Michael asked with a smile, but I could tell from his eyes he was scared. It was obvious that if I insisted, we'd get pregnant even sooner. He turned off the light laid back in bed.

"OK, we'll talk about it again in a year." I heard Michael sigh in relief.

"I hate my office." Sometimes I really couldn't figure out how I ended up in that office. I just went from school, straight to my internship and then to the office. It was effortless; I didn't have to think about it. I just went with it. But life had suddenly stopped, and I had to reconsider my life choices.

"I know," he shut his eyes.

"If it weren't for Sarah, I would have already left."

"I know."

"If life is too short then maybe I shouldn't have to suffer. Maybe I should look for another place."

"OK, I'll support any choice you make. You know that."

"Do you think I should also tell my dad about the test?" I waited for an answer but he didn't reply. "Michael?" I turned to him and saw that he had already fallen asleep, even without taking his glasses off. I placed them on the window ledge above our bed.

I envied him for being able to fall asleep so fast. I laid next to him and looked at him. When he slept, he looked like Adam. I pitied him because he married me and got screwed over. Well, we couldn't have known what life would throw our way.

I laid on my back and looked at the dark ceiling. I tried to make a list in my head of all the appointments I should make; breast surgeon, gynecologist, ultrasound, blood tests. Despair.

I wanted to start as soon as possible. They keep saying that early detection saves lives. So please, I thought, I hope it saves mine too.

I kept thinking that I couldn't possibly be the only woman in this situation, I also felt that no one else could really understand what I was going through. I read somewhere that one in every forty Ashkenazi women are carriers, or something like that. So, there must be other women like me. There was that young woman who had an appointment with the geneticist's right after mine. Perhaps she's a carrier? There must be more carriers.

That night I realized I should talk to another carrier. But a healthy carrier, not someone who's already sick. It's inappropriate whining to someone who had to actually face this disease. Besides, she wouldn't understand what I was talking about because she would be going through something different. She would be actually fighting for her life; being a carrier would mean something else for her. I wanted to talk to someone who was considered healthy. Someone like me. But where will I find someone like that? It's not something that you post on your Facebook feed or status; it isn't something that you would talk about with a stranger. If I could, I would have written: "Wanted: a healthy carrier for conversation purposes." But how can I post such a text if I don't want people knowing I was a carrier too?

I waited for sunrise, quietly got dressed and drove to the office for a day full of tasks that had very little to do with my being a lawyer.

CHAPTER 17

During the morning rush hour, I thought again about the woman whose appointment was after mine. I had to find someone who could answer all the questions running through my mind. When I got to the office, even before having my tea, I started researching on my computer. First, I searched for BRCA carriers. I was already familiar with most of the information that came up. The Israel Cancer Association posted information about carriers in their breast cancer tab. I decided to call them again. The last time I spoke to them, I asked for information about ovarian cancer, and tried figuring out what mom was entitled to as a cancer patient.

I couldn't believe that I was now calling for myself. After two minutes, a middle-aged woman answered the phone. "Good morning. This is Suzanne speaking, how can I help you?"

"Good morning, Suzanne. I would like to ask about whether you offer assistance for BRCA carriers."

"What carriers?" I heard people coming into the office so I closed my door.

"Carriers of the BRCA gene, causing breast and ovarian cancer. Are you familiar with it?"

"Not really, but I'll try asking someone. Hold please."

While I held the line, hearing the association's jingle playing in the background, I went over my emails - one from Nathan sent at 2:30 A.M. Doesn't that man ever sleep?

"What cancer did you say that you had?" I heard Suzanne asking.

"I don't have it. I'm a carrier of the gene, but I don't have it yet."

"Oh, we assist only cancer patients and their families."

"OK, but I'm at risk. I just want to get information about how not to get it."

"We don't have such information. If you do get sick, we're at your service," she replied as if she were a customer service representative at a phone company, and I was asking about the dangers of radiation.

"Thank you, but I don't want to get sick. I want you to help me not to get sick."

"I can't help you with that."

"Who can help me with that?" I tried staying calm but started losing my patience.

"I can give you our social worker's number. Maybe she can refer you to someone else."

"Thank you very much."

I wrote the number down and immediately called Lily, the social worker. She didn't answer, so I left a voice message and asked that she call me back as soon as possible.

It didn't make sense to me that no one was helping carriers. I felt like a drowning woman trying to clutch at straws.

It was a good time to have some tea, especially since my other option was to start working on an injunction letter for Samuel. In the kitchen, the interns were making coffee while talking about their tedious bar exam course. I would switch places with them in a heartbeat, and retake all these absurd bar exams if it meant getting rid of this gene. I didn't even try joining their conversation and when the water boiled, I took the mug in one hand and a teabag in the other, and went to hide in my small office.

I sat in my chair and stared at the screen. I could hear Sarah's stilettos annoyingly tapping from the end of the hallway, getting closer and closer. She opened the door and peeked in. Her curls were pulled into a ballet bun, meaning she had a court hearing today. It made her look very serious.

"Hey, would Michael give you a pass for a short weekend abroad?" Sarah probably didn't remember I had my meeting yesterday, which bode well for me since I didn't want to talk about it at work.

"Are you crazy? How can I leave him with two little kids? I won't have a house to come back to."

"No biggie. There's a cool Sting concert in Prague and I was thinking of going. I can still fly for free with El Al. Come on, don't be heavy. We'll celebrate your birthday in Prague." You could count on Sarah to take full advantage of her time as a stewardess.

I sighed loudly and tried explaining again, "It's not going to happen, Sarah. He won't agree."

"He will if you just stop being so miserable all the time. Come on, you've been cooped up in here for two weeks. Live a little, have fun." Sarah started dancing as if she were in some club waiting for me to jump in.

"I'm too tired. Forget it." I moved my mouse and the computer lit up.

"OK, we'll talk about it later," she said and lightly danced out of the room and into the kitchen. Seeing her skipping with those heels has always impressed me.

"There's nothing to talk about, Michael won't agree!" I yelled after her, but knew it was no use.

That truth was that Michael would have definitely agreed, but I wasn't in the mood for celebrating. Perhaps if things were different and normal, I would have jumped at the opportunity.

I shut the door again and started working on the injunction, hoping that Samuel's nonsense would distract me. Other people's troubles can be a good thing sometimes. Even if Samuel's troubles concerned things other people could only dream of.

CHAPTER 18

"Can I come over tonight?" Tommy sent me a surprising text in the middle of the day.

"Sure, when?" I replied and hoped that he might also help me around a bit.

"When Michael's home, so we can talk." What a shame, I thought.

"OK, come after 9." That's usually when I got to bed, but I didn't have any other option. Although I was constantly tired, I struggled falling asleep at night.

When Tommy came over, Michael and I waited for the kids to fall asleep. Adam and Ariel were in their beds and we stood outside their room.

"Call dad," Adam whispered to Ariel, who obviously wasn't old enough to call us, let alone say 'dad.' She could cry the most. "Call dad," Adam asked again. Michael and I couldn't stop laughing.

"See, you can't talk!" Adam said angrily and was probably very disappointed. Ariel just giggled and enjoyed his attention.

"Let's go outside," Tommy whispered to me, "so we can talk quietly."

We went downstairs and sat on the building's front stairs. The air was cool and pleasant. The street was usually silent in the evenings.

"I wanted to tell you something. I haven't spoken to mom and dad yet." Tommy played with a leaf that crumbled between his fingers.

"What?" I asked calmly, even though I suspected what this was about. Mom told me he came back home reeking of cigarettes, so I tried paying more attention. Jonathan started smoking at this age too, even though I asked him to quit. I grew up with Gabi's smoking and it was horrible. It took him years to quit and it really annoyed me that someone else would also take his chances with lung cancer. I was hoping that Tommy wouldn't take that road. It seems I was wrong.

"It's something that I've known for years, but now, I feel that I can tell you." He fell silent and I waited patiently, even though I really wanted to sleep. "I'm attracted to boys, I'm gay."

"OK," I stared at him for a few seconds. I was surprised and didn't know what else I was expected to say.

"I've already spoken to Jonathan a few days ago."

"Good," that wasn't as surprising. "Are you sure? Because you're still very young." I hugged him and he placed his head on my shoulder.

"Yes, Shirley, I'm sure." He suddenly seemed so mature.

"How did Jonathan respond?" He had that talent for being able to laugh even at serious issues.

"When I told him I wanted to talk to him he said 'as long as you're not going to tell me you're gay, no problem.' So, I said, 'I'm gay.'" We both laughed and I caressed his head, like mom used to do when Tommy was younger.

"It's very like Jonathan to react like that." I waited for a second and then turned to him. "So, what was going on with that girl you were dating?"

"I really liked her, but it didn't work out." Tommy found another leaf and crumbled it on the pavement. One of the neighbors walked in with some groceries and we moved aside.

"OK. So, are you sure?" Tommy sat down while I still stood in front of him. It was starting to get cold.

"Yes," he said and looked up at me for the first time that evening.

"OK. As long as you're happy."

"And I wanted to tell you another thing." I have to admit, I couldn't imagine what could possibly beat him coming out to me. "Do you remember when I lived at your place, how I would tell you that I'm attending scouts' meetings?"

"Yes…" I said slowly.

"I didn't really go there. I went to IGY, the Israeli Gay Youth Association."

"So, those were your friends at the time?"

"Yes. One of them was from school, but because he knew I was in the closet, he wasn't allowed to speak to me outside of IGY."

"Can I ask you something?" I said after a few moments of embarrassing silence. "That's why you never brought friends over during that year?" I always thought it was because he didn't want people seeing our apartment. It was furnished horribly, with second-hand furniture that we gathered at the last moment since all of our belongings were in Australia.

"Actually no. I didn't want them to know about mom, and I also didn't want them to see her like that."

"But why? There's nothing shameful about mom having cancer." His answer surprised me and frankly, I was a bit offended for mom.

"Because I didn't want people to pity me. I was already the new kid who came in the middle of the school year from Australia. I didn't need more attention."

"So, you're telling me that no one at school knew she was sick?" My upstairs neighbor passed through and Tommy held the door for her so she could walk in with her bags.

"I only told one friend. But later I found out that one of the teachers told all the students before I even started going there. I didn't know it back then."

"OK, look, I have to go upstairs, I'm exhausted. Thank you for telling me." I hugged him and he hugged me back, "in the meantime don't say anything to mom and dad. I'll talk to Jonathan and we'll figure out when it's best to tell them. Maybe after mom's checkup.

When we know she's fine."

"OK, Shirley," Tommy hugged me again and said, "good night."

"Good night, Tommy."

I went upstairs and found Michael sleeping in front of the TV, while the papers he was probably planning to read were scattered around him. I decided to let him sleep and tried to sleep without him snoring disturbing me. However, despite the silence, I couldn't fall asleep. I couldn't stop thinking about how we completely misread Tommy.

He had this whole other world that not only we weren't a part of, but we didn't even know it existed. If he's known this long, it means he's been keeping this a secret for years. I didn't know if I was more hurt because he kept it from me and felt uncomfortable telling me, or ashamed and angry at myself for not noticing. On the other hand, I felt I had so many things on my mind that I barely noticed other people. I texted Jonathan and we discussed when it would be the right time to break the news to our parents. All that had happened made me realize that I needed to stop being so self-involved. I seemed to have forgotten that other people have troubles of their own. I was too preoccupied with my own issues. It was very unlike me. I couldn't recognize myself anymore.

CHAPTER 19

Lily, the social worker, called me back a few days later, exactly at dinner time. I was in the middle of cooking the house specialty: omelettes with cheddar cheese.

"How can I help you?"

I told her about mom and the gene mutation we both have.

"I wanted to know if you offer carriers some form of assistance? Somewhere I could get information and talk to other carriers?" I asked while beating the eggs, trying not to spill them on the counter. Ariel was impatient and banged her plate on her high chair.

"I can hear that you're busy, so let's keep it short. We take care, for instance, of women who have breast cancer. We don't offer services for carriers. I can invite you to one of our seminars for women at high risk of getting breast cancer."

"And what if I organized a group for carriers? Would you be able to facilitate such a support group?" That's one of the ideas I had these last few nights and I was hoping the Association would cooperate.

"You know what? If you organize such a group, I'll assign one of our instructors and you could meet at our place. How does that sound?" Ariel's screaming grew louder and I could barely hear Lily.

"Sounds great. I'll keep in touch."

The rest of the evening was terrible. Adam and Ariel kept yelling, throwing food at each other and losing their minds. I was falling apart and asked Michael to come home immediately. I just wanted him to come and rescue me.

The moment he walked in, I got up, and without speaking a word, went into the bedroom. I closed the door behind me and lay in the dark. I heard Michael struggling in the bathroom with Ariel who refused to get into the shower and with Adam who refused to get out. After about an hour the house fell silent and Michael went into the room quietly.

"How are you?" he sat down and gently caressed me.

"You know how I am. I don't know what to do."

"There's nothing you can do. Just carry on like usual and have regular checkups. That's what we agreed, right?"

"Yes, but I can't just carry on like usual. I hate the office. I hate working there. If it weren't for Sarah, I would have lost my mind a long time ago. And I can't stand the kids. They keep shouting, crying and fighting. Ariel won't stay put for a second, Adam shouts and cries all the time." I moved his hand away and stood up angrily.

"He's getting used to having a little sister. It takes time." Michael followed me to the shower but kept a safe distance.

"How long?! It's not getting any better, just worse. His daycare teacher also said he's very sensitive and keeps crying all the time." I tried whispering so Adam didn't accidentally hear me.

"He's always been sensitive. He'll grow up and it'll get better."

"And what about work? I can't be there anymore." I wore my pajamas and pulled my hair back. A tired face looked back at me from the mirror. My eyes were puffy and I looked terrible.

"So quit."

"Oh, come on?! How can I quit? We have a mortgage and Ida." I turned the bathroom light off and went back to bed.

"We'll find a solution. Do what's good for you." Michael sat next to me and placed his hand on mine. I tried thinking what would make me happy but didn't know. I didn't know what I wanted. Everything seemed so unreal. Sometimes, I couldn't believe this was my reality, that this was how I was living my life. None of this was on my bucket list. And now, when I didn't have much time left, it was clear to me that something had to change. But I didn't know what exactly.

CHAPTER 20

"Shirley, are you coming?" Nathan shouted from the hallway. I took the brief and the documents I had prepared and joined him in the elevator. "The taxi is waiting downstairs."

"Great." It was 9:30 A.M. I hoped we would come back from the hostel early enough for me to make it to the daycare on time.

There was heavy traffic on the way to Jerusalem, but we weren't very late for the meeting. Joel came outside to greet us and invited us into the hostel. "We'll sit in the basement because it's quiet there. The kids have different activities and we don't want to disturb them."

The house was busy but organized. Young people kept climbing up and down the stairs. At times, it was hard to tell whether the person walking by was a patient or a therapist. We followed Joel down the stairs and entered a room that wasn't especially big and was filled with plastic chairs that used to be white.

I sat next to Nathan and looked at the parents around us. They seemed worried and tired. They looked at us with hope in their eyes. It was clear that if we didn't get the case dismissed, the hostel would shut down and the kids wouldn't have anywhere to go.

"These are our lawyers from Tel Aviv, Nathan and Shirley. They came to answer all your questions. So, please, ask away."

Nathan stood up in the middle of the room and had a big smile smeared on his face. He loved being at the center of attention but mostly liked hearing his own voice.

"Good morning everyone. As you know, I have prepared a detailed plea and filed all our statements. Shirley will now hand out copies of all the documents so that you have an idea of what we have done up to now."

I took out the copies and handed them out like a graceful stewardess. They thanked me and some even shook my hand.

"We're waiting for the hearing next month. We'll appreciate that as many parents as possible will attend." Some of the parents nodded and Nathan continued. "It's safe to assume that this hearing won't be the last, since we need to cross examine the witnesses which might take some time."

"When will there be a decision?" asked one of the moms who looked as if she had just raced in a marathon.

"It can take a year. The judicial system is not as fast as they show in the movies." Some of the parents laughed and Nathan seemed proud of himself.

"What will we do if they shut the place down? Where will our children go? It's hard when my son is home. We can't survive without the hostel," she continued, and the other parents nodded in consent.

"Don't worry, if it gets to that, we'll find a solution." Joel stood up and tried calming down the parents who were now talking to us and one another. The echo here was exceptionally loud and it was hard to figure out who was saying what. "Let's be quiet and listen to what our lawyer has to say."

It took a few minutes before Nathan could continue. "We believe the case will be dismissed, but we're still up against one of the biggest law firms in Jerusalem, and we shouldn't underestimate them. Next week, one of the news channels will come to cover the story and it would help if you agree to take part in it."

Nathan barely finished his sentence and the parents started talking again. From what I could pick up, it appeared that most of them agreed to participate, and asked us to keep them posted about the time and date. Joel promised to notify them and Nathan continued his one-man-show. "In short, the process will take some time, but we believe we can handle it so that the hostel remains in its current location. You may address Shirley with any question. All documents have the office contact information, feel free to reach out."

The parents still seemed uneasy; even when the meeting was over. They followed us out and kept offering their help. I thanked them and promised to contact them if I needed anything.

"We have to win this case," I whispered to myself on the way back, perhaps also to Nathan.

"Of course we will." Nathan looked back at one of the concerned parents, and then settled in his seat. "By the way, have you written the new motion in Samuel's new case?"

CHAPTER 21

I thought this would be yet another regular semi-annual checkup. But I left with an urgent reference for a breast ultrasound..

"Due to your history, we need to be on the safe side, although I think the lump might be breastfeeding related," he said. "I'll get the results. and then we'll see."

With trembling hands, I dialed Michael's number, who immediately offered to come with me. But I preferred having mom with me. I was scared of the results, but I was equally afraid of the test itself. After all, the word "biopsy" immediately makes you think of cancer.

My appointment was scheduled for the very next day. Apparently if you use the letter combination BRCA, things move a lot faster. I spent the night thinking of all the things they might find. Although the doctor said he thought it was benign, I still couldn't calm down. Doctors make mistakes. Cemeteries are probably filled with people who were told 'it's benign'. On the other hand, the test was frightening in itself. The thought that they would stick a needle in me, made me extremely anxious.

I didn't tell anyone in the office, except for Sarah, of course. She was asked to replace me in an urgent meeting with Samuel with yet another unnecessary dispute he got himself into.

"Do I need to pay?" I asked the receptionist who scanned the reference and then highlighted with a yellow marker the word 'urgent'.

"As a carrier, you don't need to pay for these tests. It's free for you."

"What a shame," I replied and thought that I would have been willing to pay if it meant not being a carrier.

Mom waited outside with Ariel, and I was taken into a dark room. I was asked to take my top off and wear a weird paper see-through apron, though I wasn't sure about its purpose. It didn't cover anything nor did it keep me warm.

The doctor came in and asked the technician to show her the file. I was trembling on the bed and couldn't calm down.

"Breathe," the technician said in a Russian accent, and I nodded but couldn't stop shaking. I could hear Ariel and mom sitting outside, and it soothed me. For a short moment I was able to concentrate on listening to Ariel and not think about where I was – in a hospital bed, moments before having a biopsy.

"I'm giving you a local anesthetic," the doctor felt my left breast and looked for the right spot. "Take a deep breath."

I was so nervous I couldn't speak, so I just closed my eyes and waited for it to be over. It wasn't so bad, but I felt the needle inside my body and the substance spreading in me.

When I opened my eyes the doctor held another needle, even scarier than the first. This time not even Ariel's screaming could distract me when the needle went into my breast and made weird clicking sounds.

She repeated that process, and I felt I was about to faint, even though I didn't feel the needle at all.

"I'm taking several samples," the doctor explained patiently, and the technician caressed my hand, trying to calm me down. "That's it, we're done," she said, and then I could actually breathe. "It seems it's just breast milk, so you have nothing to worry about. You'll have the results in two weeks."

For now, I thought. I have nothing to worry about, for now.

I stepped outside and hugged Ariel tightly.

"It's going to be fine sweetie," mom whispered and hugged me.

We stood in front of the secretary, three generations, all three of us crying, each for her own reasons.

CHAPTER 22

It was my birthday, and this time we asked Natalie to babysit so we could go out and celebrate. It was, after all, a big one – my 30th birthday; a perfectly legitimate reason to go out and have fun with my family. My biopsy results came in negative, which immediately brought joy back into my life after two sleepless weeks, in which I excruciatingly waited for a call from the doctor's office.

We met at a restaurant that mom particularly liked, and that also served food that was up to her new dietary standards which she up-held since getting sick. I wasn't sure whether the healthy and organic food (she bought at insane prices), actually improved her health, but if she believed it did, it was good enough for me. Jonathan joked about our inheritance being spent on organic carrots and juice machines. In response, mom sulked at him and Gabi added that we shouldn't count on an inheritance because they plan on enjoying life to the fullest..

When we got into the restaurant, I saw mom happily smiling next to Gabi. She had a loving look in her eyes. It was touching to see them. Their wedding was one of the most emotional moments in my life. The military chaplain almost fainted when she stood under the Chuppah with a red pants suit. For a minute, it seemed this last year was nothing more than a bad dream. She looked healthy and vital. Her short hair was the only give away, to those who knew her, that she had chemotherapy. After she got sick, her hair grew into thick curls and her straight hair disappeared. But she was still gorgeous and noble, and had a natural beauty I could only dream of. Michael once told me, that when he met my mother, he knew I had good genes. I wondered if he still felt the same.

I hugged her tightly and sat beside her. Mom took out a long white envelope and placed it in a bag with a small box. "I brought you a little something," she said. "I hope you like the card."

I opened the box. Inside was a thin golden necklace with a round pendent set with tiny diamonds.

"It's amazing, mom. Just what I like; gentle and beautiful. Thank you."

"I chose it, but Julie helped me," Gadi said proudly.

"Good job, I see mom started delegating her responsibilities" I kissed him and mom and then read the card.

I took the envelope out of the bag and slowly opened it. On a piece of lined paper (that she probably ripped out off one of Tommy's notebooks) was mom's handwriting:

"My one and only beloved daughter,

You have blessed me with thirty years of your light!

You were there through my most difficult moments. Mature, confident and loving, my rock.

I know you possess powers, that you may have inherited from your grandmother, you're a rare blend of sensitivity, humanity, wisdom and strength, that would surely help you throughout the following decades with your wonderful family.

I love you very much, my sweetheart, and wish you the best the world has to offer. I wish myself, to be with you for many more years. I'm so lucky to have you,

Mom.

P.S., I handwrote this so you can keep it for when I won't be around here, with you…"

I took a deep breath and hugged her so tightly. I hoped it would never end.

"So? Should we eat something?" Gabi interrupted our emotional outburst, it wasn't really his thing. To me, he always represented rationality. I would always ask for his advice about important issues and decisions I had to make.

When I would come back to Maccabim

on my weekend off from the university, we would sit in the kitchen and talk through the night. Gabi would pour himself a glass of whiskey (and keep the bottle close to him). We spoke about school, classes and actually, about everything. He would tell stories, lecture, and add some inappropriate jokes. We made a lot of decisions during those conversations, and I would wait for them the entire week.

However, the next day, on Friday morning, Gabi would wake me up so I could help out; sweep the front road, water the plants or just use fertilizer on the grass. Those were the moments during which I regretted coming home to visit, but in hindsight, I didn't regret them as much.

When the food came and everyone was busy with their own plates as well as tasting from others, I read the letter again. Mom had never written such words to me. It was the most poignant birthday card I ever got. I knew I would keep this letter close to me, forever.

Tommy sat next to mom and gently leaned his head on her. Mom caressed his hair and he closed his eyes like a kitten. He did this ever since he was a baby and never grew out of it. I guess it's one of the advantages of being the youngest in the family.

I really loved the necklace, and instantly wore it. But I loved the card even more. When we got back home, I put the letter in the drawer next to my bed. Then I took it out and read it again.

That night, I dreamt I was celebrating my birthday with all of my family. Tommy, Jonathan and Gabi sat and talked. Grandpa Yokannan spoke to Adam while Ariel ran around him. I looked for mom. I kept asking everyone where she was but no one knew. But then the door opened and she walked in. She wore a short blue dress, showing her long legs, her hair was like it used to be, strait shoulder-length with bangs. She came and hugged me. And we kept hugging one another while everyone around us disappeared. It was just the two of us and the world fell silent.

"Mom, are you asleep?" I opened my eyes and saw Adam standing next to me and looking at me. "I'm hungry."

I was pulled back to reality, and went to look for a snack-pack in the fridge. A new week had begun.

CHAPTER 23

"Listen, it's getting unbearable. That place isn't good for me. It's all stress and nerves. One good case isn't enough for me to survive that the office." Michael was pushing the stroller uphill. On Saturdays, when the weather was nice, the park was packed with parents trying to keep their kids busy. Adam ran around on the grass and Ariel tried breaking free from the stroller.

"So, quit." We stopped and I freed Ariel, who was now screaming.

"Come on, be serious."

"Seriously. What's the problem? You'll find another job."

"But we were talking about having another child. I don't want to postpone it. We don't know how long I have left." Ariel chased Adam and every now and then fell down.

"Stop saying these things. You're not sick and everything is fine. We can wait with the pregnancy until you find a different job and work for a couple of months."

"But I don't want to wait. I want to have another child now, so I can spend enough time with it. We don't know what's going to happen to me."

"Stop stressing for nothing. You still have time to find a different job." Michael looked at me desperately, and then turned to Adam who tried getting his ball back from Ariel.

"Of course I'm stressed. I want to finish having children as soon as possible, that's also what the doctors recommended. You realize that if something happens to me, you'll have to find someone else, right? You won't be able to handle them on your own."

"Now, you're talking."

"Stop fantasizing. You'll have to wait a bit until I actually die. Adam, come back here, stay close." Adam wouldn't listen and kept walking towards the petting zoo. Every time we came here, we had to visit the animals. When he was much younger and wanted to look closer at the animals, he would ask me to pick him up because he was afraid of them. Now, not only was he not scared, he actually tried feeding them. Ariel wasn't afraid of anything, and nearly shoved her hand into the sheep's mouth. I think the sheep was in fact scared of Ariel, because it ran away.

Even though Adam was two years older than Ariel, she gave him courage and he often followed her lead. When she wanted something, she was unstoppable. Ariel tried making the terrified sheep come back to the fence, but her yelling only scared the sheep more.

After a few hours outside, we came back home tired, but the kids were still hyped up. After lunch, they threw their toys around and the living room looked like a jungle gym. Ever since Ariel stopped taking her afternoon naps, we could no longer rest on Saturdays.

I looked at the oven, that was actually more useful as a clock. It was 2:30 P.M. How would I survive this day without a power-nap?

"I need to do some work," Michael said after having organized the dishes in the dishwasher.

"Go ahead. I also have something to go over, but I'm too tired." I vegged out on the sofa and Ariel sat next to me. Nathan asked me to have something ready for tomorrow, but I didn't even get a chance to look at the documents. Natalie was sick this week and I couldn't stay late at work. Mom worked a lot and couldn't help me. Gabi still hadn't found a job since they came back from Australia. He would occasionally pick them up from daycare, but he wasn't capable of being with both of them for more than an hour. It would also usually make him complain about my parenting, how many toys they had and how messy our home was. Sometimes, I'd prefer hearing Nathan complaining instead. Sitting there, feeling sorry for myself, made me realize that something had to change, the sooner the better.

"Come on, quit and that's it." I looked at Michael and the idea suddenly didn't seem so absurd.

"Ok, you're right," I heard myself saying.

Michael lifted his eyes at me, shocked. He probably wasn't expecting that answer, certainly not hearing the words 'you're right'.

"I'll talk to Sarah. Her parents have a friend named Alice, who has a small office in north Tel Aviv. She told me really good things about her. Maybe she could hook me up with something. It's closer, so it's also a shorter drive to work."

"Good, go for it."

"If we're going to wait on having another child, then I'll schedule an appointment with Dr. Gidron to get back on the pill. I also wanted to talk to him about that procedure I told you about."

"What procedure?"

"We start an IVF process and then choose an embryo that doesn't have the cancer gene."

"Oh, right. Isn't that dangerous?"

"Not more than any other IVF procedure millions of women have every year. If we're going to postpone having a child, we should go through with it."

"Ok, ask him, and we'll see."

At night, I turned it over and over in my mind. Maybe things won't be different in a new place. Maybe they'll also have a problem with my work-hours. I realized I had to make a change, but maybe finding a new job, wasn't enough. I couldn't keep being miserable all the time. It was nice working with Sarah, and the ALUT case was also very important to me. But it wasn't enough. I decided that, first I should find a new job and only if things don't work out, I'll plan my next step.

There was something about having this gene that made me reconsider things, realize that I don't have time to waste on things that's weren't important to me or be where I wasn't happy. I didn't want to wait for retirement to do the things I wanted, because I didn't know if I would even have time to retire.

These thoughts kept racing through my mind until the first rays of sun lit the room. I decided to give up sleeping and get ready. I wanted to get to the office and talk to Sarah. I also wanted to update my CV, so she could give it to her parents' friend. I was so concentrated on these thoughts that refused to leave me, that only when I reached the office, did I notice the radio was off the entire drive to Tel Aviv.

CHAPTER 24

"Hi, I'm calling from Alice Kaplan's office. Am I speaking with Shirley?"

"Yes."

"Good morning, Alice would like to schedule a meeting with you. Can you come tomorrow at 10:40 A.M.?" I couldn't believe they called me so soon.

I checked my schedule and replied, "sure."

"Great, I'll send you an email with our address, just confirm you've received it. See you tomorrow."

Wow. It was only yesterday that Sarah had given them my CV. This was a good sign. After calling Michael and excitedly telling him about the news, I quickly went to Sarah's office and closed the door behind me.

"Alice's office called and we scheduled a meeting for tomorrow. Did you tell her not to tell anyone? I can't have Nathan hearing about this until it's a done deal."

"Yes, of course I told her. She promised to be discrete."

"Perfect. I really hope this works out."

"How can you abandon me here with all these lunatics?!" Sarah dramatically sprawled on her desk and almost spilled her coffee. "Don't leave me."

"Sorry… I can't handle having lunatics at work. I have enough of them at home."

"Stop it. Your kids are adorable."

"Look at you, such an expert. Wait until you have kids of your own." I thanked her for her help and went back to my office.

Even though I was now working more hours, I still had the smallest office next to the interns' room. I hated it and felt as if I was being punished. I sat down and started thinking what would I say tomorrow at my meeting with Alice. Her being friends with Sarah's parents, wouldn't help me. I had to make a good first impression and close the deal as soon as possible.

When I returned home, I found mom playing on the carpet with the children. Ariel was sitting on her lap and Adam was running around with plastic work tools. He was wearing a yellow Bob the Builder helmet and tinkered around with his push car. "Did you see the surgeon I recommended you?" mom asked as I sat next to her on the carpet.

"Yes. Two weeks ago. He said everything was fine and told me to have an MRI." It was actually nice that carriers were eligible to have such expensive tests. Sarah told me that even though her mother already had breast cancer, she couldn't have an MRI. I tried really hard finding something positive about this screwed up gene.

"And did you make an appointment?"

"The insurance company needs to call me back." I kissed Ariel, who in return pulled on what hair I had left after my postpartum hair-loss.

"Good, it's important. Did they also tell you to take blood tests?"

"Yes." These tests were my only chance for an early diagnosis, and I wasn't planning on skipping a single one.

"Great." Mom looked relaxed after I answered all her questions about my bi-annual checkup.

I looked at the three of them, and my heart expanded with joy. Despite all my anxieties, here she was, with us, playing with her grandchildren. All we need is a few more cancer-free years and then we'll know it's behind us. I have everything I need, and having a new job made things seem better.

Ariel kissed mom on the nose, she laughed out loud and asked that I take a picture of them together. Only when I took the picture did I notice that Ariel has mom's ears. Never mind, I thought, she can hide them when her hair grows longer.

Adam came back with his push car and started banging on it with his hammer. There's nothing like coming back to a quiet home after a long day at work. I had to make something to eat – no way around it. Luckily, Adam wanted "Cathy's omelet", I stood next to her and tried telling her about my interview. However, as usual, Ariel found something dangerous to do the moment you looked away. I found her lifting the push car up on the table and trying to climb it. I missed the days she would stay in one place.

***

I decided to take the morning off, and told Nathan I wasn't feeling well and will come in later. I think he suspected I was pregnant or something of the sort, but was too scared to ask. It's better this way. I woke the children up, got ready and started walking to the daycare.

The weather was nice and they were happy to walk to the daycare. I had forgotten how fun it was spending a stress-free morning with them, and mostly, having an hour for myself at home. I couldn't wait to drop them off in daycare and have some 'me time'. I hadn't had time for myself in four years, since Adam was born. Besides, it was nice staying home in the middle of the week for no particular reason.

Ariel grabbed Adam's hand and they walked together. Every now and then he would stop and show her something on the ground or the fence. Ariel looked at him with an admiration, in a way only a little sister could. I was overwhelmed with warm feelings. These moments were clearly worth it. I really felt like canceling my interview and my appointment at the gynecologist and just have another child. However, the thought of having to spend another year with Nathan made me sick to my stomach, and I decided there was no other choice but finding a new law firm. Who would hire a pregnant lawyer? It was hard enough finding a job with two children, let alone while being pregnant.

Tammy, the daycare teacher, was exceptionally happy this morning. "It's so wonderful to see you!" Tammy hugged me with surprising enthusiasm, "I never see you since you went back to work."

"Yes, I know. I come home late."

"I see Natalie every now and then. She's really sweet. We have moms looking for a babysitter, does she have any free days?"

"I don't think so." That's the last thing I needed, someone stealing Natalie from me. I would have given Michael's number before I gave hers.

"OK, if she does have some free time, let me know."

"Definitely." That is, I will definitely not.

I said goodbye to the kids, actually just Adam, because Ariel hung up her bag immediately and ran to play with her friends in the ball pit. Adam whined a bit, and Tammy made point of mentioning that he wasn't used to seeing me leave in the morning because I never take him to daycare.

I walked slowly back home, and rehearsed some sentences I thought were important to mention in my interview with Alice. I decided emphasizing that I wanted to work closer to home, rather than saying something negative about my current firm. After all, she might ask Nathan for references.

My alone time passed too quickly, and was mostly wasted on choosing the right outfit for the interview. I was looking for something that didn't seem like I was trying too hard, but would still look professional. I chose a black knee-length skirt, and a buttoned eggplant-colored shirt. I even wore high heels.

When I entered the building, I could already feel there was something different about this place. It was a small and modest office building, nothing like the monstrous skyscraper I worked in. I went up to the third floor and rang the buzzer. A middle-aged woman opened the door, she was dressed in jeans and a worn-out ACDC shirt. Next to the office front door was a small sitting area with two long powder-blue fabric sofas and a long wooden table. On the table was an empty pickle jar with flowers that seemed to have been picked from the backyard. There was a packed bookcase behind one of the sofas. It was as if I had walked into someone's living room.

"Hey, I'm Shirley. I have a meeting with Alice." I threw a quick look at the sign again, to make sure I was in the right place. It said "Kaplan & Associates, law firm." This was it.

"Nice to meet you, Shirley, I'm Alice. Our secretary is off today, so we're trying to figure things out. Let's go into my office and talk a bit." This wasn't a good start. I didn't recognize Alice, who looked completely different from her picture on their website.

"With pleasure." I followed her and thought it was pointless wasting those thirty minutes on choosing this buttoned shirt. Maybe this was her day off. On our way to her office we walked by a few offices and every lawyer we passed by, smiled and said hello. One of the lawyers even introduced herself. The office was quiet and no one was shouting across the hall. I suddenly noticed there were only women in the office, which might have explained why it was so quiet.

"Would you like anything to drink?" Alice pointed at the small kitchen.

"Thanks." I took a glass of water while she waited by the door. Then, I kept following her, until we reached the last room in the office.

It was a spacious room with a large desk, but Alice sat on the sofa at the corner of the room and pointed at the armchair next to it. Her green All Star shoes stood out against the purple sofa. I have never seen a lawyer coming to the office wearing All Stars. I sat down and placed the cup on a small round straw table. The office was so much warmer and more pleasant than other rooms I have seen in different law firms.

"So, I understand you're looking for a job."

"Yes, I'm currently working with Sarah, but I'm looking to make a change. I heard good things about you and thought I could learn a lot from you."

"Thank you. Sarah also told me great things about you, but I'm afraid she's not up to date about the changes I have made. I don't work as much in the office, because about six months ago I decided to focus on my PhD. I always wanted to be Dr. Kaplan."

"That's great," I smiled at her and immediately started thinking how the changes she made would affect me. The thought about this job as a life vest that kept me afloat throughout the last week, but now I felt as if I was drowning again. I tried to keep smiling and hide the disappointment growing inside of me.

"Actually, you came right on time. I'm looking for a research assistant and also someone who can help me with some cases I still have open. We will obviously get new cases, but I'll try not to take on too many. I'm not sure that's what you're looking for, but if you're willing to consider it, I'd love working with you. From what I heard and read, you'll be a great addition here."

"It really isn't what I had in mind, but it actually sounds excellent." My smile grew wider and I could breathe again.

"I hope you realize I can't pay you like they do in big firms, right?" she didn't wait for my response, "of course you'll get all the other benefits. Our work hours are convenient and the other lawyers here are lovely. How does that sound?"

"It sounds wonderful. I would obviously have to give my 6-week-notice, so I can start then. Is that OK?"

"Of course. Take all the time you need. No rush. Just let me know the date. Come, I'll show you where you'll be working." Alice stood up and I followed her enthusiastically.

We started walking back, towards the entrance, and she stopped in front of a closed door, "take a look, this is going to be your new office." She opened the door and I saw a small office with two desks. The one next to the window was covered with papers and dossiers; it was clearly taken. The second table was closer to the door, and was empty and clean.

"Is this the new girl? Nice to meet you, I'm Anna." A young woman, about my age, walked into the office and shook my hand. She held in her other hand a large file full of papers. Anna wore the usual lawyer uniform – a white buttoned shirt and tailored black pants. Completely different from Alice. There was something familiar about it. But then I noticed she was wearing red flip flops.

Anna must have noticed me looking. "Ah, I hate wearing high heels. When I'm in the office I wear these, they're super comfortable."

"You are completely right. Nice to meet you, I'm Shirley. And yes, I hope I'm the new girl." I peeked at Alice and saw she was nodding in approval. Everything suddenly seemed so simple.

"OK, I'll leave you two to chat. I'm off to a meeting." Alice turned to me, "It was a pleasure meeting you and I look forward to hearing from you."

I spent half an hour with Anna and found out she was absolutely charming. She was a mother of two girls, slightly younger than my own, and told me that the work hours were 9 to 3, and usually they didn't have to bring their work back home.

"We're all moms here. Except for Alice, she doesn't have kids." Anna said. "She's nice but it's a bit difficult working with her."

After working with Nathan, I wasn't so easily scared, but I wanted to hear more. "What do you mean by 'difficult'?"

"Look, she's very professional and has a lot of experience. She even served as a judge for a while. But she's not an easy person. She demands from others exactly what she demands of herself."

"Like what?" she made me worry, I needed to know what I was getting into. I didn't want to repeat the same mistake I made when I took the position in Nathan's firm just because I couldn't believe I would find something better.

"When you write something and send it to her, it should be well-written and final. She won't accept a draft that needs editing. You have to stick to citation rules and add all references. She expects a finished product."

"OK," it sounded strict yet doable. "What else?"

"She comes in late and stays late, so she sends a lot of emails at strange hours. Don't be surprised if you come in the morning and find a huge pile of papers on your desk."

"Anything's better than my current job."

"Great. I would love it if you came. I get bored alone in this room." Anna smiled and her phone rang. I waved goodbye and left.

I couldn't wait to get back to Nathan's office; just so I could tell him I found a different place and was leaving. The salary wasn't important to me, as long as I could leave that tiny office and stressful environment.

I called mom before I had even left the building.

"I just finished. There's such a nice atmosphere there, you won't believe it. Everything is calm and quiet. Everyone is so nice. They're actually all women, and they're so friendly. Also, most of them are moms. And work is until 3 P.M. And it's much closer to home. I'm just so excited to get started."

"That's great, sweetie. I'm happy to hear it, but I'm about to have a conference meeting in a few minutes and everyone is already here."

"OK, we'll talk later."

Mom hung up and I called Michael, who was very happy and gave his blessing. "Never mind about the money, as long as you're happy."

"I will be happy. It seems like a great place for me."

It was the first time in many months that I walked into the office with a smile.

Nathan actually handled the news well and asked me to write a resignation letter. He asked that I brief Sarah on all my cases and we set my final date at work. No one could have been as happy as I was when I signed that document.

CHAPTER 25

"Hey, mom told me some guy tried hitting you? What happened?" I called Tommy on my way home from the office so we could talk quietly. I wanted to hear all the details. Mom called in the afternoon and sounded really upset. She told me someone attacked Tommy last night.

"Dan and I were at a scouts' meeting."

"Wait, is this actually scouts, or IGI again?" when mom told me he was at a scouts' meeting I thought he was hiding something again.

"No, this time it really was scouts."

"OK, go on." I was truly surprised.

"So, yesterday was the first introduction meeting between two different groups, since they're supposed to merge into one unit in the army. We were planning to go to the beach in Herzliya. I just joined them to keep Dan company." Tommy sounded really calm.

"OK," I replied and waited to hear the rest. Dan was Tom's best friend, which explained Tom's sudden interest in the scouts' activities.

"When we finished, we looked for something to eat and found a kiosk. We walked in and after us came in 3 or 4 drunk Russians. They were about our age, and started asking us where did we come from and what were we doing. They teased us and were probably looking to start a fight. Frankly, I couldn't keep quiet and smarted off something. That only made them angrier." I didn't speak a word and let Tommy finish his story.

"Dan noticed things were going south, and he started taking everyone outside. We walked away and called a big taxi for the other group. One by one they got into the car. While I was standing next to the taxi, someone threw a glass bottle that smashed on the car, just an inch away from my head. I turned around and saw the Russians walking towards me, the biggest one was holding a metal rod." Tommy sounded as if he was telling something that happened to someone else. If it were me, I wouldn't have been able to speak in complete sentences.

"Sounds terrifying, how did you get out of there?"

"The taxi driver stepped out of the car, he was angry and scared them away. I was a bit shocked from it all, but Dan told me to get quickly into the taxi and hide. Then the driver took me back home."

"Good thing that driver was there, he literally saved you. And also sounds like Dan is a good friend." I tried sounding calm.

"Right."

"But you have to be careful with what you say. You're not in Australia anymore."

"Yes, I realize it now."

"OK, I need to go. I'm at the kids' daycare. Stay out of trouble." I grabbed my purse from the passenger seat and started running.

CHAPTER 26

For some reason, my insurance company thought it was a good idea to schedule my MRI at a hospital in Jerusalem hospital. I was very nervous about the test and was happy that Michael took the day off and came with me. We left early in the morning thanks to Natalie who came to take the children to daycare. By the time we reached the clinic at 9 A.M., I was irritated any hungry. I still couldn't figure out why I had to fast before having the test.

After registering and the usual wait, I went into the doctor's office and Michael stayed in the waiting room.

The doctor inserted an IV tube to inject the dye, and asked me to remove my top and wear a hospital robe with the open side in front. I tried covering myself as much as I could and went into the exam room. In the middle of the frozen room stood a huge machine. I started shivering. Maybe because I was cold or scared, or maybe both. Although I was taken to the bathroom before, I felt I had to go again, but it was too late.

"Do you have a blanket or something? I'm really cold," I said to Boris, the technician, who instructed me to lay on my tummy on a weird plastic device and place my hands next to my head. A woman came in and arranged my breasts so that each was respectfully inserted into a separate plastic hole. The nurse connected me to an IV hanging on a device by the bed side and shoved yellow earplugs into my ears. I lay with my eyes closed and took slow breaths to calm myself down.

"We'll cover you soon," he replied. "No moving please."

They covered me with a blanket, but it was no use. I was still freezing. "It's warmer inside the machine," a female voice calmed me down.

After the preparations were over, I heard Boris' muffled voice, "we're moving you into the machine. You have a rescue button in your hand." I felt something being shoved into my hand "But if you press it, we need to stop the test, and that's a problem." Boris pushed the bed and I felt the machine closing in on me.

"Ok," I answered quietly and was doubtful whether anyone heard me. I heard a door close.

I opened my eyes and found out there was a mirror through which I could see the technicians' room. I saw Boris get into the room and sit down.

"We're starting," I heard a voice from inside the machine. Boris didn't wait for an answer.

A loud ticking noise scared me for a moment. The machine started making loud noises that not even the earplugs could block. I took a deep breath and tried really hard not to move. The technicians were talking to each other (I thought I could see Boris snacking on a yogurt). To them, this was another day at the office. To me, this was a fateful day. Today might be when they find my tumor, I thought to myself, and then everything would change. I wouldn't be able to start a new job, and struggle juggling two kids with all the treatments. I might even need a surgery. It would definitely make mom sad. I didn't want her to feel guilty. I felt a tear roll down my frozen cheek.

I shut my eyes. I have to stop, I thought to myself. I'm panicking for no reason. I'll wait for the results before I start freaking out. I tried calming myself down, but felt one tear following another. And another. And another. I tried thinking how I would react when I get the results. Would they send it by mail or call me? If they find something, they'll probably call.

I felt the machine closing in on me and all I wanted was to get up and run away. I needed to get out. Escape. I looked at the technicians sitting in the control room and drinking out of cheap plastic cups. No one looked in my direction. I almost pressed the button, but just before doing it, I thought about all the trouble I would have to go through to come again to Jerusalem. The drive, the kids, the traffic, parking. I couldn't go through all of it again. I didn't have a watch so I couldn't tell how much time had passed. It felt like eternity. I hoped that at least half of the test was behind me.

"Shirley, is everything all right?" the machine fell silent and I could only hear Boris' muffled voice.

"Yes," I whispered.

"Let's keep going. We don't have much left. I'm starting to inject the contrast dye."

I took a deep breath and tried finding something else to think about. I felt the liquid seeping into my veins. It hurt, but I couldn't move. Why did no one tell me it hurt?

I decided to think about all the tasks I had to brief Sarah about. There was a new file I was recently assigned and barely had time to start reading, and summaries I needed to write, and two depositions. Surprisingly, thinking about work soothed me. Still, my thoughts occasionally wandered back to the test. Mostly to its potential outcome. The doctor explained that they get plenty of false positives results because this test is very sensitive. So, regardless of what happens, I would have to follow up on this checkup. I couldn't distract myself any longer so I tried focusing on the strange sounds the machine was making. I couldn't find a certain rhythm to it, but it helped killing time.

The machine fell silent, but I couldn't tell what was happening so I was afraid to move. I opened my eyes and the technicians' room was empty. I heard a door open and then someone pulled the bed out. I took a deep breath, a real one this time. That's it, the nightmare was over. Boris disconnected my IV and taped a cotton ball over it.

"You can get up," he took the blanket off me and threw it into a big basket at the corner of the room.

I leaned on my hands and lifted myself up. At the first chance I got, I closed the robe and slowly slid off the bed. I took my shirt and bra from my assigned locker and changed as fast as I could. When I walked back into the waiting room, I found Michael sitting on a chair at what seemed to be, the most remote corner he could find.

He stood up when he saw me and immediately approached me. I clung on to his chest and he hugged me. We stood in the middle of the hall, Michael holding on to my bag and me, hiding between his arms, forcing myself not to collapse in front of everyone.

"Come on, let's get out of here," I said when I felt I had calmed down a bit. "I'm starving, should we grab a bite?"

"I'd love to. I haven't eaten anything today except for a doughnut."

I wanted to ask him when did he get a chance to eat, but instead, I chose to tell him what happened in there. "You can't even imagine how terrible that test is. That machine is insanely loud and although they stuck earplugs in my ears, it was awful. And staying like that for half an hour, without moving. It felt like forever."

"Come on, you're passed it. The most important thing is that we get good results."

"This still hurts," I took off the cotton ball and could tell the bleeding stopped. "I hope they don't find anything."

We walked towards the elevator but then I stopped. "Oh, I didn't ask how we get the results."

"I did. They send by mail within three weeks." Michael kept walking. He was pretty bad at navigating, but it was obvious that if someone would know how to get to the cafeteria, it could only be him.

"It's such a long time. How can I wait for three weeks? Do you think that if the results are bad, they call first? After all, if I have cancer, every day counts, right? They'll probably call if something's wrong. Right?"

"Shirley," he stopped and looked at me. He would only use my name when I really annoyed him. "I'm sorry, but I really don't have a clue. They only said that the results would be sent by mail within three weeks."

We walked into the busy lobby. Some of the people wore hospital pajamas and the others were visitors. There was a small coffee cart in the center of the hall. All the sandwiches had tomatoes, so I asked for a butter croissant (point me to the idiot who decided all sandwiches needed to have tomatoes in them?) Michael took another doughnut, despite my disapproving expression.

We sat on the bar stools facing the view outside. The hospital was built at a beautiful location in the mountains. I ate my sticky croissant in silence, and every now and then sipped my diet coke. It was just like the old days, when we would sit together at the university cafeteria between classes, no real worries. Our biggest concern was how much we would score on the criminal law course. I would go back to those times in a heartbeat.

Michael and I met on our first day at the university and ever since then, we've been together. We got married on our third year and after our internship we bought a small apartment in Herzliya. I wonder if Michael would have married me if he knew about my defective gene. When I asked him once, he said that he would, but I guess I'll never know.

I thought about how the genetic test had changed my life. Just the thought of having to take that terrible MRI every year, made me cringe. On the other hand, if that's what it takes to keep me alive, then it's worth it.

"And what if they find something?" I asked Michael quietly, while still looking at the Jerusalem view.

"They won't." Michael crumpled the doughnut napkin into a ball and shoved it into the ashtray on the table. He stood up.

"But what if they do?" I looked at him and tried so hard not to cry in the middle of the cafeteria.

"If they find something, which they won't, then we'll deal with it. Come on, let's go."

"You make it sound so simple. But it really isn't. One day I'll take the test and they'll tell me that they found something. If it's not this test, then it'll be the next. And if not on the next one then on the one after that. It's a matter of time, but it's almost a sure thing."

"That's not true. You were the one who told me that there are carriers who didn't get sick." Michael started walking and I followed.

"Didn't get sick in the meantime. I repeat, in the meantime."

"But there are such carriers. So, we can't know for sure what would happen." Michael kept walking and I walked slowly behind him.

"If you had an 80% chance of winning the lottery, you would by a ticket, right?" I stood and Michael turned to me, "because you would know that you have a pretty good chance at winning. This is just like that."

"It's not the same thing Shirley. Are you coming?"

"You don't realize what it's like living like this. Waiting for an inevitable nightmare. It goes both for me and my mother. They say that only after 5 cancer-free years she'll get off the danger list, but it's barely been two years."

"Exactly. So let it go and live your life. You have to move on."

"I can't move on. It's a part of me, wherever I go. This ghost, haunting me. This anxiety from the cancer, that one day will strike. You can't even begin to understand what's going on through my mind."

"That's true. But maybe we can talk about it in the car on our way home?"

"OK," I said, but I was too tired to try and explain myself again. Michael spent our drive back home taking work calls and I tried thinking who should I call first if the results are bad. By the time we got home I had already decided that I would call Michael. Not because there was anything he could do, but mostly so I could tell him: "I told you so."

CHAPTER 27

My last month at Nathan's office went by quickly. I sat with Sarah as much as possible and introduced her to all my clients. Sarah occasionally complained, but was mostly supportive. The MRI results came in too, and according to the doctor, everything was fine (if a benign finding could be referred to as 'fine'. I preferred they found nothing at all).

The kids' daycares were closed for the summer, so Natalie would come every morning. I notified Alice's office that I would start working at the beginning of the school year. Alice understood and even suggested that I start a few days later, so Adam could adjust to his new daycare. I was shocked at first, and then willingly accepted.

On my last day at the office, Nathan decided he would go the extra mile, and host a festive goodbye lunch party for me at a good restaurant. That was the first and last time I ate with Nathan (and the second partner, who still wouldn't talk to me).

"As you all know," Nathan stood and enjoyed the attention. "Shirley is leaving us today."

"Bad girl" Sarah whispered to me, and I didn't even bother trying to conceal my huge smile.

"We can say a lot of good things about Shirley," Nathan continued ceremoniously, "but we can also say other things." I was shocked but kept quiet. Sarah looked at me with a horrified expression. "She was one of the first lawyers to join us when we started the firm, and took a big part in shaping it as you know it today. She's moving on and we wish her all the best." He raised his wine glass and everyone joined him.

"Thank you very much for everything," I said when I was asked to say a few words and didn't have much of a choice. What I really wanted to say was that it was a stressful period in my life that made me think every day about changing a career. But I was able to put things delicately. "It was a special period of time, and maybe, we'll work together again sometime."

Nathan gave me a present from the partners – a jewelry box. If he would have bothered to try and get to know me, he would have known that it was the most redundant gift he could have given me. I only had the necklace mom gave me and I wore it all the time.

I had a few free days before starting my new job, which I spent desperately trying to keep two small kids busy. Michael took a few days off and we both ran from one air-conditioned place to another, in an attempt to keep our sanity. We were exhausted and crashed into our beds every evening. Mom promised to help me one of these days, but something would always come up at work. Her employees were also away with their children.

One afternoon I was suddenly hungry and asked Michael to get me a pita with shawarma. I swallowed the entire thing within seconds. After I soothed my crazy appetite, I realized how strange it was. In the evening I sent Michael for yet another mission, this time to the pharmacy.

The next morning I woke Michael up with a cup of coffee and a white stick with two blue stripes.

CHAPTER 28

"Hello, this is Shirley Moshe speaking. I have an appointment with Dr. Gidron in two weeks from now. I wanted to know if I could perhaps have an earlier appointment? I just found out I'm pregnant so it's a bit urgent." I opened the door, and told mom to come in. She was glowing with joy. I called her earlier that morning to tell her and she said she would come after work.

"Congratulations. I don't have any available appointments at the moment, but I'll write down your number and get back to you if I have any cancellations."

"Thank you. It would be great if I could come in earlier."

I gave the secretary my phone number and hung up. I turned to hug mom, who was already hugging Adam and Ariel. They proudly showed her all their drawings. They were both covered in markers on every imaginable spot, but it was a small price to pay for a few minutes of silence.

"So, how are you feeling?" mom asked.

"The same, I think. It's probably still very early." I took her aside because I didn't want the kids to know. Adam was old enough to understand the word 'pregnancy.' Half of the moms in daycare were pregnant and the other half had just given birth. "Let's talk in the kitchen."

"What's the matter?"

"I wasn't planning on getting pregnant now, mom. I planned on checking with Dr. Gidron about the procedure I told you about. Where they choose a healthy fetus, without the gene. And in any case, I'm supposed to start a new job in a week. And this apartment isn't big enough for three children. You know I wanted another child, but this really is a bad time."

"It's never a good time," mom hugged me tightly and kissed my forehead. She was taller than me and I still felt like a little girl when I was with her. She told me that when I was younger, I asked if she could give me her clothes when she died. We would joke that to this day, her clothes were too big for me.

"I know, but it's not really what I planned. I wanted to make sure that I hadn't passed on the gene to anyone else. I want to save Adam and Ariel from this thing. I wanted to at least to spare our next child this concern. How can I live with myself knowing that I could have stopped the gene from passing on and didn't?"

"You don't know whether it did. Maybe none of them got it."

"Oh come on, what are the chances that all three don't get it?"

"There's always a chance. Don't think about it now. Just focus on the things that can be helped. Like buying a new apartment."

"Yes. And what about Alice? What do I tell her? 'Hey, Alice. In a few months I'll be on maternity leave.' She'll kill me. She's been waiting for me for almost two months, and now I'm pregnant?"

"You said she was nice, right? So, she'll understand. And in any case, you would have gotten pregnant in a few months. It's just a bit sooner than expected. She'll get over it."

"She'll fire me, and I haven't even started yet." Michael opened the door and came in with the groceries. The kids ran to him and yelled "Popsicle! Popsicle!" and tried looking through the bags for the popsicles he had promised them. They weren't familiar with the term 'patience'.

"Hey Cathy, how are you?" Michael loved mom, and it was mutual.

"Everything's great." Her smile said 'I know.' Mom kissed him on the cheek and then wiped off the lipstick. "Come, kids, sit at the table and eat nicely."

They followed her, each holding their popsicle, like goslings following mother goose. Adam sat on the chair and Ariel insisted on sitting on mom. I told mom she would get dirty, but she didn't care. She ignored me and placed Ariel on her knees. I kept the wipes close by. Chocolate popsicles are infamous for staining. I should know.

I looked at them while Michael put the groceries away. The kids looked at mom with admiration. They smiled and were on their best behavior. Ariel even sat in one place for more than 5 minutes. At that moment I thought things might actually work out. Maybe we can handle three kids. The only question that remained unanswered was what would we eat when Alice fires me?

CHAPTER 29

It was my first day at the new office. I dressed as well as I could and even wore some makeup. I asked Michael to replace me and be with Adam that morning, since the first days in his new daycare were harder than expected.

I came in unusually early, even for me, and the office was still empty. Only Dina, the elderly secretary Anna told me about, was there. She was tough but nice. At least, that's what Anna had told me.

"Welcome," I thought I saw a smile, but it was a faint one. "I prepared some stationary on your desk. If you're missing anything, there's a supply closet behind me with everything you'll need."

"Thank you." I smiled and headed to my office. Anna told me that I shouldn't annoy Dina by asking too many questions. That was one of the first pointers she gave me.

I walked into my new office (finally, an actual room and not a jail cell). There were a few pens on the desk, two legal pads, that for some reason, all lawyers use. Beside them was a white mug wrapped in cellophane. The mug said "Shirley", and on a note attached to it "welcome to Kaplan & Associates.'" I opened it with excitement and went to make some tea in my new mug. When I waited for the water to boil, Anna came in with one of the lawyers I saw the last time I was here.

"Hey, Shirley, it's so great to have you. This is Lea. She's in charge of real estate." It was a good thing Anna introduced us, because I couldn't remember her name.

"Hi, nice to meet you," we formally shook hands. "Thank you for the present, it was a pleasant surprise."

"You're welcome. We each have a mug with our name, spares us doing the dishes. It was Dina's idea." Anna made a silly face and laughed. Lia took a cookie and left, I waited for Anna to make her coffee. We went back to our shared room and I waited for Alice to come and give me something useful to do.

After an hour, Dina told me Alice was running late, so I decided to use this free time to make some phone calls I was prevented from making while I was home with the kids. Calling the insurance company requires time and patience; which I had none of while the kids were on their summer vacation.

"Dr. Gidron's clinic," his secretary picked up almost immediately.

"Good morning. I have a slightly weird request. Dr. Gidron sent me to take some blood tests. He made note that I was a BRCA1 carrier. I would like to ask that you erase that from my file."

"What? What do you mean?"

"I don't want my file to say that I'm a carrier because it might make things complicated for me. So, I need you to erase that sentence for me," I tried again.

"Erase the blood test request from your file?" she asked. That's it. I gave up.

"Could you please ask him to call me back?" That was probably the quickest way to resolve the issue.

The secretary wrote down my details and all I could do was hope that she gave him my message. No one explained to me what it meant having that comment on my file, and it made me anxious. I decided it was best not having that comment at all. Everybody kept saying it was discrete genetic information, but it's written everywhere. So how was it discrete exactly?

I hung up and charged my phone. Anna approached me and sat

on one of the chairs in front of my desk. "Sorry to barge in, but I couldn't help hearing your conversation."

"It's fine," I smiled and tried making Anna feel like everything was OK. In any case, I wanted to consult with her about when and how I should tell Alice I was pregnant.

I tried not talking to anyone about being a carrier. Not just because I didn't want the kids to hear about it, but mostly because it was exhausting. People didn't really know what to say. It was even worse when they started recommending different things and sending me every possible article about it.

Anna asked if I knew Mia Miller, a lawyer from the Cohen & Associates firm. I shook my head no. "She also found out she was a carrier a few years ago. I was the opposing council on a case we had, and she was really nice. She just had the surgery, which is how I found out. If you want, I could ask her if you can talk to her. Maybe she can help you."

"That would be great, thank you."

"With pleasure." Anna smiled and went back to reading an injunction file.

My thoughts wandered off and far from the office. But it was my first day and it was important to make a good first impression. When Alice came in, she handed me two files and asked that I read them carefully and familiarize myself with the details. She asked Dina to schedule meetings with the clients two weeks from now, so I would have enough time to catch up. I immediately thought that if this were Nathan, I would have gotten the files on our way to the meeting.

**

That very evening, Anna gave me Mia's phone number and we scheduled to meet the next day for lunch. We found a nice café in a small commercial center, where mostly senior citizens sat at this time of the day. Mia said I would recognize her by her glasses, and sure enough, when I walked into the café, I saw her sitting by the table with a menu. Big red glasses weren't something you could miss. She had a short and edgy blond haircut and was dressed as if she were nominated for an Oscar no less; a fitting black dress and silver high heels. I now understood what Anna meant when she said Mia was an impressive woman.

"Hi, I'm Shirley." I sat in front of her and shook her hand. Each of her fingernails was painted in a different color.

"Nice to meet you. Have you been working at Alice's for a long time?"

"About two days," I opened the menu and looked for something light yet satisfying.

"So, when did you find out about the gene?" Mia asked without beating around the bush.

"Almost two years ago. That's what the universe gave me for my 29th birthday. And you?"

"About five years ago. I took the test because my mom passed away from cancer at a young age. They didn't have the genetic tests back then."

"Did you do you anything about it, other than the regular checkups?"

"I removed my ovaries about a year ago. I decided not to touch my breasts. Seemed a bit unnecessary."

"I was also thinking about removing my ovaries. But only when I turn 40. How old are you?"

"I'm forty-three, just a bit older than you." Mia smiled. She looked much younger, which surprised me since I knew early menopause kicks in after the surgery. It seems that it didn't affect her much.

"A bit, but I'm not as young as I look."

"Are you keeping up with your regular checkups?" When she asked this question, Mia reminded me of my mom.

"I try." These checkups became challenging with me being pregnant, but I didn't think this was a good time to share this information with Mia.

"Good. That's the most important thing. You should have a checkup every 6 months. When you're done having children, you should just go for it, remove your ovaries. Don't wait. What cancer do you have in the family?"

"My mom had ovarian cancer, but she's fine now."

"No such thing as fine with ovarian cancer."

"What do you mean?" I was shocked by what she had said. I knew there was a chance it would come back, but it's been two and a half years since mom was told she was cancer-free.

"That thing always comes back. Always. I don't know anyone who survived that type of cancer." A waitress came to take our order. Mia inquired about their vegan options.

I didn't know what to say. Ever since mom finished her treatments, she was back to her regular self. She even went on a ski vacation. She worked a lot and visited Gabi in Australia. Everything was back to normal. Gabi was also about to start a new job. Tommy started having friends at school and preparing for his GMATs. Jonathan finished his military service and started considering his options. Mom was even talking about buying an apartment and settling down somewhere once Tommy graduates from high-school. After such a long time, things felt normal.

"And what will you have, Shirley?" Mia interrupted the thoughts running through my mind, forcing me back to reality.

"A chicken Cesar salad, please, and a diet coke."

We kept on talking for while, as if we were old friends, and agreed we would stay in touch. It was so nice, for the first time, talking to someone who had been through it. I didn't want to talk to mom about it because she would immediately become sad and begin apologizing, as if she had personally chosen to pass on this gene to me. Whenever she brought the subject up, I would simply say that everything was fine, my checkups were fine, and generally speaking, I was fine.

But I wasn't fine at all. The fact that I couldn't have any checkups because of the pregnancy, made me really nervous. I couldn't wait for the pregnancy to be over. More so, I couldn't wait for them to tell me that I have a boy. A boy would make everything easier. Ok, maybe not everything, but a lot of things. After all, this specific mutation didn't have the same affect on boys. Even though men can also get breast cancer, or other types of cancers.

So, I decided to try and hope it was a boy. What else could I do but wait for Dr. Cooperman. I decided that only after he would tell me that everything was fine, I would tell Alice about the pregnancy. Unless I show. Well, that was why I ordered a salad, wasn't it?

CHAPTER 30

It was nice working for Alice, all in all. Even though, every morning I would find on my desk a pile of papers with red pen markings, her corrections were professional and to the point. Her emails were somewhat overbearing, but I made sure to answer each and every one of them meticulously and patiently, and in most cases, she accepted my answers. Also, when we would disagree on something, we stayed professional and never personal, which made working with her even easier. In fact, I successfully changed her mind a couple times.

I would work all morning without taking a break and go out at noon to grab a bite. I was so hungry I couldn't wait for my pasta take out. I guess I could blame the pregnancy for that too.

This time, I sat at the bar and waited to get my order. I casually flipped through the newspaper that was left on the bar. I couldn't remember when was the last time I had the opportunity to sit in the middle of the day with a newspaper for no particular reason. And then I saw the article.

It was called PGD. Preimplantation Genetic Diagnosis. It sounded scary, but that was exactly what I was planning to do. To choose a healthy fetus. The article was about a carrier from Jerusalem, about my age, who went through this process during her IVF treatments. She chose a healthy fetus and was about to give birth soon.

I read the article several times and the tears just starting pouring uncontrollably. I was so mad at myself. How could I have not done it?

How could I have disappointed my child? Why did I not prevent it?

I could barely hear the bartender call my name, and just grabbed my purse and ran back to the office with my lunch. I sat in my chair and started crying. Anna was in the room, she immediately stood up and closed the door.

"What happened? Is everything all right?"

"Yes, yes, it's nothing." I kept crying and started looking for tissues in my drawers. Anna went to get me a glass of water from the kitchen.

I blew my nose and took a few deep breaths to calm myself down.

"What happened? You're making me nervous." Anna sat on the desk, close to me, and placed her hand on my shoulder.

"I'm pregnant. And I just read about a procedure that would have prevented me from passing this gene on to my baby. There's nothing I can do for the others. But this, I could have done. This pregnancy was unexpected. I was going to look into it before I got pregnant and missed it." The more I spoke, the more the tears poured, "and Alice will probably kill me when she hears about it, because I was already pregnant when I started working here."

"She won't kill you. Pregnancies are a good thing, a great thing. Don't think about that gene."

"How can I not? I could have spared it this burden. This sense of anxiety that follows me everywhere. And now, everything is screwed up." I was overwhelmed with guilt. I was such an idiot for not having planned this properly.

"Actually, you were the one who was screwed, right?" Anna smiled and so did I, both laughing and crying at the same time.

"Stop, everything is going to be fine and you'll have a healthy child. Do you know if you're having a boy or a girl?"

"No, I have my scan next week."

"Great, and don't worry. Alice will be happy and supportive. Most lawyers here take a one-year maternity leave, and no one bats an eye. Really, you shouldn't worry about it. You need to worry about your health and the baby's." She placed her hand on my belly and smiled. All I could think about was that I was finally at the right place at the right time. Maybe I did get a bit lucky.

***

It turned out, Anna was right. Alice took it well. Actually, very well. I apologized about a hundred times, saying it was unexpected, and Alice calmed me down and said everything was OK. Even though she still returned everything I wrote with plenty of corrections, she said she was happy with my work and I had nothing to worry about.

After the scan I called Sarah to tell her what the doctor had said. It wasn't like we spoke every day; I just kept her posted about the important things.

"So, I have a girl. Another girl," I told her unenthusiastically, which she could hear in my tone.

"Why so sad? Why aren't you thrilled?" I heard her chewing something. She was probably having the call during her lunch break.

"Eating sushi again?"

"Of course. So, what's going on with you? What's eating you?" Some things never change.

"I was hoping it was a boy."

"Nonsense, what difference does it make? You already have a boy and a girl."

"That's not the point. I wanted a boy because the gene doesn't affect them as much. With a girl, I have to worry about it for the rest of my life. It's enough having to worry for Ariel."

No one understood why I was so disappointed, and since I hadn't told most people about being a carrier, I couldn't even explain myself.

I generally wouldn't tell people about being a carrier. No one understood what it really meant, and what it meant living with it. So, I simply kept it to myself, except for family and a handful of really close friends.

I had a complex relationship with this shadow that followed me everywhere while I tried ignoring it as hard as I could. But the frequent checkups and the endless bureaucracy before and after gave this shadow more attention than I intended to. Mostly at nighttime.

However, from time to time, I couldn't help it. Like at the Hanukkah party at the daycare. A mom sitting next to me told me that someone on her father's side had breast cancer. I immediately thought about mom who got the gene from her father, and wanted to tell her that she should get checked as soon as possible. But I kept quiet. I didn't want to make her nervous, and also didn't want the kids to accidently hear about me being a carrier. That was the last thing I needed. So, I didn't say a word.

A year later, the daycare teacher told me that the mom I spoke to got breast cancer but they found it in time. I felt so guilty that I didn't say anything because I was selfish. If I had told her of the risks, maybe I could have raised her awareness. Our daughters are at the same age, and I kept thinking it could have been me.

I went to visit her only after she recovered, simply because I couldn't look her in the eye. She told me the worst part was over, and she had pulled through it, but all I could do was hope she didn't remember our conversation from Hanukkah. She didn't bring it up and we finished the conversation by wishing each other good health.

But I could tell Sarah anything. She didn't always fully understand, but she always listened and tried her best.

"Maybe by the time she grows up they'll find a cure," Sarah tried to cheer me up. "But in the meantime, how about we go away for a week, just us girls? I'm dying for a week in London. Come with me. Don't be heavy."

"That's something that you never say to a pregnant woman."

"It'll be years before you get to go again. This is the right time. Let's go in two weeks, be spontaneous."

"I'll check with Michael."

"But this time, actually check with him. It's a once-in-a-lifetime opportunity, trust me."

"OK, we'll talk later."

When I hung up, I thought about Sarah's offer. If Michael comes home early a few days and my mom helps out a bit, and Natalie is free, then maybe I could go. It really was an opportunity to go on my own for a change, without Michael or the kids. I liked the idea of having a vacation, just us girls. I wouldn't be able to travel in a few months, so I decided to talk to Michael about it that very evening. Good thing we already sold our smaller apartment and bought a bigger one. This time, I didn't have any excuses why I couldn't go away.

Michael was all for it, after I promised someone would help him with the kids and that I'd buy him a lot of cool shirts for work. Apparently, bribes worked on big boys too.

CHAPTER 31

"Do you, by any chance, know someone in the army?" I asked Michael while the kids chased one another around the table.

"Why? Are you looking to enlist?" Michael smiled and picked up his coffee mug from the table, after Ariel almost dropped it when she chased Adam with a sword.

"Very funny. Tommy called mom and told her they were giving him a hard time." Ariel hit me on the head with the sword, so I took it away from her.

"In basic training camp?" I could barely hear Michael because Ariel started screaming and Adam ran into the other room.

"Yes. They keep intimidating him, teasing him and kicking his things. It's a real nightmare. He told his officers but they won't do anything about it," I said loudly, trying to speak over Ariel shrieking.

"I'm not surprised." Michael said and gave her the sword back so she would stop screaming. She smiled with victory at me and ran out of the living room.

"Is there something we can do about it? Mom is so worried it keeps her up at night." I wanted to use the few quiet moments we had to ourselves. "Is there someone we can talk to?"

"Maybe, but by the time they take care of it, he'll be done with his training," Michael said, and was probably right. "He just needs to man up and get through it."

"It's easy for you to speak, you're a giant. Who would want to mess with you? He's a gentle boy, not a bully. He told mom that he is the smallest guy there, which is why they pick on him."

"Mom!" Adam yelled from the bathroom, "Ariel is doing pee pee on the floor!"

Michael and I ran to her and saw Ariel standing by the toilet, with her pants pulled down, trying to pee pee standing up.

"Why are you doing that?" Michael asked and picked her up from the puddle she was standing in, then put her in the bathtub.

"Pee pee like Adam!" she said proudly, and I went looking for the mop.

CHAPTER 32

It turned out to be a project like no other. For every day I was gone, there was a meticulously detailed daily schedule. Everyone was assigned a part and had to confirm they knew it. Natalie and mom split shifts and Gabi was also on standby, because he had started a new job that week.

I left for the flight at night and promised the kids I would bring them lots of presents. Ariel said she wanted dresses. It was a good thing I packed lightly. I felt like I was running away from home, running to my freedom.

Sarah came on time and the flight was great (with several bathroom breaks). My baby bump helped cut all the lines short. In England, they respected pregnant women. On our first day we mostly walked around and, in the evening, saw an insanely hilarious show. Every evening, we ate at a different restaurant that Sarah heard good reviews about, and generally, I was in a euphoric state, which I haven't felt in a long time. Having the freedom to wake up on my own, to eat when I was hungry and go wherever I wanted was intoxicating. The thought of having to go back depressed me (I really did miss the kids, but I was willing to stay longer).

"Shopping time," Sarah posted a picture of us carrying shopping bags while resting at a café before our next Oxford street take-over. I had a slight feeling this post would urge Michael to put in a few more hours at the office.

I used this time to call mom.

"The kids are wonderful, absolutely amazing," she said proudly.

"That's great," I said, and thought how I wished they were so well-behaved with me.

"And, how are you girls? Having fun?"

"Yes, we're having a great time. But it's freezing outside, we have to wear gloves and a hat."

"Good thing the shops are warm," she laughed. "I wanted to let you know I asked Natalie to replace me tomorrow because I have a CT scan at 5 P.M., and I can't pick up the kids."

"Why are you having a CT scan?" I couldn't remember there being a reason for such an urgent scan.

"Do you remember I told you I was struggling to raise my arm? So, the doctor sent me to have a head CT." I didn't understand how her head had anything to do with it. "But it's just to be on the safe side, there's nothing for you to worry about."

"Ok, keep me posted." I hung up and felt how something started weighing on my chest.

We kept walking around the shops, Sarah, me and my aching chest.

***

The next day mom didn't pick up her phone. I called over and over again, but kept going to voicemail. Michael said he hasn't heard anything and Natalie said the "the kids are awesome, so sweet!"

I checked the time; it was already 9 P.M. in Israel. She must have finished by now.

After an hour I called Gabi. He answered right away.

"Hey, what's going on?"

"Hi Shirley, are you having fun?"

"Everything is great. What's going on with mom?"

"I'm here with her, and everything is fine," but something about his voice wasn't right.

"Should I call you later? So we can talk?" I thought I figured out what that voice meant.

"Yes, that would be great. We'll talk."

Gabi hung up. I couldn't go shopping anymore and went back to our hotel. Sarah kept walking around. She knew every corner in the city from her time as a stewardess, she was the best partner for a trip like this.

"What's going on Gabi, I'm losing my mind here," I told him when he called.

"Mom doesn't want you to know because she doesn't want to ruin your vacation."

"Know what?" I was yelling by now, although I knew it wasn't his fault.

"They found something on the CT scan, some finding in her head. They're having an urgent MRI tomorrow."

I was at loss of words and the only thing I could say was, "what?"

"Don't tell her anything. She can't know that you know."

"Ok, I'll check with the airline when's the earliest flight back and I'll come home as soon as possible."

"No need. We'll know more only after the MRI, which will be only tomorrow night. And then it'll take time before the doctor gets the results. We're trying to schedule an appointment at the Jerusalem medical center, with a neurosurgeon Eric knows." Gabi's brother always knew all the important people, even doctors.

"OK, in any case, I'll check when the next flight leaves."

"It's really unnecessary, but do as you please." I think that's what parents say when they realize they can't change their children's decisions.

"OK, I'll keep you posted."

I hung up and simply burst into tears. I was glad to be alone at that moment. I couldn't believe this nightmare was starting all over again. Mom kept saying that if it would come back, she wouldn't survive it. And here, it's back. All these terrible thoughts kept passing through my mind. I tried imagining a day without her and couldn't.

I got into the shower to calm down, and when I came out, I decided to start taking care of things. First, I called Michael and told him everything. I asked him to switch shifts with my mother and not tell anyone anything. Then I called the airline and got a flight one day earlier. I didn't want to stay here, but coming back the next day wasn't good either. I obviously wouldn't have time to process it at home. I preferred to have another day for myself, to cry and be mad at the world for a little while. I deserved it too.

When Sarah came back, I told her everything. We simply sat in silence, hugging one another, and in the evening, instead of going to a restaurant, Sarah brought us some take out. This time, she didn't even bother saying I had nothing to worry about, or that things were going to be fine.

I spent my last day filling my guilt-ridden suitcase with clothes and toys for the kids.

CHAPTER 33

I came back home, hugged Michael and the kids, and left immediately to see mom. I left Michael with the big suitcase of presents for him to hand out, because that was what the kids actually cared about.

As he did every evening, Gabi sat in the living room with a glass of whiskey, while listening to some intellectual discussion about yet another political corruption scandal. Mom was watching TV in bed. I took my shoes off and lied next to her.

"How was it?" she asked and tried to squeeze out a smile.

"It was wonderful. I bought a lot of clothes for the kids."

We hugged and I didn't know what to say.

"I know that Gabi told you." She looked so fragile and terrified.

"When is your appointment with the neurologist?"

"Sunday morning."

"It's going to be fine, mom. We'll get this tumor out and everything will be fine. Do you want me to come with you? I can take another day off."

"No need. Gabi will be there."

"Ok. What about Tommy and Jonathan? Do they know?"

"Sure, we told them right after the MRI."

"I'll talk to them, too."

"Thank you, sweetie. I'm happy you had some free time and enjoyed your vacation. You deserve some time off. Soon you'll be very busy again." She placed her hand on my tummy and left it there.

"What's the deal? Every time I get pregnant you get cancer. That's it. I'm not having any more children." Mom smiled. "You know how they say that bad things happen to good people? So maybe you should like rob a bank? That would make things better."

"You always cheer me up," she said with a smile, kissed my forehead gently and slowly got out of bed.

That moment, I realized what job I should take on – cheering her up. Making sure she's always happy and laughing. The question was, how would I do that?

"I can't believe I have to give up my ski vacation. I was really looking forward to it. Do you think they'll give us a refund?" I couldn't believe this is what bothered her.

"Sure, tell them that you're cancelling because of a brain tumor. What would they even say?"

She laughed. "You're right. Now I can get away with anything."

***

"I can't believe it's happening again," I told Michael while we were in bed. "of all people, my mom needs to get this cancer again? It's so unfair."

"Other people have troubles too, but you're right, it's frustrating and unfair."

"She had very slim chances to none, to get out of this. And they don't even know if they can operate. And I don't even understand if it's a new cancer or if it has something to do with her ovaries. How does her brain have anything to do with her ovaries?"

"I have no idea."

"I also can't figure out how they didn't find it sooner. From what Gabi told me, it's been there for a while. Why didn't they check her head? No one said anything about her head. I just don't get it." Michael didn't answer.

We kept laying there in silence. I didn't know what he was thinking about, but I was mostly thinking about our children who had to face this. Perhaps, I was also feeling sorry for myself. I decided to talk to Jonathan the next day and make sure he was aware of what was going on. During my previous pregnancy, I tried staying away from hospitals, as much as I could, but this time I knew that I wanted to be with mom as much as possible and didn't care what she had to say about it. This time, she won't get rid of me so easily.

That night went by as slowly as the scary nights I used to have when mom and Gabi went out when I was a child. I used to be afraid that something might happen to her and I would be left alone. I wouldn't fall asleep before hearing her heels tap around the house. If I felt I couldn't stay awake I would purposely fall asleep in the living room so Gabi would carry me to bed. That's how I knew they came back and everything was fine. I feel uncomfortable admitting that I kept doing this until I was too old for Gabi to pick me up. He had to wake me up and send me to my room. And now I was scared in my bed again, scared of losing mom, once again.

CHAPTER 34

I came to work on Sunday with a box of chocolates and everyone asked about what we ate, what we did, and mostly what we bought. I decided not to overburden anyone, and told only Anna and Alice about mom.

At noon I went to the National archives, to track down some data about the Workers Unions in the 1920's for Alice's PhD research. I was mostly happy for the opportunity to be alone before I get back to my usual afternoon with the kids. The archive had a musky smell, and the old AC was as loud as a truck. While I opened an old moldy file, filled with pictures and old letters, my phone vibrated on the table. Mom probably finished her meeting.

I left everything on the table and went outside to talk to her.

"What did they say?"

"They said that they need to operate, but they're not sure if they can. They scheduled another MRI for next week because they want to have their own tests."

"OK, I want us to get a second opinion. It seems pointless waiting another week and then making a decision."

"Where will I find someone on such a short notice? I got this appointment fast thanks to Eric's contacts."

"I'll talk to Alice, she told me that she had a friend who was married to a neurologist."

"Try whatever you can. Thank you, sweetie."

I hung up and called Alice straight away. That very day, we scheduled an appointment with the head of neurology at the Tel Aviv Medical Center before 8 A.M .the next morning– it doesn't get any better.

***

"I felt like a celebrity," mom told me after her appointment with Alice's friend. "They greeted us so nicely and treated me so well."

"That's wonderful. What did he say?" I gathered some of the pages scattered across the table.

"On Saturday I'll be hospitalized and Sunday morning they'll operate. He says he can remove the tumor and then take a biopsy."

"Great," I felt there was still some hope for us.

I immediately called Jonathan and we decided that he'll come over from Jerusalem for mom's surgery.

"Listen, we're about to go through some difficult times. Mom is nervous and dad is working, we have to figure out how he can keep going to work and not lose his job. We'll have to help more."

"Of course, but I'm studying and I'm in Jerusalem. It's a bit harder for me to come over. Now I have my exam period, so I'm more flexible, but later, I'll be very busy again." He sounded tired. It was 9:30 A.M. but he wasn't a morning person.

"I'll talk to Gabi and see how we can work things out. In any case, let's agree that I'll share with you everything he tells me, and vice versa. I don't want us to miss anything. We can decide together what we'll tell Tommy, deal?"

"Deal. OK, I'm going back to bed. We'll talk."

Anna, who sat quietly and pretended to read something, stood up and sat in front of me. "Do you need help with anything?"

"Thanks, but I think I got it figured out. I won't be here on Sunday. We'll see what happens after that."

Alice also offered to help and asked about my mom. I thanked her over and over again, because I felt that thanks to her we've earned some more 'mom time.'

I decided to leave early and spend some time with the kids. After all, I was about to have some busy days at work and with mom.

I went to pick up Adam from daycare and the second teacher, Rebecca, greeted me with a smile, "Hi mom. I see that a congratulations is in order," she smiled and pointed at my bump. "Adam's in the yard, I'll go get him." She put down the broom she was holding and went outside.

When I walked in, I hugged Adam and told Rebecca how much he loved her and Lina.

"We love him too. I keep telling Lina how clever he is. He told me today about all the things he builds with his play mobile." I saw how proud she looked.

"He really is smart. Ok, I have to make it on time for my daughter's daycare. Thanks for everything."

"Bye Adam's mom." I wonder when I'll get used to that title. When I heard the word 'mom' I still thought of my own mother.

CHAPTER 35

Mom's concerns dissolved when she found out the surgery would be under general anesthesia. She was scared that she might have to stay conscious during the surgery and it kept her up all night. We were there at 6:30 A.M., because we were told they would take her in at 7.

I smiled at her when the orderly took her to the surgery room and we all went to the waiting room. Eric and Grandpa Yokannan came to keep Gabi company, while Jonathan and I had breakfast at a mall nearby. We decided that Tommy shouldn't take days off for the time being.

When we came back, the waiting room was crowded and smelled bad. Everyone stood by a socket to charge their phone. There's nothing like stuffing dozens of people into a window-less room. It was a good thing people noticed my baby bump, so someone gave me their seat. After a few stressful hours the surgeon came into the waiting room.

"The surgery went well, and we removed the entire tumor." We all breathed a sigh of relief, he continued, "I think it's a c-met from the ovarian cancer, and not a separate one." I wasn't sure whether that was a good or a bad thing. Or, actually, did it make things worse.

"What's next?" Gabi asked, and we all looked at the doctor.

"She'll soon be moved to recovery, and then we'll see how her rehabilitation goes. I can't tell to what extent her brain has been damaged, but from what we saw, there was no substantial area affected that might impair her functioning."

"Great, thank you so much, doctor," Gabi said, and although he was trying to keep himself together, his voice disclosed his stress and excitement. The doctor was gone in seconds and Gabi turned to us. "You can leave if you want. It'll take some time before they move her to her room."

"Sure, I'll be back in the evening," I said and hugged him tightly. This time, he hugged me back.

***

Mom woke up completely paralyzed. She couldn't move her legs and needed round-the-clock help. Julie saved the day once again, and arranged shifts with all their friends who came from all over the country to take their turn at the hospital.

Natalie came every day after working in the supermarket to be with the kids. I think she paid for her driving license just from working for us. She started saving for a car.

After a week at the hospital, mom was discharged home with a wheelchair. She didn't want my help with anything, because she didn't want to burden me. She kept sending me home to rest and be with the children. I explained over and over again that when I'm with her, I rest more than I do at home; that put her mind at ease.

At home, she moved around with a walker, while her phone hung on her neck plugged to her earphones. Trying to avoid radiation seemed a bit pointless after they had found a tumor in her head, but she insisted. Just like that phase when she used only natural deodorants, special cleaning products for her vegetables and ecologic shampoo. We just went with it and used chemicals and radiation far away from her.

As the weeks passed by, things became better and mom was recovering. She obviously went back to work the moment she could drive to the office. Only her appetite was still lacking and she was weak. I would joke that even though I was eating for two, it didn't mean she should stop eating. She didn't think it was funny.

CHAPTER 36

I went into labor in the middle of the night, but couldn't reach Natalie. It was Pesach vacation and she was probably sleeping in. Eventually, my contractions were getting closer together and I had to call mom so we could go to the hospital. Home birth wasn't really my thing.

Michael dropped me off at the labor emergency entrance and went to the park. I got off the elevator and slowly walked to the reception desk.

"I think I'm in labor," I told the nurse, who handed me a form.

"If you're walking around like that, I don't think you are, but let's check," she said, and the only thing that crossed my mind was that I woke mom up, who wasn't feeling too well, at 4 A.M. for no reason.

They connected me to the monitor when Michael walked in. "Anything new?"

"We just started the monitor, let's hope there really is something." My guilt started bothering me more than the contractions.

Michael sat on the 'husband-chair' and napped. The monitor beeping didn't wake him up.

"You have regular contractions two minutes apart, but still not dilated enough," the nurse announced. "We'll find a free delivery room for you."

I was shocked, but also relieved. I didn't wake mom up for no reason.

The on-call doctor came in when the shift changed. "How are things going?" he asked the delivery nurse.

"Three centimeters dilation and regular contractions."

"I want to have a natural birth" I said before they could decide for me.

The doctor looked at me amused. "Everyone says that and then cries for the anaesthesiologist."

"I didn't say that you should send him home" I replied.

Only after confirming that Natalie was with the kids, could I think about the labor itself. But in fact, all I could think of, was that mom wasn't there. I sat on the physio ball crying, finding it impossible to believe that she wasn't there with me. This was my first time in the delivery room without her. The thought of it filled me with pain, almost greater than the contractions. Michael was running around, bringing water, massaging me and calling the delivery nurse over and over again. But contrary to what the doctor had predicted, I did just fine without the anaesthesiologist and this time, Michael wasn't wounded during the birth.

When Romy was born, she didn't cry. The delivery nurse placed her on me and the baby looked at me with her big eyes.

They picked her up so she would cry and get her color back, then gave her to me, all pink and crying. I held her and cried even when she had already stopped. We both probably wanted our mom.

In the afternoon mom and Gabi came to see Romy. Mom wore make-up and nice clothes. She covered her bald head with a peach-colored fabric, that matched her shirt. Romy quietly slept in her cot. Michael also came with the kids, who suddenly seemed so big. Unlike the rest of the guests, they weren't as excited about our new addition.

My dad came too, and announced that the baby looked just like his mom. I actually thought she looked like my mom, but said nothing since he was so excited.

Two months later, we moved to our new house and Romy finally got a proper cot, which we didn't have room for in our previous apartment. We could now change her diaper on a changing table and not on the computer desk. I hoped we weren't spoiling her too much, after all, she was a third child.

CHAPTER 37

My maternity leave went by too quickly, and the day of my return to the office was slowly approaching. Although I loved working with Alice, I didn't feel like going back to work. I was still trying to wrap my head around the idea of having to work full time while taking care of the house and kids.

I used the Sukkoth holiday to have a morning alone with mom in our regular café. I sent Michael with the kids to the park for some daddy quality time.

"When are you going back to work?" mom carefully tasted the soup she was served. It was nice meeting her like this, alone, without the kids, without my brothers. Just the two of us. These were truly rare moments and I cherished them. It was amazing how this disease made me appreciate things that were otherwise taken for granted.

"After the holidays, as people say. Alice doesn't mind." I mixed my salad and added some salt. I was still hoping to lose my baby weight before I go back to work.

"That's nice of her."

Ever since the cancer came back, mom tried eating healthy again. She stayed away from sweets and tried eating a lot of vegetables and fruits. I also tried, and lasted for about two months, but she somehow managed.

"Have you had a checkup recently?" I stopped eating and looked at her.

"Yes, about a week ago, everything is fine. Dr. Carmi said he was really pleased." Mom smiled a big victory smile.

"Good, because I had a terrible nightmare the other day." I turned back to my salad.

"Oh, don't start. I can't even think about it."

"Then don't, it's nothing, just my personal fears." Of which I had plenty. Sometimes I dreamt I was running through the hospital halls looking for mom and not finding her anywhere. Sometimes I would dream that Gabi called and told me she was gone. The dreams changed, but the ending was always the same. I would wake up, my pulse racing and my eyes tearing, and usually I couldn't go back to sleep.

"What do you want to do for your birthday? I can't believe I have a thirty-two-year-old daughter." Mom placed her hand on mine and looked at me in a way only a mother could.

"I can't believe it either., I would be happy if we just all went together to eat somewhere." It would also be Gabi's birthday. We always celebrated together and I thought he would agree to this arrangement. We both didn't like crowded gatherings.

"As you wish, sweetie. Make reservations to wherever you want." Mom finished her soup and peeked at the display window with the delicate handmade cakes.

"But without the kids. I really want to eat quietly." I saw that she kept staring at the desserts, so I suggested, "would you like to share one with me?"

"You know what? Order one and I'll take a small bite."

I ordered a vanilla cream raspberry tart, which was one of her favorites. When the tart came, I took a small bite and let mom have the rest. If I was about to ruin my diet, might as well do it at the best bakery around.

CHAPTER 38

Mom called to tell me she probably won't make it to my birthday. She didn't sound so good over the phone, and wasn't feeling well for a few days. Her back ached and she kept coming in and out of the hospital, trying to figure out what it was.

"If you're not coming then I'll cancel, there's no point celebrating my birthday without you." I signaled Michael to come and take Adam from me and moved away from the dining table.

"No, don't cancel. Gabi will come."

"No way." Adam stood up and took his plate to the sink. I was so proud of him.

"OK, sweetie. I'll take something for the pain and try to come."

"Thanks, mom. I want both of you there." I looked at the oven clock and saw we had to leave in two hours. That was enough time for the pill to work so that mom could come. I couldn't imagine her not being at my birthday celebration.

When we arrived at the restaurant, everyone was waiting. Grandpa came with Eric and Ruth, and stood up for us when we walked in. Always a gentleman, even in his eighties. We chatted and laughed, the food was great too.

But I couldn't help notice mom moving uncomfortably in her chair, I could see the pain in her eyes. Although I felt guilty and childish for dragging her down here, I realized I couldn't really celebrate my birthday without her. I could see Gabi was concerned. He smiled and made his regular jokes, even threw in a dirty one, but he kept looking at mom and constantly asked her if she wanted to leave.

She really tried putting on a brave face and held up. They left during dessert, and little by little so did everyone else.

"Mom isn't doing well, did you notice?" Michael opened the restaurant door and stepped outside to the cold night. That is, I was cold and Michael wasn't, as usual.

"Yes, she doesn't look too good."

"I don't know what to do, or how I should help her." We held hands and walked alone down the dark road.

"What can you do? They told her it was a urinary infection."

"I don't think that's true. She's been taking her antibiotics for days and nothing seems to get better. I told her I think she needs to see an Orthopedist, maybe it has to do with her back and not the kidneys."

"Maybe, I have no idea." Michael took out the car keys and handed them to me with a smile. "Come, take me home."

Michael turned on the radio and put a station that only played old Israeli songs. I rolled my eyes, but kept quiet. In any case, I needed some time to think. Sadly, most of the thoughts crossing my mind were grim. I hoped I was just being hysterical. When we got home, I texted mom the phone number of the closest Orthopedist, who usually had available appointments. I hoped she would take my advice and go see him.

"Happy birthday!" Michael said when we got into bed and the whole house was dark.

"I wish. Something terrible happens every year on my birthday."

Michael didn't answer. I looked closer and saw he fell asleep. His ability to fall asleep within seconds, kept astonishing me. There were several things I loved about him; this wasn't one of them.

CHAPTER 39

I picked Romy up from the nanny and the kids from their daycares. Having three different pick-up stops was time-consuming, which is why I was always the last to arrive to Tammy's daycare to pick up Ariel.

"You know I can't ask the other teachers to stay until the very last minute?" Tammy caressed Adam's head, he then ran straight into the ball pit. He really did miss this daycare.

"Yes, I'm sorry. It just takes a long time taking them in and out of the car, over and over again." Ariel grabbed her bag from the hanger and ran to me.

"There are other moms here who have more than one kid," she looked at me and forced a smile, "but Ariel is really great." Tammy hugged Ariel, who had a proud expression. There was play dough tangled in her curls and her mouth was smeared with chocolate. No wonder she likes it here.

When I became a mom, I swore I wouldn't be one of those moms who came last. My mom was one of those. She finished working at 4, which was also when the daycare closed. I used to wait with one of the cranky teachers outside, and hear her ranting to herself. Every day mom came heaving and apologizing. Back then, divorced women weren't referred to as "single moms", and didn't have any support or understanding. So, I did my best to make it on time, or at least make sure someone else came on time, but it didn't always work out.

The kids loved Tammy's daycare. Adam had mentioned several times how he missed Tammy's cooking. He would only eat the vegetables and meatballs Tammy made, since I couldn't make them as well as her.

When I was in the first grade, mom found a private after-school-care for me, with someone who lived right next to school. Her name was Bella and I remember not understanding why they would call such an ugly woman 'Bella', but it seemed rude to ask. I would walk from school to her house, and have lunch at her place. Once a week, she would make pasta with tomato sauce. The sauce congealed into sticky lumps that clung on to the thick pasta. To this day, I am sick to my stomach when I smell that pasta. Perhaps that's what made me hate tomatoes, who knows.

We were about to leave the daycare when I suddenly realized something. "Ariel, these aren't your shoes." I could barely bend over with Romy in my arms as I tried taking those shoes off Ariel's feet. "Where are your shoes? You were wearing sneakers today."

Ariel pointed at the sparkly pink ballerina shoes on her feet and smiled innocently.

"She said these were her shoes. Now that I think of it, something weird happened today, because Leah did tell her grandfather that she came without shoes today." Tammy and I looked at Ariel, who joined Adam in the ball pit. I felt awkward asking who Leah was, but Tammy noticed my bewilderment and said, "Leah is the nice doctor's daughter, Dr. Rubinstein. He really is charming. He works a lot, and so does his wife" (they came on time, I guess).

"Ariel, are these Leah's shoes?" I yelled to her, but she didn't reply. She ignored me.

"I'm really sorry," I said to Tammy and placed Romy on one of the sticky mattresses. "I'll look for Ariel's shoes so we can leave Leah's shoes here."

Tammy looked in the jungle gym and I looked through the toy

box. Adam thought this was the perfect time to try and play catch with Romy, who could barely catch her own pacifier.

I suddenly thought I should check Ariel's bag. Her shoes were hidden under some drawings and spare clothes I would always send with her. I pulled her out of the ball pit and put on her shoes. I left Leah's shoes on one of the chairs. The entire floor was covered in balls and Tammy picked them up, one by one with Adam. Strangely, she only had to ask him once, and he immediately starting cleaning up and putting the balls back into the pit.

"I'm truly sorry. Please also send Leah's parents my apologies." I picked Romy up. She had already rolled from the mattress to the floor and succeeded grabbing one of the balls. I wiped her spit off of it and threw it back into the pit. Tammy looked at me and politely smiled. We left about 15 minutes after closing time.

Tammy left with us and hugged and kissed the kids goodbye. I was hoping that despite it all, in the future she'd take Romy too. But after this day, I didn't have a good feeling about it.

When we got home, I felt as if I had completed a marathon. I sat on the sofa and the children scattered around the house. Romy was placed in the play-pen for her own safety. I called mom to ask when she was coming over, but she didn't answer.

I wanted to slice one of Ariel's favorite apples for her. But sadly, the knife made a single cut, and it wasn't the apple. While I climbed up the stairs to look for the iodine, Gabi called.

"Hey, Gabi, what's up?" I put the finger in my mouth so I wouldn't drip blood everywhere.

"I have some bad news." He sounded so serious that I simply stopped walking. "They found something in mom's spine. They told her to go back to the hospital."

"What does it mean?" Adam and Ariel were fighting about something and I got into the bathroom and closed the door. Gabi hated talking to me with the kids screaming in the background, and it was important to me that he kept talking.

"It means that the cancer is back, Shirley. That's what it means." He raised his voice, but I knew it wasn't personal.

"Can't it be something else?"

"I don't think so. He didn't say anything else." He spoke quietly again. "You realize what that means, right?"

"Yes, I have to go. I'll call you back when I can talk quietly."

I locked the door, and sat on the bathroom floor, trying to replay the conversation in my head. A single tear rolled down my cheek, and then more followed. I cried like Ariel would when someone refused to obey her.

"Mom, Ariel bit me." Adam shouted and tried opening the door. "Mom, open the door."

"In a minute. Stay in your room. I'll be right there." I needed a few moments to myself.

I texted Jonathan to call me back and then called Michael.

"The cancer is back. That's it. It's over."

"I'm sorry…" Michael said softly and the typing in the background stopped.

"I don't know what to do."

"Just be there for her." He understood what I said, despite the tears.

"I knew there was a chance it would come back, but why so soon?" I saw Jonathan had sent me a text. He wrote that he knew and would talk to me later.

"Maybe there's some treatment?" Michael said hesitantly.

"I don't know. We'll see what they say at the hospital. But I don't think so." Adam yelled and then Ariel joined him. "I have to go, we'll talk in the evening."

"OK, hang in there."

"Come back as soon as possible, OK?"

"I'll try, but I really have to finish this and I…" I couldn't let him finish his sentence because I heard a loud bang and then silence. I threw the phone, opened the door and ran downstairs.

It took Ariel a few seconds to realize she fell, and she screamed so loud that my ears rung. It was the first time she tried jumping off the dining table. Sadly, it wasn't the last. It's a shame I still hadn't found the iodine.

CHAPTER 40

The next day, I told Jonathan over the phone that the hospital had suggested administrating the chemotherapy directly into mom's spine. They were starting immediately.

Our conversations were concise, just as with Gabi, but usually much funnier. I loved his sense of humor. Last week, he got the results from his genetic test. He wasn't a carrier of that shitty gene. I was happy for him, but was also boiled with anger. I was furious about how unlucky I was, at my screwed-up genetics, about not being able to spare my children from this gene.

When I left the parking lot, I stopped at a café and got mom some freshly-pressed orange juice. It was shocking that by simply crossing the road from the mall to the hospital, you would step into a different world. The smells change, and so do the sounds. The smiles also disappear once you cross that road.

I went up to the Neuro Surgical Ward and met Gabi in the hallway. He seemed worried and tired, but to me he would always be the handsome man I had met as a little girl. He was a standing army soldier when he came into our lives, and always wore his white air-force uniform. I thought he was the most handsome man in the world. He was a tall man (at least in the eyes of a 4-year-old), his hair combed to the side, one green eye one blue. Something of that first impression would always stay with me, I guess. Even the years that had passed and his little potbelly, didn't make him any less handsome.

"Thank you for coming. I just really have to go to that meeting," he gently patted me on the shoulder. He wasn't a hugger.

"Of course, call me anytime you need. Alice knows what's going on and doesn't mind me working from home."

We walked into the room, I hugged mom and sat next to her, as close as I could.

"Cathy, I'm going," Gabi kissed her and left.

"We'll talk," I said, but he didn't turn to me, just raised his hand so I would know he heard me.

"I'm really afraid of the chemo," mom said, and I held her hand. "They inject it into the spine. Like Epidural."

"Can't they do it differently?" I hated needles.

"They could operate and place a tube in my head. But I preferred doing it without the tube." She smiled, but she was obviously trying to comfort herself, not me.

"I'm sure they're very experienced. Don't worry."

We talked some more about the kids and how smart they are, until the doctor walked in with a small group behind him.

"This is my daughter, doctor," mom introduced me, and I stood up and smiled.

"OK, Cathy, we're about to start your first chemotherapy session, by injecting into the epidural space. Please turn on your side and fold your knees up." My presence didn't seem to bother Dr. Bloom. As if I wasn't there. Mom slowly turned over and I moved to the other side of the bed so I could stand in front of her. I held her hand and she squeezed it tightly.

"Take a deep breath, it'll soon be over," I leaned over and whispered in her ear.

I'm cleaning the area and we'll soon start the treatment." Dr. Bloom went on to instruct the other doctors what he needed them to prepare. The nurse kept walking around the room bringing one thing and then another. Mom looked up at me with a scared gaze and I kept holding her hand. I smiled at her and tried looking calm. Everybody recommended him and I really hoped he was as professional as he was unpleasant.

"OK Cathy, we'll first take a sample for a pathology test and then we'll start the injections. You might feel a bit of pressure."

Mom sighed and her expression was agonizing. The process was rather short and when it was over, the doctor removed his gloves and placed all his tools on a tray that the nurse took away.

"I need to give her a prescription. Can you please come with me?" the doctor said to me and then left the room without waiting for an answer.

"I'll be right back," I said to mom and grabbed my purse. I found the doctor signing something at the nurses' desk and stood next to him.

"Let's take the elevator," he said, still not looking at me. I followed him to the staff elevators that weren't as nice as the regular ones. Orderlies were walking around with different patients, and it felt as if I had stepped into the hospital's backstage. I followed him in silence.

"We don't really know how to treat this type of cancer. Sadly, the prognosis isn't good. I told your dad too," he spoke to me, but kept looking at the elevator electronic screen.

"I know. I've done some reading. Which is why I intend to have an oophorectomy first chance I get."

"Do you have children?"

"Yes. Three."

"Good." The elevator stopped and he stepped out quickly.

I tried memorizing the way back since I could barely keep up as I followed him through the hallways. It was like a maze. We walked into a small room and he scribbled some unreadable words on a small piece of paper and then stamped it. I waited in silence, thanked him and then left. I went back to mom, who in the meantime had sat up in bed and drank water. She smiled when she saw me walking in and wanted me to sit next to her.

"The doctor said there's a chance it'll help, but I don't think I'll beat it this time."

"Don't say that, of course you will. You've already beat it twice and you'll do it again. This cancer's got nothing on you. Come, can we go now?" I was such a terrible liar and I knew the best way to avoid this conversation was by changing the subject.

"I think so. Maybe you should tell Gabi that we finished?" Mom placed her cup on the small side table and took the blanket off.

"Call him from the road. I'll take you back home. I just want to get out of here."

I helped mom stand up, and five minutes later we were already in the elevator on our way to the mall. We walked from shop to shop and looked at different shoes and clothes. I felt like any other woman, just spending an afternoon at the mall with her mom; in the middle of the week, for no reason whatsoever. We tried on some shoes. Even when I wore heels, I wasn't as tall as her.

"They look great on you," mom stood behind me and hugged me. For a second, I forgot the cancer and felt like a little girl whose mother was buying her shoes.

I dropped mom off at home and went to pick up the kids. On my way home, I called Gabi.

Recently we spoke on a daily basis. It wasn't something we did before the cancer. Sometimes our conversations were concise and to the point, about mom and her treatments and about what the doctors said. But sometimes we would have long conversations about different subjects. Gabi would tell me about his fears, his thoughts, about what mom tells him when they're alone. These conversations were rare and I cherished each one of them.

"Hey, I dropped mom off at home and now I'm on my way home."

"Thanks, how was the session?"

"Pretty quick, but she was in a lot of pain. I hope it helps."

"It's hard to tell. There's nothing much they can do now." Gabi spoke quietly.

"Yes, Dr. Bloom told me. We spoke in private, and he told me the prognosis is not good. Did he say anything to you?"

"Yes. I didn't know whether I should tell you, but he said they don't really know how to treat this type of cancer."

"Did he tell you how long we have left?" I was afraid to ask but I needed to know. I had to wait a few seconds for Gabi to reply.

"A few months. But don't tell mom anything. She didn't ask, so I don't think she wants to know."

I didn't know what to say. The stinging pain in my heart turned into actual physical pain. I assumed this was our last battle against the cancer, but I didn't think it would be this short.

"Ok, I have to go. We'll talk." Gabi broke the silence.

"Ok, bye." The tears poured down my cheeks as I tried to drive home safely. I tried imagining the first day without her, and I couldn't. I couldn't comprehend how this could happen. How could I ever go on without her? How could the world go on without her?

When I parked the car in front of Romy's nanny, I blew my nose so many times that I looked like a beaten-up clown; red nose and puffy eyes. I took a few deep breaths and stepped outside. Life went on.

CHAPTER 41

When I came into the office the next day, Anna enthusiastically told me that the office lunch was going to be at a really fancy restaurant.

"I'm really not in the mood for this lunch thing." I put my purse on the desk and flopped into my chair. I moved aside the pile of papers Alice had left on my desk during the night and fell onto the table with despair.

"It'll be fun. You should know we don't celebrate every year, but this was a good one. New shoes?" Anna almost hovered with excitement.

"Yes."

"What's the matter?"

"Nothing. The whole thing with my mom, her doctor said there's nothing much they can do."

"I can't believe it." Anna sat down and her enthusiasm deflated like a popped balloon.

"Yes, it's very sad. I was with her during chemo yesterday and it was terrible."

"Shirley, I'm so sorry."

"Thank you."

My phone rang and I started digging through my purse. I was surprised to see Nathan's name on the screen.

"What does he want?" I mumbled to myself.

Anna kept sitting in front of me with a sad expression. "Who is it?" she asked. I showed her the screen and she scrunched her face with repulsion. She probably remembered everything I told her about him.

"Hey, how are you Nathan?" I asked in an energetically confident tone, which was completely opposite of what I was really feeling that moment.

"Everything's superb, how about you?"

"Everything's fine. Is there anything I can help you with?" Sometimes he would call to ask where was this or that file, or ask me to remind him what we did on some case.

"Actually, no. I called to update you about the ALUT case. We just got the verdict and I wanted to tell you that we won."

"That's great, I'm so happy," I said enthusiastically and actually meant it this time.

"Yes, the good guys won again. I thought you might want to know."

"Thank you for calling. Really, I'm so glad. Give Joel my best of wishes."

"Sure, is everything fine with you? Michael? The kids?"

"Yes, they're all great."

"Good, have a happy new year."

"You too."

It was one of the nicest conversations we have ever had, especially since I left his office. The good news made me smile again.

I came home a little late. Natalie, who by now had already bought a small car, picked everyone up and waited for me at home.

Romy practically jumped into my arms and rested her head on me.

"Rough day at daycare," Natalie gestured with her head at Adam's direction, he was busy playing with his play mobile. " The teacher asked that you call her today."

"OK, do you know what happened?"

"He didn't say anything, and when I asked him about his day, he said just it was 'OK." Natalie collected her things. "Do you need me on Friday evening?"

"No, I don't think we'll go out. Thank you, honey."

Natalie left and I wondered if I would ever find the time to call Jonathan. He tried calling me earlier and I didn't answer. In truth, I was avoiding talking to him. I promised to tell him everything about mom. I wasn't so sure it would do him any good knowing what Dr. Bloom told me yesterday. I wasn't going to tell Tommy, that's for sure. He started working at a camera store, and wasn't at all interested in what was going on; as if he chose to shut his eyes to it. But Jonathan was more mature and I made a promise to him. I knew I had to keep this promise. No matter what.

I played the *Mamma Mia* movie for the kids. They didn't understand the plot, but they liked the songs and the dance moves. They imitated the dancers; it was hilarious. Romy sat on the floor and clapped while Ariel danced on the sofa. Adam wore a pirate costume and tried imitating Ariel.

Mom took me to see that movie a few months ago, when she was still feeling well. We went together one evening and Michael stayed at home with the kids

"It's a sweet movie. It's just been running for a while," mom tried explaining why the movie theater was empty. It was just us and about 5 other people, all of which were elderly.

"It's OK, mom. I like their songs."

The movie really was nice and amusing. "Look at Meryl Streep, she moves so well for her age," mom whispered. "I wish we all could." I had to agree with her. Meryl Streep really did look very good for her age. In fact, she looked good even regardless of her age.

After a few days, she smilingly gave me the DVD of the movie, and the kids loved watching it over and over. They called it "Cathy's movie."

I used this relatively quiet moment when they were busy, and nervously called the teacher. Adam was running around the coffee table and laughed his cute laugh as Ariel followed. It didn't look like he had a rough day.

"Good evening," Rose the teacher said with a stern tone.

"Good evening, Rose. This is Shirley, Adam's mom. I was told that you asked me to call you."

"Right. I'm happy that you called, because I don't get to see you in daycare." Unlike Tammy, who every now and then would still be there when I came over, Rose almost never saw me.

"Yes," I was overwhelmed with familiar feelings of guilt. Not every mom has the privilege of having a short workday.

"I just wanted to let you know that today was a difficult day for Adam. He wouldn't sit with all the other kids at circle time. And during music class he wanted to sit in the kitchen." She spoke in a didactically tiring tone.

"OK," I also would have probably run to the kitchen, if I were expected to sit in a room with thirty-three children playing with flutes.

"I just wanted to make sure that you are aware of these issues and that they are being taken care of." Adam and Ariel jumped together off the sofa when everyone in the movie jumped into the water. That part always made me laugh, but I couldn't laugh while Rose was on the line.

"OK, thank you." I hoped the conversation was over.

There were a few moments of silence, but Rose wouldn't let it go. "So, are they being taken care of?"

"Look, I think he's just nervous about my mom's situation." I pulled out the cancer card. "She's been fighting ovarian cancer and she's not doing so well. He might be responding to that. We're having a tough time as a family and Adam is really close to her."

"Oh, I had no idea. I'm really sorry to hear about your mother."

"Thank you." Adam and Ariel were lying on the floor and waving their arms. I had to stop myself from laughing again.

"That might be the reason, but if this keeps happening you should probably get a professional opinion." Rose kept insisting.

"Of course, thank you."

"Thank you for telling me. All the best to your mother. Good night."

"Good night," I hung up and looked at Adam. He seemed just fine. He didn't like this daycare from the very beginning. He kept saying that his teacher, Rose, didn't like him. I hoped that all parties involved would survive these last few months before Adam started school.

It was dinner time. I took out the eggs from the fridge and tried thinking how I could change dinner up. One day the kids would say that omelets and cheerios with milk reminded them of their childhood home. I chose the easier option and made eggs sunny side up.

While the kids were eating, I tried gently poking around. "How was daycare today, Adam?"

"Fine." Adam kept dipping his bread in the egg but didn't actually eat anything.

"Good. Why didn't you sit with all the kids at circle time?"

Adam kept playing with his food as if he hadn't heard me.

"Adam? Why didn't you sit with all the kids at circle time?"

"Because it was too crowded." He took a bite from the bread and then handed me his leftovers, "it's too runny. I don't want it."

"So next time don't dip it so many times in the egg."

Ariel had just finished eating and went to finish watching the movie in the living room. Adam ran after her while yelling at her to wait for him. Romy was in her high chair, so all she could do was throw her plate to the floor. Yet another successful dinner completed.

When Michael came back home, the kids were already in their beds but I could still hear them chatting. I went downstairs to find Michael leaning over the counter and eating Adam's leftovers. We'd finish Rachel's food by Monday or Tuesday, especially when Michael took some to work.

"I spoke with Rose today." I started picking up the plates from the table.

"Who?"

"Rose, Adam's teacher," I tried saying without sounding judgemental, but probably failed.

"Oh," Michael avoided talking to her when he dropped Adam off.

"She said Adam is having a rough time in daycare. He won't sit with the other kids, and he doesn't participate in other activities." I tried cleaning the egg, but it was stuck to the table. I decided that from now on I would only make omelets because they were easier to clean.

"Of course he's having a rough time, he hates it there." Michael didn't like this daycare either. The building was old and Michael said that the teachers never said hello to Adam when he dropped him off in the morning.

"Yes, but I couldn't tell her that. I blamed the cancer. That shut her up."

"They won't take his nonsense when he gets to school. Everything makes him nervous." He looked at me and added with a smile, "just think about what happens when he'll take his SATs…"

"Are you seriously trying to annoy me right now?" Any chance mom got; she would tell Michael how stressed I was when I took my SATs. To her, that was my most challenging period. By now it was already a family joke that everyone would mention on different occasions. I didn't think I was exceptionally anxious compared to other students; it's just that I needed to do well on these horrible exams so that I wouldn't have to retake them. That's it. When Tommy hardly studied for his SATs, I reminded mom of how much she complained about me. She answered that she didn't know which was better; my unnecessary hysteria or his annoying laziness.

We sat quietly and heard Ariel singing in bed. It was a good thing that Romy and Adam fell asleep so easily. Michael was reading something for work while I stared at the TV screen.

"OK, I'm done. I'm going to take a shower and then go to bed."

I stood up and looked around me. Romy's toys were scattered all over the floor and Ariel's clothes were spread on the sofa. I decided I would take care of it tomorrow. In any case, when it's dark, no one sees how messy it is.

Even though I was exhausted, I couldn't fall asleep. I thought about how we would tell the children about mom. I knew it was a matter of time, but I didn't know how much time. It was best to be ready. Thinking about the day after, made me sick. I gave up trying to fall asleep, and watched some *Seinfeld* reruns. I probably fell asleep at some point, because when I woke up, it was morning and the alarm clock went off.

CHAPTER 42

"So, what do you think?" I asked Anna. We were working together on a big case Alice had to present in the supreme court. I asked her to go over a precedent I had found, but I wasn't sure whether we should use it. I was trying hard so for once Alice would be truly pleased with what I had prepared.

"I think it would help the opposing council more than us."

I erased that part from the document and hit save again. "Do you think I can hand this to Alice?" I panicked every time I sent her an email.

"Sure," Anna went back to her desk and sat down.

It was a relatively boring case that dealt with budgets from the Ministry of Culture, and the way they were divided among different theaters across the country. David, our client, owned a small theater that didn't get any budget at all. He was a nice man in his fifties, an art enthusiast, who would tell me every time we met about his travels from one art gallery around the world to another. Our conversations were fascinating, and definitely livened up dealing with this case. His unique wardrobe could be a whole other conversation topic in itself.

I was working on rereading the document before sending it to Alice, when a knock on the door made me jump.

"Hey." Mia came in with a big smile on her face. She wore an elegant beige-colored suit and shiny black heels. Next to her, Anna and I looked like students on spring break.

"Hey you!" I stood up and hugged her. We became good friends, and made sure to have lunch together every other week. She gave me recommendations for good doctors, and we kept each other posted about test results, mostly MRIs. I always felt comfortable talking with her about these things. After all, she was the only other BRCA carrier I could talk to.

Mia hugged Anna and then sat in the chair in front of me. Even the way she sat down was elegant.

"I have a meeting in an office nearby, so I just dropped by for a minute. I have good news for you."

"Yes?" I leaned forward, just waiting to hear something good. I needed to hear something good. Anna realized we needed some privacy and went back to her desk.

"Do you remember that I once told you about someone named Lisa, who was starting a foundation for carriers?"

"Of course," I saw that Anna was listening, but she didn't say a word.

"She started a foundation called 'Bracha.' You have to talk to her. She's having a symposium for carriers."

"When?" I couldn't believe it finally happened.

"I don't know. You should talk to her, here's her number." Mia put on my desk a yellow post-it with a phone number in her handwriting. "I have to go."

"Thank you, Mia," I said with excitement, "that's great. I'll talk to her in a little while." I walked her to the front door and hugged her again.

I ran back to my office and immediately called the number Mia had given me.

"Hello?" I heard a distinct Anglo-Saxon accent.

"Hello, Lisa?"

"Yes?"

"My name is Shirley, I just got your details from a friend. I understand that you started a foundation for BRCA carriers.

"Right, how can I help you?"

"I feel uncomfortable calling you like this so early in the day, but you can't imagine how happy I am to speak with you. I've been looking a long time for someone who can help healthy carriers, I even thought of starting something myself. It's just that my mom got sick, and I have small kids, so I don't have the time for it."

"No worries. I'll be glad to meet you. A lot of women call me, even men. We're holding a symposium at the end of the month; would you like to come? There's going to be a lot of important information. We'll also have doctors that will be answering all your questions."

"That's great. Sure, I would love to come."

"All the details are on our website. No need to register, just come. When you're there, feel free to introduce yourself, so I know who you are."

"Great, thank you, Lisa. I'm so grateful that you did this for us."

I hung up and immediately called mom to share the good news.

She was at work. I was amazed at how despite it all, she was business as usual. My mind, however, would constantly wander and I found myself reading the same sentence over and over again.

I tried reaching Michael, but he said he couldn't talk, so I gave up and kept going over personal stories on the foundation's website. Many had the same thing in common – their mother had died of cancer. Sometimes it was their sister or aunt. Sometimes, it was both. The stories were sad, but for some reason, they didn't upset me, but rather made me feel I belonged. I felt I could see myself in each of these stories.

I wrote down the symposium date and sent Natalie a text asking her to save it. It was unbelievable that my entire plans, eventually relied on a twenty-two-year-old.

CHAPTER 43

"I want you to go to the lab and give the Armenian specialist a blood sample," mom said, while I was struggling to give Ariel a shower. Romy sat in her bath seat and Ariel kept trying to pour water on Romy's head.

"I have no idea what you're talking about" I replied, and tried stopping Ariel from getting my phone wet.

"Do you remember I told you about the Armenian who tests blood for viruses? He's in Israel for the next couple of days. Ian from the council knows him and will give him your sample. Can you go now?"

"Mom, I'm with the kids giving them a shower. I could maybe do it tomorrow, on my way to the office."

"OK, I'll ask Ian to come by and collect it. Just let me know when you're in the office."

"OK, I'll talk to you later."

Ever since mom got sick, she kept trying different things. There was a time when she went on a very strict diet, and took special vitamins. Gabi became a real expert at importing vitamins to Israel. Every day, she drank fresh juice made of different orange vegetables, until she turned orange herself. Then, she did the Armenian's plant extracts. She heard about him a year ago, and sent her sample to him in Jordan. I have no idea how she pulled that off. After a few weeks, she got a small box with bottles in it, and for a few months she took the Armenian's magic drops. That's what she would call them. The cancer was back, so apparently, they didn't work.

However, despite my skepticism, I went the next morning to the lab. I assumed that she wanted to try and save me, in any possible way. When I came to the office, Ian was already waiting for me in our small front lounge.

"Nice to meet you," Ian stood up and gently shook my hand, "you look very much like your mother. It's uncanny." Dina looked at him suspiciously, but kept quiet. A courier came to deliver something and he was waiting for her signature.

"Thank you," I said, for the lack of something better to say, "so, you're taking the sample to the Armenian?"

"Yes, Dr. Dickran is in Tel Aviv this week. Did you know he's a famous specialist?"

"Mom told me about him," I answered quietly, because I didn't want everybody to hear our conversation.

"It's a shame he couldn't help her. Maybe it was too late when we found him."

"Maybe. Anyhow, thank you for all your help, with my mom's issues and mine." I knew he went above and beyond his position when it came to helping my mom.

"Of course, I adore your mother, she's an amazing woman," Ian said with a smile.

"I agree." I gave Ian the box with the lab sample.

"I'll give him your number and he'll call you. He doesn't know anything about you, he gives a diagnosis only based on your blood." Ian peeked into the box, and seemed to see what he was looking for.

"OK, thank you again." We said goodbye and I went back to my office.

Anna was slowly drinking her herbal tea and looked up at me when I came in. "Who was that?" she asked with curiosity.

"Someone who works with my mom and took my sample to some Armenian virus specialist."

"Sounds interesting. What does he do with it?"

"He claims that every cancer starts with viruses, so he looks for viruses in your sample, and gives you medicinal extracts that are supposed to treat the virus. Then the cancer recedes. I think it's nonsense, but it's important for my mom. So, I just went with it."

"Cool," Anna went back to sipping her tea.

"Yes, we'll see what comes of it." As long as I wasn't forced to eat things I hate, I was willing to try anything. Well, almost anything.

CHAPTER 44

The Bracha foundation's symposium was held at the Tel Aviv Medical Center, so I decided to stay in the city instead of driving home and back.

At 7 P.M., I drove to the hospital. Lisa had arranged parking spots for participants, and when the executive parking gate opened, I felt like a V.I.P. The hall was in the basement, next to the operations rooms, that I was all too familiar with. I had never been to the hospital for no reason whatsoever, unless it had something to do with my mom.

A big table of sandwiches and salads was surrounded by women who happily chatted with one another. It looked like a high school reunion, and not a cancer symposium. I registered and proudly made a donation. I tried finding out who Lisa was, but there were many women, and I felt uncomfortable asking.

It was impossible finding a sandwich without tomatoes, so I took a few crackers and walked into the hall. There were only a few women sitting scattered throughout the hall. Some looked like mothers and daughters, while others like sisters.

A long table was placed on the stage and on it were signs with doctors' names. I was very happy to see Dr. Carmi's name between two other doctor names I was unfamiliar with.

At about 8 P.M. most of the women were in their seats. The hall was still half empty, but someone standing on the stage asked everyone to sit down. The lights were dimmed, and a good-looking blond woman, who looked slightly older than me, appeared on the stage. When she started speaking, I could hear her accent and understood she was the famous Lisa.

"Welcome to the 'Bracha' professionals' symposium," Lisa spoke ceremoniously, and I could tell she was excited. "I'm so happy to see familiar faces as well as new ones. Tonight, sitting in the audience, we have some healthy carriers as well as some survivors."

I looked around and saw everyone smiling at Lisa. Some looked at her with admiration, of which she was definitely worthy. There was a small number of men in the room. Sometimes I forgot it concerned them too.

"When my mom got sick, no one told us that we need to get tested. Several years later, my sister got sick too and then I found out I was a carrier. I had my breasts removed just before my sister passed away. I am a proud previvor. My sister couldn't save herself, and I knew that I should allow each and every woman the opportunity to help herself. Instead of sitting and waiting for the disease to come – actively preventing it.

The doctors will soon tell you that the surgery can't prevent cancer from developing, but only reduces chances of getting sick. While this is of course true, what matters is that you have the option to do something that would significantly reduce your chances of getting sick. You will all make your own decisions, but I want you to know that the foundation is here to answer any question you may have."

The doctors of the panel spoke and answered questions. Dr. Carmi was there and spoke in a calm tone about ovary removal surgery. I didn't ask anything. I only sat and listened. From what I heard, I realized that losing a mother, was something that many of these families had in common. I didn't know whether I should be happy that my mom was still alive or sad because our time with her was limited.

Everyone clapped when it was over, and the lights turned back on. I approached the stage to introduce myself to Lisa and waited patiently until she could speak. It felt like I was waiting in line to meet a celebrity.

"Hi, Lisa. I'm Shirley, we spoke over the phone." I assumed I wasn't the only one who called to ask for her help.

"I remember. It's so great that you came." Lisa hugged me as if we've known each other for years.

"It was amazing. I learned so many new things tonight. Thank you for putting this event together."

"I'm glad. We're having another meeting at my house, for Purim. You should come."

"I'd love to. Thank you again, we'll be in touch."

That night I dreamt I was walking down the street only to find I was surrounded by women with breast implants, and they all looked like Barbie dolls. I think that for Michael, my nightmare would have been a wonderful dream.

CHAPTER 45

A few days after the symposium, Dr. Dickran's assistant, Josef, called to give me the results of my blood sample testing. I was at work, having a meeting with David and I realized I had completely forgotten about all that Armenian voodoo.

"The doctor said that he found a virus related to breast cancer in your sample," Josef said.

"What does a virus related to breast cancer mean?" I asked.

"It means that now you don't have cancer, but you might potentially get sick."

"What about ovarian cancer?"

I heard him mumble something in a different language, and after a few seconds, he said, "there's nothing related to ovarian cancer. Just breast cancer."

"OK, good. What do we do now?"

"I'm coming to Israel in about a week and then Ian will give you some of the doctor's extracts. You take 10 drops a day, morning and evening. When you finish them, send over your sample again and we'll check."

"OK, thank you."

I hung up slightly shocked. So many thoughts ran through my mind: what would I tell mom? What do I do with this information? That's it? Something has already developed? How do I stop it? Will those voodoo drops help?

"Perhaps it's not my place to say," David said, "but I accidentally overheard your conversation." He squirmed in his chair and kept looking at his papers, as if he was reading.

"It's OK," I replied quietly, it wasn't really his fault. He knew that my mom was sick, because I had moved around some of our meetings to take my mom to radiation sessions. He had asked me once if we tested for the gene and I confided in him about being a carrier. It seemed that he was well informed about this topic, but I never asked him why.

"I didn't tell you until now, because I didn't want to make you anxious, but perhaps I should."

"I think I can handle it." I didn't think I could be more anxious than I already was.

"My wife's mother passed away from breast cancer. She also was a carrier. They lived in the U.S., where there's more awareness. They checked her the moment she was diagnosed, and so did my wife and sister. My wife's sister, Jenny, found out she was a carrier of gene number 1. My wife found out she wasn't a carrier."

David fell silent and I sat down in front of him. He sighed, and then went on. "Jenny was really young, not even thirty years old. She took all her tests strictly by the book. She had a checkup every 6 months. She had the best insurance you can get and went to the best of doctors. On one of her tests, I think it was an MRI, they found a very small cancerous tumor. Really tiny, only a few millimeters long. She had a surgery to remove the tumor. It was successful, and she kept going on her regular checkups."

David fell silent again, as if he had run out of battery. His fiddled with the papers. I slowly drank my tea and waited for him to go on. The room was so quiet we could hear the office noises outside; Anna's flip flops tapping, phones ringing and Dina typing. David's phone rang and he silenced it.

"Anyway, she kept going on her regular checkups because she

was told she didn't need any treatments after the surgery. When she turned thirty-three, she started not feeling so well. When they found out she was sick, it had already spread to her bones, and I think her lungs, too. There was nothing more they could do, and she passed away after a few months."

"I'm very sorry to hear. I didn't know," I said to him and put my cup down on the table.

We sat in silence a little longer. Both with our own thoughts. David continued reading and correcting the notes I had prepared, and I couldn't stop thinking about everything I had just heard.

The delivery guy had already brought lunch and the kitchen was now full with hungry lawyers who raided the bags as if they hadn't eaten in years. We collected our papers without saying a word and got into my room.

"Listen," David said, "never mind the budget nonsense. What really matters is your health. Take care of yourself. You have little children and you can't neglect your health. If you want, I can give you my wife's number. You can talk to her. She will be happy to help you in any way possible"

"Thank you, I'll think about it."

"I have to go. I think we've gone over the important things. If you have any more questions, you can call me." David shook my hand and left.

I couldn't focus on anything. I leaned backwards in my chair and looked at the ceiling. It had small mold patches. I didn't know what to do with this new information. I felt as if a huge weight landed on my chest and I struggled to breath. I took a few deep and slow breaths, trying to calm down, but couldn't. I pressed my head against the table and cried as quietly as I could.

I pulled myself back together, but kept thinking about Jenny, and was overwhelmed with sadness again. This year I turn thirty-three, like Jenny was. I tried wrapping my head around how she had gotten to that situation within a few short months while having regular checkups. How could they have not found the cancer when it came back. Her sad story frightened me like hell. After all, I was counting on these checkups, and now my entire theory has collapsed. Then, I decided to check something that I hadn't thought of until that very moment.

I googled "recurrence of cancer among BRCA carriers," but couldn't find anything. I wasn't sure whether anything could comfort me. I was thinking about my children, and how badly I didn't want them to experience what I was going through with my mom. I didn't want them to constantly be worried. If I get sick, how will I look them in the eye and tell them I knew this could happen but did nothing? That I knew I was at risk and waited.

Until that very moment, when I encountered previvors, carriers who removed their breasts or ovaries, I couldn't understand why they did it, why having checkups wasn't enough. Now, when I finally understood why, I realized something needed to be done, I can't idly wait. It's not that I was about to amputate a healthy organ. It was an organ that was literally endangering my life.

If until that moment I thought that checkups would be enough to save me, Jenny's story completely changed things for me. I understood I had to save myself, and fast. I want to be a previvor. Not a survivor.

***

When Michael came back home, the children were already asleep and we could talk quietly. While he ate his late dinner, I told him about my conversation with David.

"I want to look into having that surgery."

"We said you'll have it at 40, right?"

"That's the one for my ovaries. I'm talking about removing my breasts." That was the first time I spoke those words out loud, and it scared me.

He lifted his eyes from his plate and said, "if that's what you want to do, I'll support you."

I was surprised by how well he responded to this statement. As if I said I wanted to pull out a tooth.

"You realize it's irreversible. I'll have silicon instead." I pointed at my reckless breasts and wanted to make sure he understood.

"I understand what it means, Shirley, and I support any choice you make."

"I want to do it this year. After the holidays, so that the kids are at school and not breathing down my neck." I was restlessly pacing back and forth in the kitchen.

"OK," Michael stood up and hugged me. "I told you, anything you want."

"And I want to do it in a private hospital, so I can choose my own surgeon." I said decisively to his face.

"Of course, it will cost what it will costs. We'll get you the most beautiful boobs out there."

"Don't count on a size enlargement," I smiled.

"What a pity. Oh well, I'll have to get over it." He kissed me and we stood hugging in the kitchen for several moments, as if this was a cliché 1950's American movie.

"And if I have this surgery and it helps, then you'll be stuck with me for many more years. You might not have time for a new young wife."

"What can you do, life is all about compromise." Michael kissed me gently and loosened his grip.

"But at least when we get to a nursing home, I'll have the nicest boobs." I turned off the lights and we went upstairs.

"That's good. All the other grandpas will be jealous of me."

"But I don't want the kids to know about it. We'll talk about what we should tell them."

"Of course." Michael was also happy to avoid awkward conversations with the children.

Although I wasn't sure he comprehended how important this was, I decided to let it go and allow it to sink in. After all, it would have a small impact on him too.

After taking a shower I stood in front of the mirror and looked at my body. Before today, I rather liked it. I didn't love it, but we liked each other a fair amount. But now, I felt my breasts were an enemy that I had to defeat. I wanted to pull them off me that very moment. If it wasn't this late, I would have called Lisa that very evening. However, I decided to wait for tomorrow. Unfortunately, my breasts weren't going anywhere.

CHAPTER 46

In the morning, I called Lisa from the parking lot. It wasn't a conversation I wanted to have at the office.

Lisa answered immediately, which surprised me. I definitely wasn't the only person calling her.

"Good morning, Lisa. I hope I'm not disturbing you."

"Good morning, Shirley. It's so great to hear from you. Of course you're not disturbing me." She was a genuinely nice person, and it wasn't just her British politeness.

"I started looking into the breast surgery and wanted to get recommendations for doctors that deal with these issues."

"That's great, excellent choice. Some of the experts working with the foundation are also hospital surgeons, but there are obviously other good doctors. We have a lot of information on our website, as well as on our closed Facebook group. Have you joined it?"

"Yes, I'll write there and ask for recommendations." Before, I was avoiding logging into it. I was afraid of reading scary stories and being even more anxious than I already was. I didn't want to hear stories from women who had the surgery before I decided to have it. Maybe because I was scared of the surgery itself. Maybe because I was jealous of their courage. But I didn't have much of a choice and had to know as much as I could before moving forward.

"I'm sure you'll get some names from the group to get you started."

"Great, thank you Lisa." Talking to her helped me relax a bit. It made me feel like I was doing something normal.

"Are you coming to my Purim get-together?" Lisa would occasionally email me invitations to different events she organized, which I have never attended.

"Sure, next Thursday at 8, right?" Seeing as I have decided to have the surgery, I should start hearing stories first-hand.

"Yes, great. I'm glad that you're coming. I'll see you then. Have a good day, Shirley."

Our conversation gave me strength and I quickly went up to the office. I passed by Dina and got into my office. Anna was already there working on a document, so she casually said 'good morning' without even looking up. I immediately logged into the *Bracha* group and asked about experts for the amputation and recreation. I couldn't believe I was writing these words. It was gradually becoming real.

I had a hard time focusing. At that moment, I felt as if everyone else had disappeared, and I didn't actually care how much funding David's theater would get. But still, I started going over the file and editing the document. Every now and then I checked whether someone had answered my post.

Only when I came back from my lunch break, did I find a comment from someone named Lia. She recommended someone in Jerusalem. I didn't want to drive all the way to Jerusalem, let alone have my surgery there. But I thanked her for commenting and kept waiting.

After an hour, someone named Grace, recommended Dr. Katzman from Tel Aviv. Grace wrote that Dr. Katzman is a plastic surgeon who works with several other surgeons, from which I can choose. Minutes later, I was already talking to his secretary, and with a trembling voice, scheduled a consultation meeting. Worst case scenario, if I change my mind, I can always cancel the appointment.

When I drove to mom's that evening, I felt the process had begun. I was afraid of her reaction because she was always in favor of the regular checkups. Once a month she would question me to ensure I wasn't forgetting to have tumor marker blood tests, and that I had an appointment for my annual MRI. I felt guilty. I could still save myself, she couldn't. If she wouldn't have gotten sick, I doubt whether we would even know about the gene. I felt as if she had sacrificed her life for me, which is why I had to do something, and not idly sit by. As if this way, her sacrifice wouldn't go to waste. But for the most part, I knew that without her support, I wouldn't be able to go through with it.

When I got there, their door was open. Gabi was watching TV in the living room. A cup with the grapefruit juice he loved so much (which I thought, tasted more like a detergent than anything else) was placed on the glass side table next to the armchair. He said that mom was in bed, and I rushed to her. On my way I took a spoon from the kitchen so mom could eat her favorite tart that I had picked up from her favorite café. Recently, she gave up her health diet.

Mom was watching a silly American sitcom and lowered the TV volume when I came in.

"Hey mom, how are you? Sit up, I brought you a treat."

"Thank you, sweetie, you're spoiling me." And then she added quietly, "instead of me spoiling you."

"Oh, nonsense. Come, I'll fix your pillow." I straightened the pillow behind her as she opened the box and savored the fresh raspberries.

"Delicious." Mom took a bite, and a small red berry fell and stained the blanket.

"It's the best desert ever," I held the berry and ate it. This time I didn't get myself anything. I was overexcited and lost my appetite.

"Where's Tommy?"

"He's out with some friends."

"How's he doing these days? I haven't spoken to him in ages." Jonathan kept me in the loop, but whenever I came to visit, he was either away or asleep.

"He's trying to shoot a film, that's what he does all day. It's driving everyone insane."

"I see, I'll try talking to him." I paused for a second and then thought this was a good time to bring it up. "I want to tell you something.

"What?" mom raised her eyes from the tart.

"I decided to have the breast surgery. I mean, I'm looking into it, but I'm seriously thinking of having it."

"Wow, that's a big decision. What happened?" She went back to eating her desert but occasionally looked up at me.

"I'm starting to realize that an early diagnosis isn't enough, and that it can come back – big time. Besides, I have a 90% chance of getting sick, and I would have the surgery in any case. I decided to have it at a time that suits me, and as a preventative measure before I'm actually sick. It puts the odds in my favor, at least I think it does."

"Makes sense," she surprised me and took another bite. Another berry rolled my way. Perhaps it was something that she wanted me to do, but didn't feel it was her place to say.

"I made an appointment with a highly-recommended doctor, and I'll also ask other previvors who had the surgery. It does scare me, but I think it's the lesser of two evils."

"I also think it's best. Maybe we really shouldn't rely on these checkups." She finished eating and placed the empty box on her knees. Her face was smeared with powdered sugar, and she looked like a little girl who had been at a birthday party.

"I didn't get a chance to tell you that the Armenian doctor called and said he found breast cancer viruses. That's also what motivated me to start looking into the surgery. He said that he would give Ian extracts for me. Maybe you should talk to him." I gave her a tissue and signaled she should clean herself.

"Start asking around and I'll talk with Ian tomorrow at the office." I couldn't figure out how she was still working.

Lately, she stopped driving. We thought it was best that she doesn't sit behind the wheel, considering all the pain killers she was taking. For the past couple of weeks, her employees have been picking her up from home in the morning, and then dropping her off at the end of the day. Sometimes, she couldn't stay the whole day, but no one cared about how many hours she worked.

"So, what's new with the kids? Tell me something nice." Mom leaned back again and I fluffed her pillow. She was clearly trying to change the subject.

"Everything is fine. Adam is still struggling in preschool. Thank God it'll be over in four months. Next year he'll start first grade and he's very excited about it."

"And what about Ariel? She's probably running the place by now." A big smile spread on her face, and her eyes sparkled.

"She wants to. In the meantime, she's giving them a hard time because she refuses to nap and all the other kids won't sleep either. It's a good thing she's starting a different daycare next year."

"It's unbelievable how time flies." The smile wiped off her face and she looked away at the TV.

"Yes…" I replied, and continued, so that she wouldn't sink deeper into herself, "and Romy, such a cutie, she's practically walking. Come, I'll show you."

We sat in bed and watched some video clips together on my phone. Mom was excited and laughed, it seemed to distract her. After a while, I could see she was tired. I was exhausted too. I said goodbye and drove home.

On my way, I thought I should visit her more often. I don't know how much time she has left. But then I felt bad for even having these thoughts. Still, I obviously couldn't ignore the facts. I felt as if I started realizing the reality of the situation. Mom soon won't be here with me. And me? I had to save myself. That was the way things were and it was time I handled it properly.

The house was dark and quiet. The kids were asleep and Michael was watching TV in the bedroom. While I looked at Ariel sleeping, I wondered if she would even remember my mother.

CHAPTER 47

"Tommy, are you sleeping? Weren't you supposed to go to work?" It was 11 A.M. and I had already been to two meetings at the office.

"I'm up…" he answered but sounded half asleep. "I'm not going to work today. I called in sick earlier."

"OK, don't they mind that you're skipping work?" It's unbelievable, he found a way out of his one and only responsibility, I thought to myself, but still chose my words carefully.

"What do you want from me?" he barked at me with anger.

"I'm just worried that you might lose your job, why are you so angry?" Anna walked in and placed a slice of Dina's birthday cake on my table. I smiled at her and mouthed 'thank you'.

"I'm just tired, Shirley. You might not be aware of what's going on here at nights, it's terrible," Tommy answered sarcastically. Frankly, I had no idea what he was talking about.

"What's going on at nights?"

"Mom keeps going to the bathroom, and then falls down. Every night, again and again. And some nights, more than once. I wake up from the sound of the fall and then wait to hear if dad wakes up," Tommy replied tiredly.

"And does he?" One of Gabi's famous army stories was about the time he didn't wake up during the War of Attrition, when his station was bombed. But I hoped he could at least hear mom.

"Eventually he wakes up and helps her. I don't get much sleep."

"If you hear her falling, why don't you just help her?" I asked, and was pretty surprised that he simply lies there and waits.

"I don't want to embarrass her," he said quietly.

"I see your point…" I didn't even know that she was falling this much, and I didn't think about how this was affecting Tommy. Sometimes, I would forget he was just a kid, a recently-discharged soldier who was living with his dying mother. It was happening right in front of him. He couldn't avoid it. I could at least look away every now and then, and focus on smaller problems; Ariel ruining Adam's drawing, Romy refusing to take a pacifier. Normal things, that happen in normal families.

"Can I go back to sleep now?" Tommy asked, but didn't wait for an answer and hung up.

CHAPTER 48

The Foundation's Purim party came. I chose a Tinkerbelle costume and drove to Lisa's house. When I got there, I saw a lot of women but didn't recognize any of them. The party's agenda included a laughter yoga class.

Lisa introduced Lea to me, the woman who responded to my post. She was really nice and slightly older than me. She had the procedure two years ago, and was now back to her usual self.

"Except for breastfeeding, I can do everything," she said, "at first it was hard, but with time, things worked out. I recommend you have a lymphatic drainage massage after the surgery. It really helps with recovery, but only after they remove the surgical drains." She mentioned so many things I barely understood, and despite being scared to ask, I knew I didn't have much of a choice. I needed to know what was going to happen.

"What are surgical drains?" I asked in the calmest way possible, hoping I didn't sound hysterical.

"Tubes placed during surgery to the drain liquids from the area. They're placed under your armpits and about a week later, they're removed."

"Oh…" I was getting a bit weak and dizzy from all these details, and thought it was best if I stopped asking questions.

"Don't worry, things work themselves out pretty quickly. There's also a special bra you should buy and use after the surgery. Don't forget, no heavy lifting for about six to eight months." Lea poured herself some soda and grabbed a home-baked cookie.

"I suppose picking up children is considered heavy lifting, right?" I leaned against the wall near the table and sighed.

"Of course, you're not allowed to pick them up during that time. It can do a lot of damage. You'll need plenty of help."

"OK," I couldn't tell whether her tips reassured or stressed me. She pointed out little things that I didn't even consider when I decided to have the surgery. The only thing I could think about was stopping the cancer. I never thought about how I would handle myself after the surgery. And then I realized the person I should be talking to about the date of the surgery was Natalie.

The yoga class started, and it was awkward and embarrassing to laugh for no reason whatsoever. But after a few minutes, I was able to let go, and it really was amusing. We rolled on the carpet and laughed hard. I looked around me, at the previvors who already had the surgery, and they all looked happy. Maybe it was just my imagination, but there was something serene about them. I envied them for having finished the procedure. They didn't look so crazy to me as they did in the past, and then I realized having this surgery might actually make me sane again.

CHAPTER 49

"Did you have fun at Julie's yesterday?" I called mom from the office to ask how she was doing.

"Yes, it was nice, everyone came, and Johnny was there, too." Mom sounded quiet and tired. I didn't know Johnny was visiting. Mom told me that when they were little kids, Johnny always followed her when she met with her friends, and constantly asked to join them. Now, they were older and he joined Gabi and mom's friends and met with them when he came to visit in Israel. I couldn't see that happening with Jonathan. My friends would probably bore him.

"That's great. The Foundation get-together was also nice. I'm really glad that I went. I got a lot of useful information." I opened the file I had been working on for the past week.

"I'm happy to hear it, sweetie," but she didn't sound happy at all.

"What's the matter, mom?"

"Nothing special. Everyone kept talking about their plans for the summer, booking flight tickets, looking for hotels... and all I can think of is that I don't have a future. I have nothing to make plans for."

I fell silent. I felt the sadness in her voice and simply kept quiet. I didn't want to lie to her but I also didn't want to annoy her. I wasn't sure what was the right thing to say.

"I didn't mean to upset you," she finally said when I didn't respond. "I'm exhausted, my back hurts and I can't sleep. Gabi is supposed to get me sleeping pills from the doctor today."

I promised I would get her an appointment at a pain clinic as soon as possible.

Mom fell silent but then asked, "did the kids wear a costume today?"

"Yes! they were so cute. Adam went as a soldier and Ariel as Little Red Riding Hood. We dressed Romy in the old elephant costume, the one Ariel had, remember? I'll send you some pictures." Adam was so excited to wear his soldier costume, and announced he was going to be a warrior. With all his medical issues, it would be a miracle if they even recruit him, but I didn't want to ruin it for him.

In the evening I called mom to tell her I got her an appointment for tomorrow at a pain clinic. I wished it would at least give her some hope. That was really the only thing I could do for her.

CHAPTER 50

Passover eve came, and we were obviously going to spend it together. I offered mom to have the Seder at our place to make things easier for her. She promised to make some soup and I promised to cook as little as possible. Just because the Israelites suffered through the desert, doesn't mean people had to suffer again from my cooking. I had some cooked food delivered from a place Anna recommended. I made some salads and mom made her kneidlach soup.

Jonathan came early to help me set the table. When mom came, he took the pot of soup from her since she seemed to struggle climbing up the front door stairs. She looked so fragile. Even though her hair grew out a bit, her puffy yellow face gave away she was sick.

When we served the soup together, she spilled some and nearly slipped.

"It's OK, mom, I'll give you some soup." I refilled her bowl and served it to her. She didn't try to help after that.

Gabi read the Hagada, or at least the important parts of it. Romy sat on her high chair and broke her hard-boiled egg into small pieces. Ariel sat on my other side (I mean she mostly stood on the chair and sang holiday songs throughout the entire dinner). Adam insisted on sitting next to mom, who cut up his kneidlach. Grandpa Yokanan sat smiling in front of him, and didn't say much, as usual. He didn't mind the kids being noisy. His hearing impairment must have helped. Jonathan was the only one who dressed for the occasion and wore a white buttoned-down shirt.

"Michael, come here and take some pictures," I told Michael, who was in the kitchen as usual, stressed there wasn't enough food.

"Don't take pictures of me!" mom tried fixing her hair but it was too short, "I look terrible."

"You look great," I told her and signaled Michael to include her in the picture.

It felt awkward. I was happy we were all together, laughing and having fun. Jonathan made us laugh as always, and constantly teased Tommy. Gabi laughed and looked happy, perhaps thanks to 4 glasses of wine. One might have thought everything was normal. But I couldn't stop asking myself over and over again – was this our last holiday with mom?

CHAPTER 51

After Passover, the birthday season began. The kids' birthdays were close to one another, so we would always throw one party for all three, sometime between April and June. We had all the family over on a Saturday afternoon at the beginning of May, when the weather was suitable for an outdoor party.

Everyone came to celebrate Romy's first birthday, Ariel's fourth and Adam's sixth, who told everyone proudly that next year he'll start the first grade. Adam took pictures of people holding the "happy birthday" sign he hung on our front door, and ran around excitedly holding every present he got. Ariel opened every present she was handed even before the guest walked into the house. The front door area was covered in colorful wrapping paper that flew around in the wind.

The home phone rang and I saw Gabi's number on the screen. Except for charities, no one called this number.

"Hello, Shirley," Gabi said in a formal tone he only used for de-livering bad news. "Mom isn't feeling very well, we won't be coming today."

"What happened? I spoke to her in the morning and she said you were coming." Adam got a Lego set and shouted happily. I went to look for a quiet spot.

"She started having really bad back pain and nothing helps. We tried everything. I don't know what to do anymore."

"Do you want to take her to the ER?"

"Maybe, we'll see. We'll talk later, OK?"

"Yes, I'll come over when we're done here."

I hung up and looked for Jonathan. He sat on a plastic chair at the corner of the yard and smoked. Tommy stood at a safe distance from him. We both hated cigarettes. All our attempts to make Jonathan quit, failed miserably.

"Mom and dad aren't coming, mom isn't feeling well," I told them with disappointment.

"That's a shame," Jonathan put out his cigarette, and Tommy sat next to him. Jonathan took a sip from his soda and gave me a look that said 'don't make a big deal out of everything.'

So this is how it was going to be from now on, I thought, we are going to celebrate without mom. "I really wanted her to be here with us," I said and they both nodded.

"It can't be helped. That's the way it is." Jonathan looked up at me, "so, this is how you see the world? You're such a midget."

Tommy laughed and Jonathan added, "what are you laughing about? You're also a midget." It was really unfair that only one of us hit the genetic jackpot in terms of height.

Tommy and Jonathan kept teasing each other and went back into the house to help clean up, so I could go to mom the moment everyone left. I looked at all of our family – Michael's parents sat with Ariel and listened to her stories about daycare. Apparently, Ariel was surprised she wasn't allowed to hit other kids with a rolling pin.

Romy crawled on what little grass we grew, and every now and then someone helped her climb the red slide. It was a good thing she knew how to keep herself busy. Adam was having a long conversation with my father, who came with his new wife. My dad looked happy, and still, when I saw him with Adam, I felt a twinge in my heart. Mom and Gabi weren't here and I couldn't believe it was all happening without them. To me, no one could make up for their absence.

When the last guest left and the house was almost back to normal, I drove to mom's. I took the camera with me to show her the photos I took. Perhaps so I could feel she took part in the birthday party. I brought some leftover cake and hoped it would make her happy.

The entire drive I felt something burden my chest. I let the tears pour and when I arrived at their place, I felt more relaxed. I took a few deep breaths and walked into their building.

They moved here a year ago, so I didn't get to spend a lot of time in this apartment, but somehow it felt like home. Maybe the weekend we stayed here, for a lack of any other option, made things easier. Last winter rain leaked into our fuse box and caused a short circuit. We obviously couldn't get through the weekend without power. In a matter of minutes, we packed mattresses, a foldable playpen for Romy and some clothes, and we all went to mom's place.

Tommy's room was big enough for all of us and we stayed there for two nights. Michael felt uncomfortable troubling mom and Gabi, but we didn't have much of a choice, we couldn't stay home for two days without power. On Saturday morning we decided to give them some quiet and visited friends so mom could rest. But Adam refused to come and insisted on staying with her. This was the only place he agreed to stay without us. It was so fun spending that weekend with them, despite the challenging circumstances. I was half sad to go back home on Sunday.

I knocked on the door and Gabi opened with a look that said it all. "Things aren't good, Shirley. Not good."

"I know," I hugged him tightly and we simply stood there for an unusually long period of time.

Mom sat in bed and watched TV. "Hey sweetie," she said when I walked in, and muted the TV show. The laugh track was silenced and mom signaled me to sit next to her.

I slipped into Gabi's side of the bed and pulled out the camera. "How are you?"

"Not so great. Julie was just here, you missed her by a couple of minutes."

"Never mind, I'll see her next time. I brought you pictures from the party." I wanted to tell her that she was missed but didn't want to make her even sadder.

"So cute." She browsed at the pictures with a proud grandmother smile on her face. It was so nice seeing her smile. "Your dad gained some weight, ha?"

"Maybe, I don't know. He looked the same to me."

Mom looked at me with a concerned expression and then went back to the pictures. When she finished, she gave me back the camera and took her glasses off. "You must be very tired from the party. You didn't have to come today."

"I wanted to be with you," I said and moved closer to her. She hugged me and we stayed quiet for a while. She turned up the volume and we watched a silly American sitcom rerun. "Lately, I only watch nonsense. I can't handle anything else. I have enough drama going on in my real life, so whenever I can, I prefer comedies," mom said when the episode was over. She probably felt she needed to justify her choice.

"I understand," I looked at the time, it was getting late, "I think I'll go. I have a long day tomorrow."

"No worries, sweetie. Go rest."

"Do you need me to get you anything before I leave?"

"No, I'm fine. Drive safely," and then, when I walked through the hallway, she called out her usual sentence, "both eyes on the road…"

She was right about driving carefully. It was hard driving with tears in my eyes.

CHAPTER 52

"How was yesterday?" Anna came in refreshed after having rested over the weekend.

"It was great, but my mom wasn't there." I put down the tea I had made earlier.

"Why wasn't she there? Is she at the hospital again?" Anna hung her bag on the hanger behind the door and sat in front of me.

"No, but she wasn't feeling too well. It's getting worse from one week to the next."

"That's so sad."

"Yes, very. I think this was the last birthday party she could have been to, and she missed it too."

"Don't be so pessimistic. These treatments might give her some extra time, perhaps even years."

"That's not what her doctor said. She has a few months."

"I find that hard to believe."

"I know, believe me, it's hard for me too. If it were possible, I would have been with her all day."

"Why don't you take a day off every now and then to be with her? I'm sure Alice would be happy to give you the day. You can also work from home"

"She's still working. My mom goes to work every day. Her employees drive her back and forth."

"Are you serious? That's amazing." Anna stood up and sat in her chair.

"I think it helps her keep her sanity." Mom had told me it distracted her from her scary thoughts.

"Probably, good for her. It must be hard." Anna brushed aside the curls bouncing in front of her eyes. They made her look even younger.

"Very hard. I'm actually a bit jealous of her employees. They spend more time with her than I do. It's unfair." I sounded like a little girl, but felt comfortable enough with Anna to say things as they were.

"That's understandable." Anna's phone rang and interrupted our conversation.

I tried throwing myself into my work and different assignments that kept piling up since last week. Next thing I knew, it was 1 P.M. and I was getting peckish. I went down to the salad bar, where I knew I could get a salad without all the ingredients I disliked. The line stretched outside the bar and I peeked inside to see whether it was worth the wait. And then I spotted her. Her blond hair stood out from the other hungry people lined up. It was amazing how even in a place like this she looked glamorous and noble.

"Mia," I called out and stood next to her, as if she was reserving a place for me, "how are you?"

"Everything's great," and she certainly looked great, too. She peeked at the menu, as if she wouldn't obviously have salad.

"I was planning on calling you," I was actually planning to call her for quite some time but didn't get the chance, "I decided to do it."

Mia looked at me and said with a smile, "me too."

It was amazing how she immediately understood what I meant, and even more so, agreed with me. We both understood we couldn't go into much detail while standing there in the crowded line.

After we ordered our lunch, we found a relatively quiet table. I sat in front of Mia and opened my take-away container, "so, where are you planning to have it?"

"I think at the Tel Aviv Medical Center," Mia opened her box and poured thick dressing on her salad, "I got a recommendation for Dr. Dolev, have you heard of him?"

"He was at the Foundation symposium. Such a shame you weren't there. He actually looks nice and professional. He answered everyone's questions patiently. I think he also operated on Lisa, and everyone strongly recommends him."

"Maybe I should call Lisa and talk directly to her. The Foundation get-togethers are not really my cup of tea. Except for you, I hardly talk about it with other people."

It was understandable. I didn't share my genetic information with a lot of people, either. In any case, anyone who heard about me being a carrier had something to say. One says he knows someone who got sick and suggests I talk to her (why would it help me to talk to someone who got sick but isn't a carrier?). Another says they know someone who had an operation (but couldn't remember what kind, who was the surgeon and whether or not it was preventative). Everyone had a different advice, (holistic medicine, veganism, meditation and more of the such). But what they all had in common, was the look in their eyes. They all looked at me with pity, as if I was dying.

"To each her own. Lisa is really nice and knows a lot of doctors." A piece of tomato found its way to my salad and I removed it with disgust.

"I want to find out if I'm qualified for a tissue reconstruction surgery."

"What's that?"

"They take fat from your stomach and use it to reconstruct your breasts." Mia spread some butter on the bread she got with her salad and ate with evident pleasure.

"I didn't know it was even possible."

"It's irrelevant for skinny girls like you, but I have some meat on me." Mia gently patted her belly, that didn't look at all fat to me. "Two surgeries for one, that way you don't have to replace your implants every few years, and all that."

"That really is a plus." Maybe I should have ordered the pasta instead of the salad and started growing a gut.

"Have you chosen a surgeon yet?"

"I scheduled a consultation next week with Katzman and Remez. We'll see."

"Both are considered amazing. Everything is private, naturally. Will your insurance cover it?"

"I actually don't have a clue. I didn't think about it." I felt silly not even having started looking into it.

"Never mind, as long as you find someone good. The rest will work itself out." Mia spoke with confidence and it reassured me. "How's your mother?"

"Not so good. The doctors don't really know how to treat her cancer."

Mia's mom died of breast cancer when she was really young, less than twenty, I think. Although I knew she sympathized with me, I didn't feel comfortable complaining too much, because after all, I still had a mother.

"They generally don't too much. Which is why I decided I can't rely on their early diagnosis." Mia said firmly. "I have to go back to the office, let me know after your appointments."

"Of course, we'll be in touch." I tightly hugged her goodbye.

CHAPTER 53

"Shirley, here's your file. You can see the doctor now." Dr. Katzman's secretary gave me a paper folder and opened the door leading to the exam room. I walked into the room and Michael followed me in. It looked like a private clinic from an American TV show, filled with statues and paintings scattered around. There were also some 'thank you' letters and gifts that Dr. Katzman probably received from his patients.

Dr. Katzman sat behind a large wooden desk and we sat in front of him on two leather armchairs. His short greying hair and delicate glasses, disclosed his real age. A wooden box full with silicone implants was placed on the table. You could clearly tell what he mostly did.

Next to the desk, was a door leading to a room that looked like a real doctor's clinic.

Dr. Katzman opened the file and scanned the form I had filled in. "So, I understand that you're a carrier and you're looking to have a preventative surgery."

"Right," I tried smiling to conceal how nervous I was. I looked at Michael but he was too busy examining the art across the room.

"It's not my place to say, but I think you're doing the right thing." He put the folder down and leaned back, "I operate almost weekly on two to three carriers having a preventative surgery. In the US nearly all carriers have it, we just started having them here."

"Yes," for some reason I was at a loss for words.

"Come, I'll show you what it's going to look like." He turned the screen to me and the image was split in two – the before and after. Michael looked at me with embarrassment and kept quiet. Dr. Katzman flipped through the pictures and explained who amputated just one breast and who amputated both, and how the reconstruction happens in either cases. I tried to conceal my shock with an awkward silence and polite nodding.

"Come into the room and take off your top, we'll see what we're dealing with." He stood up and went to the exam room, I followed him. Michael stayed in his chair and his alarmed look showed that he didn't know where to put himself. He wouldn't come with me to my checkups, and except for the pregnancy scans, he has never been with me on such intimate exams.

I undressed while Dr. Katzman sat on a chair in front of me and examined me. "You should know there are two options. If we decide to keep the nipples, I make the incision under the breasts. If you choose not to keep them, then I make the incision here, in the middle of the breast and around the nipples."

"OK," I was still speechless. The whole thing was too embarrassing for me.

"So, which do you prefer?" he asked after waiting a few moments.

"Oh, I think I won't keep my nipples." I could see Michael, in the corner of my eye, sinking into his chair, "I understood it reduces chances of getting sick even further".

"So they say, but it's up to you."

"Do I need to make a decision right now?"

"No, you can let me know later."

"Good, so I'll think about it."

"About the size, I'll try putting in as much as I can but I don't want to stretch the skin too much. There's not a lot of excess skin here and I'll be removing some with the nipples. You'll choose the type of implant and I'll bring a few sizes with me to the operation, and we'll see which one fits."

"OK," I nodded and Dr. Katzman stood up.

"You can look inside that box and feel them," he said to Michael, as he walked into a storage room, "there are different types of implants, but I recommend a silicone anatomic one. They get the best results."

Dr. Katzman came back with a camera and signaled that I stand on the red X marked on the floor in the middle of the room, "Come, let's take some pictures."

I felt my face turning red, but I tried to remain calm, as if I took nude photos next to my husband on a daily basis. Michael was busy with the implant box and I thought maybe I should have charged Dr. Katzman rather than paid him. All that was left for me was to hope my pictures didn't find their way to his presentation or into the dossier at the waiting lounge.

"Get dressed and let's talk." He put the camera back in its place and stepped into the office.

"So," he said as I sat in front of him (fully clothed this time), "I operate at the Tel Aviv Private Medical Center. This surgery is comprised of two parts – amputation and reconstruction. I'm in charge of the reconstruction. On your way out, my secretary will give you a list of surgeons who amputate and with whom I prefer working. I can also work with other surgeons, but those on the list are those who I trust and know their work. It's your choice to make. Also, you should either find an anesthesiologist, or use the one at the hospital. That's also up to you. If you decide to move forward with me, then you can call my secretary and she'll schedule the operation. She will also give you a list of tests you should have with you. I work with all insurance companies. If you need help handling their bureaucracy, my secretary will help you. That's it, more or less. Do you have any questions?"

"No," I looked at Michael who shook his head.

"Good, stay in touch." He stood up and we shook hands with

formality.

His secretary explained everything again as she handed us a pile of papers and of course, a receipt for the consultation.

"That was awkward," Michael said when the elevator door closed.

"It was, but that's how it is, I guess," I casually said, though still worrying about those photographs.

"What next?" Michael held the door open and we stepped outside into the sticky Tel Aviv air.

"We'll go see the other doctor and decide who we want to go forward with. Do you have it written down? It's next week."

"I think so."

"What do you think about Dr. Katzman?"

"I wouldn't meet him for coffee, but he looks professional. The surgery sounds complicated, doesn't it?"

"Perhaps, but it doesn't matter. If that's what we need to do, we'll do it. Worst case scenario, your new wife would have to replace me sooner."

"No problem, I just need to let her know in advance, so she can get ready." This time Michael went with it.

"You'll get a notice, don't worry," I said and we kept walking towards the parking lot. "Don't you mind the silicone? It won't be the same, you know?"

"I don't mind. I'd still love you with silicone." Michael pressed me closer to him and we walked, hugging.

I kept thinking about all the stories I read on the Foundation's website, about men who really struggled with their wife's surgery. Sometimes, it caused a serious marital crisis. I let it go, although I didn't think Michael really understood what this surgery meant. I was losing a big part of my femininity. I hoped Dr. Katzman was really as good as he thought himself to be.

CHAPTER 54

My second task, other than booking Natalie for the next two months, was finding someone who would stay the night with me at the hospital. Everyone said that I would need help at night. Mostly during the first night. So I decided to ask Sarah, my only single friend.

"So," I said to her on one of our short conversations, "I need your help." I closed the office door for some privacy. Anna had just left for a hearing at court which made this a good time for having such conversations.

"Of course, honey, anything you need. You name it." I could ask Sarah for anything, if she couldn't do it, she would always let me know.

"I need help after the surgery. Someone to stay the night with me at the hospital. I would rather Michael stay with the kids. Would you stay with me?"

"Sure, no problem. Text me the date and I'll save it." I could finally put Sarah's unique and flexible sleeping skills to use.

"Thank you, Sarah, so much, you're a real life-saver," I said, and I really meant it. "I'll feel better knowing Michael is with them at night."

"Don't worry, honey. I'll take good care of you. You won't want to go back to him." She laughed and I imagined her curls bouncing around as she spoke.

"I just hope that he would want me back after the surgery..."

"Of course he will. He's crazy about you. And you'll still be gorgeous with your new boobs." I hoped Sarah had closed her office door so that Nathan wouldn't hear our conversation. I hated having these conversations at work, but it was impossible having them later, "is everything ready for the surgery?"

"Not really, but I'm working on it." I peeked at the operation to-do list I had written down in the little notebook I would take everywhere with me.

"What else do you have left?"

"I met Dr. Shavit, a surgeon some girls from the Foundation had recommended, and I took the documents from him for the insurance. I just need my insurance company to approve the surgery. They referred me to their own Onco-geneticist. The surgeon asked me to have another MRI to confirm everything was fine, and that the surgery was indeed preventative, so I made an appointment for that too."

"All these procedures sound like such a pain. Good thing you're a lawyer and know what to do. I had to help my mother with these things a few years ago, because she couldn't handle it on her own. Are you getting any work done?"

"Between that and all of mom's issues, hardly. Even when I'm at the office I can barely focus. In any case, there's still plenty of time, until mid-August." I looked at the papers piled up on my desk, there was hardly any place left for my tea.

"That's a long time from now, will you get the results by then?"

"The surgery is after the holidays. There's no pressure, just a lot of bureaucracy. The only thing I'm nervous about is hoping it won't be too late." These bureaucracies felt like having a second job.

"What do you mean?"

"I hope nothing develops while I wait for the surgery. And then, instead of a surgery, I'll have chemo." I closed the notebook and put it in my bag so it wouldn't get lost on my table.

"God forbid, why would you say that?" Sarah's superstitious side took over. "Stop talking nonsense. Everything's going to be fine."

"I hope," I said. I hope it won't be too late.

CHAPTER 55

"You can take the kids into the water in the meantime. I'll just put away the food and come." Michael reluctantly took them to the pool, and I packed the leftover vegetables and hard-boiled eggs in boxes.

There weren't a lot of people at the pool, because bathing season had just begun. I placed the boxes in the cooler and slathered some sunscreen on myself. I hardly heard the phone ringing in my closed purse.

"Hey Gabi, what's up?" Michael called after Ariel who ran towards me. I signaled him it was OK. I was planning on telling Gabi I would call him back later, but he spoke before I could say anything.

"Listen, mom just fell, and she's in a lot of pain, but she won't go to the hospital."

"Do you want me to come?" Ariel was wet and clung on to me as she tried pulling me towards the water.

"I would love it if you could. When can you come?"

"Give me an hour and I'll be there."

"OK, come as fast as you can." Gabi sounded extremely nervous.

"OK, I'll see you soon."

I waved at Michael to come over and he came out of the water with Romy in one hand and Adam in the other.

"Mom fell and I have to go to her right now," I said as I handed out towels to everyone and helped Romy wear her sandals.

"OK, did anything happen to her?"

"I don't know. Gabi said she's in pain."

"What happened to Cathy?" Adam asked.

"She fell and I need to go and help her," I said as I looked for Ariel's second sandal.

"But I want to stay in the pool." Ariel started running to the pool but Michael chased and caught her.

"We can't, we need to go home." Michael tickled her to soften the blow, "I'll give you ice cream at home, what do you think?"

"Yes! Ice cream!" Adam and Ariel shouted excitedly and agreed to wear their sandals.

We rushed to the car and when we got home, I went in with them to change clothes and then left quickly. With every second that passed my nerves were about to get the better of me. Michael sat the kids down and handed them ice creams to compensate them for our change of plans. I rushed out of the house, and grabbed a sweater, just in case we find ourselves at the ER. It's always cold at the ER.

When I got to their place, Gabi opened the door. Today, I didn't waste time on niceties and ran straight to mom's room. "Mom, how are you?" I yelled from the hallway.

"I'm fine," mom was in bed, covered with a thin blanket. She had an agonized expression on her face as she shamelessly lied.

"You're not fine. Where does it hurt?"

Mom paused for a few seconds, as if she was contemplating whether she should tell me, and only then replied, "actually, my head hurts a little."

"From the fall?" I asked and sat next to her on the bed.

"Probably," Gabi walked into the room, "she fell on the door frame. I was right next to her and I couldn't catch her. I think she hit her head."

"What made you fall?"

"I don't know, I just came out of the bathroom and lost control of my legs."

I looked at Gabi and then at mom again. The pain showed on her face, even though she wouldn't admit.

"Maybe we should go to the ER?"

"What for? Waste another day? On a Saturday?" Mom twitched her face with pain. "In any case, there are only interns today at the hospital, and they don't know anything." Gabi left the room, and I could hear from the kitchen sounds of pots banging and drawers opening and closing.

"Maybe we should call and ask an on-call nurse?"

"As you wish. In the meantime, could you please get me a glass of water? I want to take something for the pain."

I went to the kitchen and saw Gabi standing and staring outside the window. He was leaning against the counter and I noticed he was wearing the silly red-spotted apron on which I had sown the word 'mom' ages ago. That ridiculous apron made me smile, even though what I actually wanted to do, was to cry.

"She wants to take a painkiller," I told him as I poured her a glass of water.

"Something isn't right with her. She's in a lot of pain. She just fell for no reason. I couldn't catch her on time." He kept looking outside.

"If that's the case then you need someone here all the time. She can't be on her own anymore."

"I guess…" Gabi said quietly as he left the kitchen and went back to mom with her water.

I called the medical helpline and within a few minutes a nurse name Rona picked up. After having a back and forth on the matter, she convinced mom to go to the hospital ER. She wouldn't listen to us, but she did listen to Rona. It was mom who actually taught me that trick. She would do the same to me, but she used grandma, who would basically repeat what mom said, without making me angry. I tried thinking who I could do that trick with, when I'll need to convince my own kids. But the ambulance came and I didn't have too much time to dwell on it.

Gabi insisted that they take her to the Tel Aviv Medical Center, because that was where she was treated. They finally agreed. I drove with mom and Gabi drove in his car behind us.

We arrived at the hospital ER. Judging by the amount of people, you would think this was the hottest hangout in Tel Aviv on Saturday noon. While the paramedics gave the nurse the relevant information, I texted Gabi that we were inside.

They connected mom to the monitor. We were already familiar with every parameter on this monitor. The blood saturation parameter was too low.

"Can someone maybe take a look at what's going on here?" I asked the on-call doctor again, who looked as if she herself needed to lie down and rest on one of the ER beds.

"I'll be right with you," she replied and kept walking away.

Gabi arrived a few minutes later. Mom shut her eyes and rested. I used the opportunity to quietly point at the low number. Gabi nodded with concern and we both stood silent by mom's bed.

After what felt like forever, a doctor, whose name I didn't catch, came over. He said mom needs a special CT to check her lungs. Each time mom looked my way, I smiled at her, when in fact, I was on the verge of a nervous breakdown.

"You can go. Take a taxi to our place." Gabi handed over my purse, that was on the bed next to mom.

"I can stay with you." I was willing to stay as long as it took. Michael was home with the kids, and he hadn't even called me, which meant everyone was still alive.

"No need. I'll let you know after the exams. It can take awhile." Gabi insisted and it was no use arguing with him, so I kissed and hugged mom goodbye.

I stepped out into the disgustingly humid Tel Aviv air. Although Gabi was there with her, I felt I had abandoned mom at the hospital.

"OK, they're waiting for a CT at the ER," I told Jonathan on my way to the taxi station.

"Yes, dad told me."

"She's in real pain." A few tears rolled down my cheeks.

"Yes," Jonathan replied and I could hear the sadness in his voice.

"I don't know what else we can do to help her," I said with complete despair.

Jonathan kept quiet. There was really nothing else for us to say or do, other than what was already being said and done. We agreed to talk later.

When I returned home, the children sat around the table, smeared with chocolate in every place imaginable.

"She wanted a birthday cake," Michael smiled apologetically.

"But her birthday is in two weeks from now..." I heard something crack and noticed I had stepped on sprinkles scattered all over the sticky floor (and the table, the counter, and Ariel's happy face).

"I'll clean up," Michael said when I walked into the kitchen and tried looking for a clean spot to put my purse down.

Egg leftovers, flour and sugar caked the counter, and Ariel's chocolaty handprints were all over the cabinets. I took a deep breath and tried to keep it together. I really tried. But I couldn't.

"Why was it so important to do it today? I can't believe you agreed to this!" My voice grew louder with every word, until I was literally screaming. The kids looked at me and then at Michael.

"I told you I'd clean up. Go rest."

"Seriously?! We need to get a cleaning crew to handle this mess!"

"Mom, we'll clean up," Adam said, as he walked into the kitchen and grabbed a rag. He started cleaning one of the cabinet doors but only smeared the chocolate everywhere.

"Leave it, I'll clean up," I said angrily, even though I tried calming down. "Finish eating."

Adam went back to his chocolate cake and I took my anger out on cleaning. I scrubbed the cabinet doors (how on earth did they get dirty on the inside?!) I rubbed the counter (if Michael would have bothered cleaning it earlier, it wouldn't be this sticky!) and I washed all the dishes they used (why did they need three different bowls?!). Mom used to say, there's some dirt only mothers see. At that moment, I understood what she meant.

Just as I opened the oven, and witnessed the horror in it, Gabi called.

"So, we just came back from the doctor," he said, as if we had already started the conversation, "and mom has a blood clot in her lung."

"How did that happen?" I gave up, what more could happen to her?

"They say it's from the cancer. She needs blood thinners again."

"I'll come tomorrow after work to visit. Will someone be with her tomorrow?" For a moment, I tried remembering when was the last time I could spontaneously do whatever I wanted, without having to check with Natalie, Alice or Michael. I couldn't.

"Julie will be here tomorrow morning and Jonathan said he'll come at noon, when he wakes up."

"OK, so we'll be in touch. Give her kisses for me."

"Shirley says hi," I heard him saying seconds before we hung up.

I put the phone down and closed my eyes.

"What's wrong with Cathy?" Adam asked.

"She fell and got hurt. She's going to stay at the hospital for a while." I caressed his hair, which was similar to Tommy's.

"I also fell today, I hurt my knee. Look," he pointed at a little blue mark on his knee and gave me a worried look. "Do I also need to go to the hospital?"

"No, honey, you're fine."

"Are you sure?"

"Positive."

"Good." He started walking into the kitchen, but then turned around and asked, "but Cathy's also going to be fine, right?"

"We hope so," I lied to him, "the doctors are doing their very best."

"Good. I love Cathy."

Adam went to play with his toys, while Ariel took another piece of cake, with Michael's help this time. I went to the bathroom, locked the door, and only then I could cry on my own.

CHAPTER 56

"You're at work?" I asked mom in complete shock. Anna peeked over her computer screen but kept quiet.

"Yes," she replied proudly. "June came with me." June was mom's new Philippine nurse, who started helping mom when things went south and we didn't have much of a choice.

"You took your nurse to the office? I'm shocked!" I couldn't believe it. I thought that after having to move around in a wheelchair most of the time, she wouldn't go to the office every day. But she wouldn't give up. Anna also had a shocked expression but didn't say a word.

"OK, good for you. I'm stunned. I wouldn't go to work for much less." My envy towards her employees reared its head again. It was unfair that they spent time with her and I was stuck in my office with a pile of files.

"I prefer keeping busy and not having time to think."

"I can get that..." I replied, "OK, so I'll come over at about 6."

"Good, sweetie, I'd like that. I have to go to a meeting. We just approved an extension in Kibbutz Einat and we're having a toast."

"Are you allowed to drink with all the drugs you're taking?" Anna quietly peeked at me again.

"That's not what's going to kill me, sweetie. Enjoy work, see you in the evening."

"What's going on with your surgery?" Anna asked when I hung up.

"I'm waiting for answers from the insurance company about the funding. But I'm planning on having it after the holidays."

"Good, I wanted to tell you that I think you're really brave." Anna gave me a surprising hug.

"Brave? I'm not at all brave. On the contrary. I'm terrified. It's just a matter of what scares me more. Once the surgery scared me more, but now it's the cancer. That's it. Balance of terror."

"All in all, logical" Anna laughed. "I still think it's a brave move."

"Thank you. But I'm really doing it so that my kids won't have to go through what I'm going through with my mom."

Anna held my hand for a few seconds, as if trying to pass on mystical powers. An insubordinate tear rolled down my cheek, and smeared the makeup I used to hide the dark circles that settled around my eyes.

"How is Michael handling the whole surgery thing?" Anna asked with caution. "Does it bother him? You know, after all, it's not really the same thing."

"He claims that he's perfectly fine with it and it doesn't make a difference to him. I think he just doesn't understand what this surgery truly means. It's going to be even worse with the ovaries. I've heard scary stories about loss of sexual drive, weight gain, hot flashes... in short, we're only getting started."

"Wow, it sounds horrible. Doesn't it freak you out, hearing all these stories?"

"If I don't read them, would it change anything? I'd rather know everything. All possible scenarios. I want to be prepared as much as possible."

"I don't know if I would have done it. Sounds scary."

"Like I said, when the other option is cancer, it's not as scary. Besides, there are hormones you can take that help with those symptoms. In any case, I have to remove my ovaries. That's something that almost all carriers do. I'm sure that if my mom would have known about the gene sooner, she would have gone through that surgery, and we wouldn't be in this situation."

When we walked into the kitchen, we joined all the girls eating their lunch standing up. I sat quietly eating my tomato-free salad and listened to their conversations. Lea was talking about taking her kids to Netherlands this summer (how can I book a flight when mom's in her current state?) Carry is going to a cabin up north (I wonder if they'd let you cancel last moment in case you need to attend a funeral?) Nancy said her parents were taking the entire family to Cyprus for a week (which we could never do, since no one could take us). But what really broke my heart, was when Emily said that she and her sister were going with their mom for a weekend in Berlin (some "girl time"). The only place my mom and I visited together, was Tel Aviv. More specifically, the Tel Aviv Medical Center.

***

"She tried dialing with the remote, like a phone," Gabi told me when we spoke in the evening.

"What?" I was just getting ready to give the kids a bath. Ariel ran away naked and I tried bringing her back with Romy still in my arms. She was getting too heavy for this.

"She tried calling you from the TV's remote control. And yesterday, she tried answering a phone call, but couldn't. As if she had forgotten how to use her phone. Something isn't right and I don't think it has anything to do with her falling down."

"So, what do you think it is?" I put Romy down and she ran towards Ariel.

"I don't know." I heard Gabi's favorite talk show in the background. Even when he'd occasionally come over to babysit, he would watch it loudly.

"Maybe you should ask Dr. Bloom? Maybe it has something to do with the cancer?"

"I left him a message and I'm waiting for him to call me back."

"Do you want me to come over? Michael will soon be here, so I can come."

Romy and Ariel were jumping on Ariel's bed. Romy wasn't wearing a diaper, so all I could do was hope we don't have any unnecessary accidents.

"You don't have to come," he didn't tell me not to come, which to me was a sign that he wanted me to come but didn't feel comfortable asking.

"I'll come over. I'll text you when I'm on my way. Bye."

I grabbed both of them and successfully got them into the shower. Ariel splashed Romy and me, and the floor. At least now, I don't need to take a shower, and I can leave as soon as Michael walks in.

I stopped at mom's favorite café to get a tart, but they didn't have the kind that she liked. I chose some éclairs and rushed to their place.

The door was unlocked so I let myself in. Gabi was sitting in the living room, watching some talk show. I gave him a kiss on the head and then went to mom.

I walked into the room and mom smiled at me. But it was a different smile. An honestly calm smile. As if she suddenly possessed a certain serenity. As if it wasn't her who was about to die of ovarian cancer. She watched a silly sitcom, as usual, and when she tried lowering the volume, she changed the channel instead. I helped her and sat next to her with the éclair.

"Would you like to have a dessert?" I asked and offered her the pastry.

"Of course, thank you, sweetie." She took a bite and then placed the éclair on her nightstand. She went back to watching TV, as if I wasn't there.

We sat there quietly for a few minutes.

"Were you at work today?"

"I think so," she replied quietly.

It was an especially weird conversation. She answered my questions, but nothing else. After fifteen minutes, she said she was tired. I kissed her goodbye and she fell asleep.

"It really is strange," I said to Gabi when I came back to the living room.

"Right?" Gabi kept looking at the TV.

"Has Bloom called you back?"

"Not yet."

"Is this what you do every evening?"

"Why not? I'm resting."

"Maybe we should go out someday? You haven't gone out in months. I'll even go with you to a concert." Those who knew me, knew that to me this was a real sacrifice of my free time.

Gabi smiled. "Not interested."

"But why?" It pained me to think he sat here alone every evening. "We'll go out and you'll get some fresh air. You deserve having some fun, too. June can stay with mom."

"I can't go out without her," Gabi said assertively, and it was clear he was trying to make me drop it, but mostly, he wanted to stop talking.

"OK, if you change your mind, let me know."

I sat with him and watched another commentator commenting on a different political scandal. At least when it came to these matters, things were predictable. At some point I noticed it was late, so I kissed him goodbye and went back home. The entire way back, I kept having this image of Gabi (sitting alone in the dark, a whiskey glass in one hand, the remote in the other,) and mom (lying in bed with that weird smile). It was hard trying to remember how things used to be. How they used to be. Everything took such an extreme turn, and the realization that things would never be the same, made me so sad...

CHAPTER 57

"I don't see the problem; we told them that we have about five shows a week for schools. Why do they keep saying they don't have all the data?" David asked with a naivety that was typical of someone who was engaged in a judicial fight against the government.

"They're just trying to make things harder, don't let it get to you." I collected all the pages with the notes I had made and stapled them together.

"So, now what?" David picked his bag off the floor and stood up. "Is there anything else I can do?"

"Not right now. I'll make a draft of our response and I'll email it to you."

"Again, thank you so much." David warmly shook my hand, "I've already told Alice, several times, what a pleasure it is working with you."

"Thank you," I think I was blushing, "it's a pleasure for me too. You're one of our best clients." I stood up to walk him to the door, but then got a text. "We'll keep in touch," I said and went back to my desk.

I hoped it wasn't a text from Natalie saying she couldn't come. We were about to have a meeting so we could divide the work load for the summer vacation. If I won't attend it, I might accidently get cases I really don't want to handle. Due to summer camp considerations, most lawyers are taking their vacation during the last week or two of

August. This year, we were trying to plan ahead and make sure there was at least one of us here every day. Despite the summer hiatus, there were still urgent matters that required attention.

"Call me," Gabi wrote, as if he was charged per word. I immediately called him.

"What happened?" I asked nervously.

"Mom fell again and we're in the ER. The orthopedic ER."

"I'm coming." I plainly stated. I organized my purse and shoved my phone charger in first.

"Tell Alice I had to go because my mom is in the ER," I told Anna as I left.

I ran to the parking lot. A familiar sense of anxiety weighed my chest down. I tried taking deep breaths and calm down, but couldn't.

***

I found mom on a stretcher in the orthopedic ER hall.

"We're waiting for an X-ray," Gabi said when I hugged him.

"Do you want something to eat or drink? I can go to the cafeteria."

"I can't eat," mom said in a weak tone, "I want to throw up."

"I'll go get myself something to eat." Gabi took a long look at mom and then left.

"Did you leave work again?"

"Of course." I looked for a chair, but they were all taken.

"They gave me a lot of liquids and I have to go to the bathroom." Mom pointed at the empty IV bag and put her hand back down.

"Are you allowed to get up?"

"I don't think you can help me. I'm too heavy for you. Could you ask for a bedpan?"

"OK, I'll go get one." I tried looking for someone who could give mom a bedpan, but all the nurses were running around. They all looked so busy and I didn't want to bother them. I wandered around the hall and then saw someone grab some sheets from a room facing the bathroom. I waited for her to walk away, and then got into the small room that was filled with sheets, towels, gloves, and many other things, some of which I didn't recognize. On one of the shelves, I found a small cardboard bedpan. I then helped mom use it. I couldn't believe this was happening. Mom and I, in the middle of the hall, with a bedpan. Despite being shocked, I kept operating on auto-pilot. Not thinking, just doing.

I looked for a place to leave the bedpan and then went back to mom.

"I can't believe you had to do that for me," she said with her eyes shut. "I was always afraid of getting old. I didn't want to become a burden on anyone. I didn't want anyone changing my diaper or cleaning after me like a baby."

"Nonsense, mom. You're just sick. It happens."

"No, it doesn't just happen. On the one hand, I know I won't get old, and on the other, I'm already at the diaper stage. It's a lose-lose situation."

"You didn't lose anything," I lied through my teeth, "when you feel better, you won't need any help. When are you having the X-ray?"

"I don't know."

Gabi came back with a bottle of water for me, and stood quietly by the bed.

"You really didn't have to come. We'll have the X-ray and then go back home. We'll just see if she broke anything." He said after a few moments.

"I'll stay a little longer, and then go back to the office, don't worry. I have an important meeting at 3 P.M."

"As you wish," mom said with her eyes closed, she looked in pain, or nauseous, or both.

"Caterina!" someone yelled, with a heavy accent.

"Here!" mom raised her hand like a little schoolgirl and Gabi pulled the stretcher into the X-ray room.

After the exam, mom was back in the stretcher, that was placed in the hall, and again waited for the doctor. I left them at 2:30, and went back to the office in despair.

**

Everyone was already sitting in the tiny conference room, but there was one spot left by the door. I sat down and took out my phone to silence it, but even before I could put it back in my pocket, I saw I had received a text.

"The doctor said she didn't break anything. They're taking her to do a head CT, because she's throwing up. They want to check if she had a concussion." That was one of the longest texts Gabi has ever sent me.

"OK, keep me posted," I replied and put the phone back in my jacket pocket.

"Is there someone who isn't planning on taking time off this month?" Alice opened the meeting. No one raised her hand.

"So, let's go one-by-one and see when each of you is taking time off so we can find the problematic days." There was a calendar on the screen and each read her vacation days to Dina, who added them to the calendar.

I kept checking my phone every minute, to see if there were any new text, but there were none.

I was trying to be the bigger person, and volunteered to come in for a few days during the last week of the month. I obviously didn't tell them that after being at home with the kids for a week and a half, I would probably prefer being in the office and resting. Michael can handle them alone for a few days.

After the meeting I called Gabi. "They're letting us go home, but they did the CT and they found a fluid buildup in her head."

"What? What made that happen?"

"Probably the cancer. I don't completely get it, but the doctor said it explains everything that's been going on."

"Her falling?"

"Not just. Also, what she did with the remote. It hurt her cognitive abilities." I heard everyone leaving and the office slowly emptying.

"So, what now?"

"Dr. Bloom said that there's nothing we can do in her case."

I was still hoping that the doctors had some sort of solution. Another way of buying some more time with mom. I asked Gabi what do we do.

"Nothing," he answered quietly, "we wait."

"Wait for what?" I insisted.

"The end."

When I heard his answer, I closed my eyes and felt everything getting dark around me. I sat down (or perhaps crashed) on the chair. I tried breathing but I felt a huge stone weighing my chest down. The office was empty and I could only hear the vacuum cleaner in the background.

"I have to go home. We'll talk in the evening. I'll try coming over."

"OK"

I took my purse and left. Even though it was still light outside, I felt as if I was walking through mist. I didn't know how I would handle the kids at home. The only thing I wanted to do was get into bed, hide under the blanket and never come out. I don't even remember the way back home, only that I found myself standing at the front door, breathing deeply and trying to muster the strength to face the world. Ariel's loud screams pulled me back to reality. I was so scared that I ran inside and towards the direction of her screaming.

"What happened?" I asked Natalie who was holding Romy in her arms. Adam and Ariel were sitting on the sofa that was once white, and watching some kids' show.

"A terrible disaster," she smiled, "Adam changed the channel while she was watching a movie."

"Can you stay a bit longer today? I have to make a phone call."

"No problem. Until when?"

"I don't know. About an hour?"

Natalie checked her phone for the time and replied, "cool".

I went upstairs and called Jonathan. We agreed before that we would keep each other posted, and sadly, this time, I had something new to tell him. I knew he had an exam this afternoon and was hoping he was done by now.

"Hi," I said quietly.

"Hi," hearing his voice, I realized Gabi had already spoken to him.

"Things aren't good. When are you coming?" I looked at myself in the bedroom mirror. You could see the sadness on my face.

"I'll try coming tomorrow for a visit."

"Good, will you talk to Tommy?" Tommy had recently become more reserved and introverted. He would only come out of his shell to lash out at everyone. Only Jonathan could get to him.

"Yes," he replied, but unenthusiastically.

"Thank you."

We both fell silent. Frankly, there was nothing left to say. The battle was over, there were no other moves left to play.

I hung up and lay in bed. I heard the kids talking, shouting, fighting and playing. I didn't know what I was supposed to tell them. I tried picturing the day after. The day she would no longer be with us. "Gone", as people put it lightly. I tried imagining how I would feel, but couldn't. It was beyond comprehension.

After half an hour I went downstairs and asked Natalie to come with me to the kitchen. Romy came with us and I sat her down by the table with a biscuit.

"My mom isn't doing too well. I'm going to need your help even more in the next few weeks."

"Oh, I'm sorry," Natalie said and hugged me, almost making me cry the tears I was holding in.

"Thank you. I'll go over the schedule and check when I need your help. I'll send you a text with all the information, but there might be other unexcepted days."

"Sure, honey, anything you need, I'm here. They can come over to my place, don't worry."

"Thank you, sweetie." I reached for my purse to pay her.

Natalie said goodbye to the kids and left.

I decided it was time to call Michael, but he sent me to voice mail and texted me "sorry, I can't talk right now." If I had a dime for every time he texted me these words, I could have paid an au-pair.

CHAPTER 58

Dr. Friedenson looked just like he did in all the morning talks shows he appeared on. He was short and sturdy, had a pleasant smile and plenty of patience. I also saw him at the Foundation symposium conference, but this was the first time we spoke.

"How can I help you, Shirley?" he asked when I sat in front of him in the medical center.

"I'm a BRCA1 carrier and I would like to have a preventive breast amputation. Since you're an onco-genetic expert, I need a letter from you." I handed him my insurance member card and he scanned it. I wonder what else my file says about me.

"Can you tell me a bit more about your family history. Who got sick?"

"My mom got ovarian cancer when she was 50 years old. That's how we found out the gene was in the family. It turns out it came from her father, because her cousins are also carriers."

"OK, I'm not supposed to tell whether you should have the surgery or not, just confirm that you qualify for the surgery because you're a carrier," he said with formality while he filled out the form. Then he added with a quiet smile, "but between you and I, you're doing the right thing."

I stared at the window while he kept filling out the form. I wonder what would have happened if mom would have asked him rather than that idiot physician who told her the gene doesn't pass on from the father's side. Maybe we would have spent the summer having a family vacation. The sound of his stamp clicking pulled me back to reality.

"And how's your mother?" he asked.

"Not so well. The cancer has spread to her spine and she was told there's increased pressure on her brain caused by a fluid buildup." I hoped I was using the right terminology because I didn't want to sound ridiculous.

"I'm sorry to hear that. It sounds like these are the last weeks."

"Really?" Even though I assumed we didn't have much more time; I didn't expect it to be weeks.

"Spinal cancer cells prevent CFS absorption, which is the spinal liquid. It causes pressure on the brain that eventually... you understand?"

"Yes," I replied quietly, "I think I understand. There is really noting that can be done?"

"Now you only need to make sure that she isn't suffering. That's the only thing you can do for her. Good luck with the surgery," he said quietly and gave me all the signed forms. I left the room and felt that I could barely drag myself back to the car. His sentence rang through my head, over and over again – "last weeks." Weeks?

***

The next day I went to visit mom the first chance I had. The word "weeks" wouldn't stop ringing in my head, and I decided I should spend every moment I had with her.

"I'm OK," she said and smiled, but didn't really look at me. She still had that different look in her eyes. A look of someone who doesn't quite understand what's going on. Someone who has no worries. That smiling look wasn't my mother's look.

"Good," I took off my flip flops and lied beside her. I rested my head on her, and we stayed there together watching a movie.

"What movie is that?" I asked.

"I don't know. I think she's in love with him." She pointed at the screen.

"OK. When did the movie start?" I said just to keep the conversation going. She didn't initiate any conversation but at least she replied.

"I don't know."

I kept lying next to her quietly. "Weeks" I thought and a tear made its way. Mom didn't notice because she kept staring at the TV and my head rested on her. She didn't say a word. The only thing that crossed my mind was that this may be the last time we watch TV together.

"I decided to have the surgery after the holidays," I said to her, "do you remember I told you?"

"Yes," she replied but didn't say anything else.

"Maybe I could bring Romy over tomorrow?" Only Romy could come visit, because I didn't want the older ones to see mom in this condition, "I'll call you in the morning and you'll tell me when to come?"

"OK."

We stayed like that for an hour. I asked something every now and then, but didn't know whether what she was saying was true. I knew my mother was somewhere in there, but the woman talking to me wasn't her exactly. It was so strange.

"She's not herself," I told Gabi when I met him the living room, "she's really not herself."

"I know, it's getting worse by the day."

"She barely talks to me."

"Julie was actually here today, and they spoke. Your dad also sat here for two hours."

"Really?" I didn't know what surprised me more. The fact that she had a normal communication with someone else or that my dad was here for a whole two hours.

"Yes, we sat in the room and spoke. Mom was relatively fine." He lifted his gaze but wouldn't look at me.

I tried thinking whether I should tell him and then decided I should. "Yesterday, I saw a doctor about the surgery and told him about mom. He said he thinks these are her last weeks."

"Maybe it's time to tell Johnny to come to Israel," Gabi said quietly and kept staring at an unknown spot.

"I think he should come as soon as possible, while she's still communicative."

"Let's call him. It's noon there now." Gabi brought mom's phone. She couldn't use it anymore.

Jonny answered after two rings and Gabi put the call on speaker so the three of us could speak. It was one of the hardest conversations I ever had. Even though it was Gabi who mostly did the talking, hearing Johnny cry made me cry too. Johnny promised to book the first flight to Israel and come.

I hoped he would make it on time.

CHAPTER 59

"Mom... mom... mom..." I heard in my sleep. I opened my eyes and Ariel was standing beside me, gawking at me, wide-eyed, "can I have a snack pack?"

"Yes," I said and shut my eyes again. Then I jumped up and checked the time. I couldn't believe they let me sleep until 8:30 A.M. I looked to my side and saw Michael had gotten up – that explains it.

I checked my phone. There weren't any new messages and no missed calls. It was too early to call mom. I tried going back to sleep but couldn't.

I waited until 10 A.M. and then called mom. She didn't answer but I expected it. She hasn't answered her phone in a week, simply because she couldn't. Sometimes, she wouldn't even realize it was ringing. I called their home and someone, who sounded like Gabi before his morning coffee, answered.

"Can you ask mom if I can come now with Romy?" I asked, "I spoke to her about it yesterday."

"Cathy, can Shirley come over now?" I heard him asking in the background, but I didn't hear her answer.

"She says that you should come later because she's taking a shower. June is helping her but it takes a while. Try calling again later." Gabi didn't wait for my answer and hung up. The heat was terrible outside and I decided it was best that we stay home. The swimming pool in the yard, popsicles (which were in fact frozen grape juice with a spoon stuck in them) and a Disney movie (with lots of popcorn) did the trick.

I called again at noontime. Gabi said he's going out to buy something and mom went in to rest, so I could come over later, in the afternoon. When Romy fell asleep, I sent Michael with the older ones to the mall, where they could blow out some steam in a cool and distant place. I went into bed and fell asleep in mere seconds. I wish I would fall asleep at night this easily.

"We're on our way to the hospital," Gabi said when I answered the phone in my sleep.

"What?" I wasn't sure whether it was yet another horrific dream or reality.

"Mom lost conscious when I wasn't here. June didn't realize what was going on and we called an ambulance only when I got home. They left and I'm on the way in my car. Will you call Jonathan?"

"Sure, I'll be right there."

I called Jonathan and immediately left for the hospital.

***

I was once again, at the ER, on a Saturday. I was once again, looking for mom from one bed to the next. I was once again chasing doctors to come and take another look. But this time, it was different. Mom wasn't all there. That is, her body was there, but she was unconscious.

Gabi stood next to her in despair.

"June thought she was resting, so she didn't call me," he said again, but we both knew it didn't matter anymore.

I caressed mom and kissed her. I could see she was wearing all her jewelry.

I took off the necklace her mother gave her, and wore it. I put grandma's wedding ring on my finger, and also the ring she received from her old aunt. With every piece I took, I felt heavier and heavier, and terribly guilty. As if I was robbing her from who she was. But my fear that someone would steal them, was greater than my guilt.

"Do you know that in the morning, she asked June to get her dressed for work? June kept telling her it's Saturday, but she forgot." Gabi caressed mom's head and then held her hand.

Every now and then, a doctor would come to check mom, but they didn't have much to say except that she was in a coma. Jonathan came from Jerusalem with Maya, his new girlfriend, Tommy came too. This time we knew it was mandatory, and everyone had to come.

We passed the time crying (but not in front of Gabi, so as not to irritate him), laughing (Jonathan managed being witty and funny even in situations like these) and eating candy (that was the only thing we could get from the vending machines).

While we sat outside with our bag of potato chips, Gabi asked me to join him inside.

"It's a good thing we called Johnny." I sat next to mom on the only chair we could find in the ER, "maybe we should let him know things got worse?"

"I'll send him an email later; we need to think what we're going to do." Gabi paced back and forth by the bed.

"About what?"

"Mom has signed a living will. I don't know whether I should show it to the doctors."

"Why shouldn't you if that's what she wanted?"

"Because then, they might not treat her as well." Gabi stood on the other side of the bed and held mom's hand.

"Do you think there's anything they can do?" I whispered, because mom might still be able to hear.

"I don't know. But if there is, I want them to do anything they can."

"So, we can wait with the document and see what happens," I said. I didn't believe there was still hope for improvement, but I didn't want to bring Gabi down more than he already was.

"OK," it seemed this decision reassured him a bit.

Mom was hospitalized only in the evening, probably just so that they don't send us home. June stayed with her at night and Jonathan got the first morning shift.

CHAPTER 60

I pretended to work all morning. I couldn't focus on anything and canceled every meeting possible. I took the next day off, because I knew Johnny was supposed to arrive and wanted to be at the hospital.

I came in the afternoon to find mom in the same condition, only in a different room. I was mad that no one told me they had moved her, because when I walked into the previous room and saw an empty bed, I was about to faint. I tried talking to her and she didn't answer.

Gabi came in the evening to replace me, and there was still no change. June spent the night with mom again and I came back the next morning to find mom in the exact same condition. No doctor came in to speak with me. They probably didn't have much to say. The nurses came in every few hours to change her position, and that was that.

I sat there with a book but read the same sentence over and over again, until I gave up. I sat next to her and spoke to her. "Mom, I'm here and soon Jonathan will come." I hoped she was listening.

Jonathan came around the afternoon. "Hey, mom," he said and kissed her as usual, as if this were yet another Friday lunch and mom would soon whip out the schnitzels and mashed potatoes.

I couldn't believe this was our reality, that this was it. The end. We lost after so many years of fighting.

My phone rang and disrupted my thoughts. An unfamiliar number. "Hello?"

"Hi, am I speaking with Cathy's daughter?" someone asked.

"Yes, this is she."

"I'm the committee's secretary, where your mom works." 'Worked', I wanted to correct her, but kept quiet. "The head of the committee is here to see her. Can you tell me which department you are in?"

"Yes, we're in ward H, room 15." I really didn't feel like having any visitors, but no one really bothered asking me.

"Thanks. He'll be right there. Tell her to feel better soon. Goodbye." I told her, but it's not that it had any impact on her.

"The head of the committee is coming," I told Jonathan who was sitting with his earphones, deeply concentrated in his terrible music.

"Now?"

"Yes, now. Where is mom's headband? She wouldn't want people from work seeing her like this."

I found her orange headband in the drawer, and tried to somehow hide her bald head. Although some hair sprouted on her head, she preferred using headbands for now. So, I covered as much as I could, and just as I was done, the head of the committee came in with his entourage.

"Hello, Cathy," he said to her and perhaps even expected an answer.

"She's been unconscious since Saturday noon," I explained, so that he wouldn't think she was ignoring him.

"I assume you're her daughter? You look very much like her." He shook my hand with formality.

"Thank you, nice to meet you. I'm Shirley."

"And I'm her son," Jonathan introduced himself, and the head of the committee shook his hand too. If we weren't at the hospital, I would have thought he was running an election campaign.

"We were very sad to hear about your mother," he said, and seemed sincere. He looked at her, and I was glad I had the chance to put her headband on. "Everyone at the committee values her work and hopes she gets better."

"We hope so too, but it doesn't seem likely," I said and hoped the doctors were right and mom couldn't hear us. For a second, she seemed to have opened her eyes, but they immediately closed.

"In any case, you should know how much we really appreciate her work and were extremely happy when she came back to us. It's unfortunate that we're meeting under such terrible circumstances, but it was important for me to come."

"Thank you for coming," I replied, "I'm sure she would have truly appreciated it." The thought of speaking about mom in the past tense, made me sick to my stomach.

The head of the committee and his entourage left the room and I approached mom so I could remove her headband. When I touched her head, she opened her eyes for a moment.

"Mom, can you hear me?" Jonathan saw something was happening and took his earphones off. "Mom?"

Jonathan stood next to me and we both looked at her and waited. But mom just shut her eyes again. I sat next to her and tried talking to her, but she didn't reply.

"Jonathan, can you hear me?" I asked him after a few minutes of silence. He nodded and took off his earphones. "Do you think Tommy will come over?"

"I think it's too hard for him."

"Could be, but he'll eventually have to come and see her." Jonathan went back to his earphones and I stared at the window. Through the blind, I saw a window of another room. I wondered if someone else's mom was there too. The AC was rattling and I checked mom wasn't cold. I covered her with another blanket, just to be on the safe side.

An hour passed (which is forever by hospital standards) and we heard Johnny's voice at the nurse's desk, asking for mom's room number. I ran out to him and dragged him quickly into the room.

"Catika," Johnny leaned over her, "how are you Cathy?" Jonathan and I stood behind him.

Mom opened her eyes and looked at him. A big smile, one we hadn't seen in months, spread on her face and Johnny kissed her forehead and sat next to her. Jonathan and I stepped outside and started crying with excitement. There was a glimpse of hope. A hope that they might be wrong. Mom was back with us. We stood hugging and crying outside her room, until we calmed down and were able to return to mom.

"Mom woke up!" I texted Gabi, and he replied, "coming."

I was planning to leave the hospital early that evening, so I could spend some time with my family, but mom had woken up that night, so to speak, and I stayed as much as I could. Before I left, I whispered in her ear, "mom, I love you so much."

And she answered quietly, with her eyes shut, "me too."

CHAPTER 61

The days passed by both quickly and sluggishly at the same time. I couldn't go back to the office. I didn't want to hear stories about grandmothers spending time with their grandchildren, about family vacations, but mostly, I didn't want to see anyone. We kept taking different shifts at mom's as friends and family members came to visit.

"Where is your mom hospitalized?" dad asked the moment I answered his call, he skipped all niceties people usually say at the beginning of conversations.

"In ward H, why?"

"I'm here at the building, I'm coming up." I was surprised. When I had told him that mom was at the hospital, he didn't react. He just asked what hospital she was at, and that was it. I didn't think he would actually come.

I fixed mom's headband. I didn't know whether she was sleeping or unconscious.

Dad walked in, I kissed him on the cheek. He stood next to me and we both looked at mom.

"Why is her skin so dry?" he said and pointed at her hands. "Doesn't she have a moisturizer?"

I opened the drawer next to her bed, but there was only lip balm, "there's nothing here."

"I'm going to get her some. Do you want anything? Are you hungry?"

"No, I already ate."

"I'll be right back," he turned around and left.

I sat with mom and whispered to her, "dad was here and he's going to get you moisturizer. Weird, right?" but, obviously, she didn't reply. I gently caressed her. Dad came back after half an hour with a bag full of the most expensive cosmetics he could find at the drugstore.

"Take this, use it on her hands," he pulled a hand moisturizer out of the bag, I opened it and gently applied it to her skin. "I got her some perfume, too," he kept taking things out of the bag and placed them on her nightstand, which was packed with water bottles and liquid food boxes.

I squirted some on my finger, and gently rubbed it on her neck. It was a different scent than that one she used, and it felt strange. But I realized dad needed to feel he was doing something for her.

"That's better," he said, "she already looks so much better."

"Yes, thank you dad." I sat back in my chair next to mom and held her hand. Dad kept standing up and leaned against the wall.

"What did the doctors say?"

"Nothing. They don't have much to say." I didn't want to tell him we were told these were her last days, since I didn't want her hearing it. It was hard telling how much she understood of what was going on around her.

"When is she going home?"

"I don't know." I was quiet for a moment, and then continued, "now that you're here, I wanted to talk to you about something."

Dad kept quiet and listened, but still looked at mom and not at me.

"I'm having a surgery after the holidays."

"What surgery?" he turned his eyes to me, half-astonished, half-angry.

"A preventive mastectomy." There's nothing more embarrassing than telling your father you were about to amputate your breasts. It was similar to announcing you were pregnant.

"What?" He asked, as if it was all Greek to him.

"A preventive mastectomy, so I don't get cancer," I patiently explained, despite my embarrassment.

"Why would you have cancer?"

"Because mom passed on the cancer gene to me. This is why she got sick, because of the gene, and I want to prevent it." Although I had told him several times, that she got sick on account of the gene and not because they left to Australia, he struggled accepting it.

"But she has ovarian cancer." Dad looked at mom again.

"It's the same gene, dad." This was also something I had told him several times, but he was probably repressing it.

He was silent for a while and then said, "as you wish."

CHAPTER 62

With every day that passed, mom communicated with us less and less, and at some point, she simply stopped waking up. One day, they told us they were sending her home the next day. "There's nothing else we can do for her," they said. In other words – she's holding up a bed, take her home. Julie was with me at the time and I looked at her in despair, but she had nothing to say. She just hugged me tightly and sat next to mom.

"Where did all these creams come from?" she asked after having updated Gabi that mom was being sent home.

"Dad bought them for her. He visited a few days ago." Frankly, I couldn't remember what day it was. It all felt like one long neverending day.

"Expensive," Julie smelled the perfume, "she really did smell different today."

"He asked me to spray it on her, although I don't really think that was what she needed." I threw out food leftovers and empty bottles, trying to clean up the room a little.

"She likes this kind of things," Julie said and lovingly caressed mom's face.

"Yes." A nurse walked in and I stood up so she could check the IV.

"Your dad must be taking this hard." Julie gently held mom's hand and the nurse left.

"I guess," I had no idea what was going on in his mind. He wouldn't really talk to me.

"He loved her very much. They truly loved each other." Julie told me once again what I had already heard plenty of times, from so many different people, yet it still managed to move me.

I wanted to ask her more questions, but Johnny came and they started speaking in Hungarian. I went downstairs to grab a bite, and then realized I hadn't eaten all day.

**

The next day, mom returned to a home hospice, and I went back to the office.

The office was quiet because half of the staff members took time off. At the moment, the silence suited me perfectly. The office that was fully occupied was mine and Anna's. She hugged me when I walked in and brought me up to speed about everything that had happened that last week. I cried and cried, until we ran out of tissues.

"Maybe you should be with her?"

"Her brother is with her today. I'll go in the evening. In any case, she won't wake up anymore."

"That's terrible," Anna said and hugged me again before sitting down.

I tried my best, but couldn't work. It was as if my head was elsewhere. The only thing I could do was sit and cry.

"Maybe you should go home?" Anna cautiously suggested.

"The kids are home with Natalie, at least here I can cry and rest." The thought of having to keep them busy at home made me nervous. Being with Ariel was more challenging than writing an appeal for the supreme court. Frankly, I was unable to do either.

I looked at my schedule for the following week, so I could see what I'd have to cancel. I then noticed; the Foundation symposium was scheduled for Thursday at the Tel Aviv Medical Center. I registered a long time ago and with everything going on I simply forgot.

I sent an email to a few clients, letting them know I was taking some time off. They responded with "have fun", and "enjoy," and other responses that had nothing to do with what was really going on. I replied "thank you", because I didn't want to tell them I was probably going to be attending a Shiva.

CHAPTER 63

On Thursday morning, after spending some time with the children, Natalie came over and I went to visit mom.

I walked into the apartment and heard a familiar tune playing on a guitar. I quietly approached mom's room, and peeked inside. Tommy was sitting on a sofa, next to mom, and playing a children's song. He looked at her and didn't even notice I was there. I was contemplating whether I should join them, but decided to let them have some time alone. June was sitting in her room and waved at me.

I stepped into the living room and looked at the photos on the packed book shelves. A picture of mom and Gabi on a Ski vacation, dressed in thick colorful snow suits and smiling at each other. Another picture of Gabi and mom scuba-diving in Eilat. Another one, which I had taken a long time ago, of them hugging and smiling on their lawn in Maccabim on Jonathan's birthday party.

"When did you arrive?" Tommy asked and startled me.

"Not long ago," I hugged him and he simply leaned his head against me. We stood there for a few seconds, quietly hugging, "what are your plans?"

"I'm going back to Dan's place and then off to work."

"Ok, sweetie, we'll talk later." I closed the door behind him and went to mom's room.

I was exhausted after not having slept in several nights, so after I kissed mom I simply collapsed on the sofa, next to her hospital bed.

I was awoken by the phone. An unfamiliar number again. I thought perhaps it was mom's office. They would call me or Gabi every now and then to ask about mom.

"Good morning," I replied politely, so I don't accidently embarrass mom.

"Shirley?"

"Yes?"

"This is Grace. Lisa gave me your number. She told me you were planning on having Dr. Katzman operate on you. He operated on me too. If you have any questions, feel free to ask away." The whole surgery business had recently been put aside, but this was an important conversation.

"Thank you for calling." I tried thinking if I had any questions for her, but couldn't think of anything, "but I would actually love calling you back some other time, because my mom isn't doing too well. I can't seem to think of anything, but I'm sure I'll have questions."

"Of course. I'm sorry to hear it. I've been through it with my mom."

"Ovarian cancer?"

"No, breast cancer. It wasn't pretty. How is she now?" Grace asked with sincere concern.

"She's unconscious. In home hospice." I looked at mom, as if to confirm that was indeed the truth.

"That's sad." Grace fell silent, but 'sad' was perfectly accurate.

"I'll call you soon, thank you," I said after a few moments of silence.

"Of course, with pleasure, call me anytime."

At that moment, I was glad I had found someone who understood me, who knew what it was like losing a mother. Someone who knew what it was like being a carrier and having the surgery. I decided I would go to the conference. It seemed like the right place for me to be.

I texted Michael I was going out that evening, he replied that he would come home on time.

I still wanted to spend some time with the kids. I took my things and approached mom. June was there and I knew Gabi was on his way. I wanted to have a moment with her, before he arrived.

I shut the door and stood beside her. I held her hand, it was yellow and thin. Mom was still gorgeous. Her skin was still tight and nearly wrinkle-free. If it weren't for her heavy and slow breathing, you could have thought she was simply sleeping.

"Mom, I'm going," I said like I always did, "I want to spend some time with the kids. They keep asking about you and say hi. I want you to know that you can let go, you don't need to fight anymore. I love you so much…" I was chocked up and couldn't speak. I stood next to her a few more moments, and then kissed her and left.

When I stepped outside, I called Jonathan. "When are you coming to visit mom?"

"Tomorrow, I think. Maybe the day after tomorrow," he said with a sleepy tone. Why did he always sound so tired?

"The day after tomorrow will be too late. You might still make it tomorrow. Try, OK?" I walked slowly towards the parking lot, because I had forgotten where I had parked.

"That bad?"

"Yes, she looks really bad." I found my car, but the thought of getting in with that terrible heat, made me linger outside.

"Ok, I will do my best to come tomorrow."

"Good, we'll talk, goodbye"

I texted Natalie, "I'm on my way home," to give her a glimpse of hope. 'Keep both eyes on the road' kept ringing through my mind. So, I drove carefully. I kept reminding myself that I needed to be careful so that my children don't become motherless. Like me.

CHAPTER 64

"I'll donate for two," I said to a volunteer waiting at the entrance for the Foundation's symposium. On my way there I had already decided I would also make a donation in mom's name.

I walked into the hall, and unlike previous symposiums, the hall was very crowded. I sat at the end of the row so I could slip out if necessary. While I was waiting for everyone to sit down, I looked around me. This time there were more men than last time (perhaps spouses, or also carriers). There were women of all ages. Every now and then I recognized a similarity between two women and assumed they were sisters or mother and daughter. Mom never came with me to these meetings, even when she was doing better. I think she was scared of hearing what was waiting for her. She just didn't want to know.

I was wondering how many women in this hall were motherless. I had a feeling I would soon feel much closer to this group of people, if that was even possible.

The symposium began and this time was mostly dedicated to questions directed at the specialists.

A young woman, about my age, asked the panel a question that voiced my biggest fear – "I'm supposed to have a surgery, but there was a finding in the MRI that requires further exams. Should I delay the surgery?"

I hungrily waited for the answer. I was well-acquainted with being scared from the possibility of finding something before the surgery and finding out it was too late to have a preventive procedure. I wanted the stressful exam to be over so I could have the surgery on time.

"In that case you should delay it," the doctor said calmly. "First finish the other exams."

Some of the people in the audience nodded in consent while others looked at her with grief. She sat down in disappointment. Someone else stood up to ask a question. She was tall and thin, and had a short haircut. I assumed she was after chemotherapy.

"I got sick with ovarian cancer a few years ago, and now they found a c-met in my liver. I wanted to know if I should do the breast surgery."

I felt like an arrow had pierced my heart. I knew that in her condition, there was no point in having a surgery, but I couldn't be there any longer. I didn't wait to hear their answers. I left quickly to the bathroom and washed my face. I took a few deep breaths and looked at myself in the mirror. My hair was pulled back in a sloppy ponytail, and black circles surrounded my eyes. I felt a throbbing pain in my head and decided to go home. This day was enough, I just wanted it to be over.

***

But it wasn't over. On the contrary. My headache wouldn't allow me to fall asleep and at some point, I took a painkiller and sprawled out on the living room in front of the TV.

At 3 A.M. I slipped into bed and closed my eyes. My phone rang and I jumped. It was mom's home number.

"Gabi?" I asked with a trembling voice.

"Shirley, mom's gone," Gabi said quietly.

I started crying and couldn't speak.

"It happened just a few minutes ago. She just stopped breathing. I don't think she was in any pain."

"I'm coming."

"You don't need to come. Come in the morning."

"Gabi, I'm coming."

My next phone call was to Jonathan. We agreed that he would come pick me up and we'd go to mom.

I stopped crying and lay back on the sofa. I tried making sense of what was happening to me. The thing I was most scared of, happened, and I felt I was shutting down. I couldn't comprehend it was actually happening. That everything was over. Michael was sleeping and I knew I would have to wake him up and tell him, but I couldn't say it out loud. I couldn't utter those words. As I lightly napped on the sofa, there were moments in which it seemed it was all a dream and when I'd wake up, I'd find out everything was OK.

But when Jonathan called to tell me he was outside, I realized it was all very real.

CHAPTER 65

The monitor indicated she had no pulse, as if we wouldn't have known otherwise that she was gone. But, as they explained to us, that was standard procedure when someone died at their home. First, came an ambulance and then the police. Who would have thought there was so much bureaucracy involved in dying? When the police officers left, we asked Tommy to come back home.

"We need to think about the funeral. Where we should bury her." Gabi sat by the table with all the forms they had left and looked at me with a puzzled expression.

"I think she would have wanted to be buried in Kibbutz Einat," I said decisively, although I wasn't completely sure. Mom wouldn't speak to us about those things.

She chose Kibbutz Einat for her father when he passed away. A few months ago, she had even told us that Ian took her to find the exact location of his grave. "Olive lane number 1," she said again and again, and I realized that was something she wanted me to remember, but I didn't say a word. A silent understanding. She never spoke about herself with regards to the day after she passed. But I assumed that if mom chose that location for her father, it was good enough for her too.

After asking around a bit and pulling some strings, we managed buying companion burial plots in Kibbutz Einat. The funeral was scheduled for 4 P.M.

Gabi went to return all the medical equipment, and Jonathan went to the civil registry office to take care of some more bureaucracy. Tommy was closed up in his room with friends who came to support him, and I was walking around the house, zombie-like. The exhaustion, sadness and pain overwhelmed me.

Her glasses rested by the bed, on one of the books she had once started reading. The drawing that Adam had made for her on Mother's Day. Her jewellery was scattered by the bathroom sink as if she had just taken if off to take a shower, and would soon wear them again. Every one of these details stung my heart and the pain was excruciating.

"At least she's not in pain anymore," people wrote to me in different texts. But she suffered enough pain these last few years and I couldn't find any comfort in that.

Michael asked Natalie to come over so he could attend the funeral. We decided we shouldn't tell the kids before the funeral in case they asked to come. They were too young.

Our family started gathering in the apartment. Eric and Ruth came with Grandpa Yokannan. Gabi and Jonathan came back after running their errands. Gabi kept telling over and over again what had happened during the night and morning. I simply sat there and tried breathing in and out. One breath, and then another, and another. I wasn't able to cry anymore, nor smile.

It was noon, and we decided on our way to the cemetery to have lunch at mom's favorite café. I reserved a table and when we arrived, a round table waited for us at the corner of the room. As we approached it, I passed by all the tables I had once sat with mom and felt the pain choking me up.

We were the quietest table at the restaurant. We ordered some food, and even tried eating some of it, but most of the plates stayed full on the table.

"It's just tragic," Gabi said. "When my mother passed away it was sad, but not tragic. This is plain tragedy." He was right.

CHAPTER 66

No, the skies did not weep, nor any other such cliché. It was a pleasant and warm summer day. The skies were blue and the birds sang. The world kept going as if nothing had happened. As if this was yet another day. As if our world hadn't collapsed that night.

When we made our way to Kibbutz Einat, I couldn't believe it was happening. I felt as if mom would soon call me and ask where were we and when are we coming over, and I would ask her how she was feeling, and she would say not so great but could have been worse. She would always say things could have been worse, but at that moment I thought it was impossible. This was our worst moment as a family.

We drove through the passageway on our way to the cemetery.

"Can you see the houses they're building here?" I said to Tommy, "mom has recently signed off on these."

"Signed off on her own neighbors," Jonathan said from the front seat.

"Yes… who thought we would be here so soon," I said, partially to them, but mostly to myself.

I can't remember much of the funeral. There were so many people from so many different periods of our lives. Julie hugged me tightly and we cried together. Sarah came, after I hadn't seen her in such a long time, even Nathan was there. All the girls from the office came and so did Alice, wearing her black All-stars. I walked among the people with a tissue in one hand and a bottle of water in the other. If we would have been elsewhere, not surrounded by graves and trees, it would have felt like a wedding, or some other happy event.

Gabi spoke first. He stood in front of the microphone with the paper he had prepared and everyone fell silent.

"This moment is too difficult for me to describe with words," a cry was heard in the distance, but Gabi kept with a trembling voice, "in the last few years, Cathy's health deteriorated, at a slow pace, but in the last year, her deterioration was fast and painful. Cathy suffered greatly from the disease, in terrible pain as well as being aware of her condition. Despite all this, she lived as if she wasn't sick at all. She worked while going through chemo and whenever she could, even a few days before her final deterioration, two weeks ago on Saturday.

"On that day, she woke up early. She wasn't at her best, but she was at a sound mind, until she asked me why her nurse hadn't arrived yet to dress her for work. On that afternoon, during her nap, she slipped into a state of unconsciousness, from which she never really woke up.

"We, Cathy and I, have been together for almost thirty years. I think we had a good life together, that only improved with time. Cathy was my best friend. We raised three successful children together, several cats, two dogs and a beautiful garden. We went skiing in the Alps every year, started new careers in Australia, and had true friends who have been with us many years.

"Cathy was everything I could have wished for myself and more. Educated, beautiful and loving. Now, Cathy has left a big hole in my life.

"This is a good opportunity to thank our dear friends who constantly helped her at the hospitals to overcome her challenging, physical struggles. Cathy and I thank you."

Gabi gave the microphone to the head of the committee, who wanted to say a few words. I cried quietly and blew my nose. Tommy sat next to me with his head down and kept quiet. I hugged him and together we listened to everyone's eulogies. Jonathan spoke after.

"I have always tried to make mom admit to me, in private, that I was her favorite child," Jonathan started, showing that sense of humour he was so well known for, "I never succeeded. She always smiled and said she loved us all, and I wouldn't be able to get it out of her. She really did love us all, and we loved her more than words could describe. I've missed you, mom, this last period. Now, I will miss you for the rest of my life. All I have left to say is thank you for everything. Thank you for the time, the warmth, the humour and your wisdom. Goodbye, mom."

After Jonathan spoke, those who didn't cry by then, couldn't hold it in any longer.

It was a respectable civil funeral, just like Gabi wanted it. I stood in front of her grave and watched as they covered her casket with sand. Maya hugged Jonathan, who couldn't stop crying, and Tommy stood with his friends. Dan, his boyfriend, stood there and hugged him. I was glad he was there. I couldn't believe it was all happening, as if it was all happening to someone else. I felt like a zombie, but still did what I was supposed to do, like a good girl.

Michael stood next to me and hugged me, everyone came to say their goodbyes and offered their condolences, and all the other things people said when there was nothing else left to say.

When it was over, it was time for the second challenge of the day, which was equally difficult. It was time to talk to the children.

***

"Oh, sweetie, I'm so sorry for your loss," Natalie hugged me when I walked in with Michael.

"Thank you dear," I told Michael to pay her and asked the children to turn the TV off.

I sat between Adam and Ariel and Michael sat Romy on his lap. "You know that Cathy has been sick for a long time, right?"

"She had a wheelchair," Ariel said, and Adam just nodded.

"Right, she had a wheelchair. But recently, she wasn't feeling very well and had to be at the hospital. The doctors tried taking care of her, but they couldn't because she had a special disease that not a lot of people have. So, the doctors didn't know how to treat her."

"But she's going to feel better soon. Right, mom?" Adam asked me with a hopeful look.

"No, my love. She passed away from her disease." I hugged him as tightly as I could and kept the tears from pouring. I wanted to keep it in a little longer but couldn't.

"But she wasn't old," Adam said. "Only old people die."

"She was very, very sick." I caressed Ariel and hugged her too.

"So now you don't have a mommy?" Ariel asked and hit straight in my wounded heart.

"Right," but my kids still have a mother, I reminded myself. They have a mother. We sat hugging each other.

"Are you going to be sick like Cathy?" Adam asked after a few moments of silence.

"No, sweetie. I won't be sick like Cathy," I said with the most decisive tone I could muster, and could only hope I was telling him the truth.

CHAPTER 67

"Want to go to a movie?" I texted Anna on Saturday morning. The Shiva was about to start in the evening and I wanted to have a nice day with the kids, after all those weekends I hadn't seen them.

"Are you serious?" Anna called after a few seconds.

"Yes, I haven't been with them all summer. I want to have some fun with them. Have your daughters seen the new 'Ice Age'?"

"No. But are you sure you want to go see a movie?"

"Certain. I need a change of scene before the Shiva. Let's go, should I buy tickets for 11:30?"

The movie was funny and cute. The children had a good time and enjoyed spending time with Anna's girls. It felt somewhat normal, which was strange. There were moments when I even felt a sense of relief. I didn't have to check whether I had any new messages. I didn't have to call Gabi to ask whether everything was OK. I could just disconnect from everything for a few hours and simply be with my children. Be their mother.

The Shiva started that evening, and it was one of the most exhausting things I have ever experienced. People came throughout the day. When we did have a break, I tried resting, but the moment I heated up some food, someone new would walk in. I ate more cakes and cookies than I had ever eaten in my entire life, and met so many people, that at some point, I stopped trying to figure out who they were and how we were related.

My dad didn't come to the Shiva. It was probably too much for him. My mother-in-law, Rachel, actually surprised me when she came, since we haven't been so close before. Who knows, I thought, perhaps now she'll come back into our lives. After all, she was the only grandmother my children had.

***

"Hello, am I speaking with Shirley?" I had just arrived at mom and Gabi's apartment. I wanted to clean things up before people started coming in for the Shiva. After the first evening, that was so busy, I realized I should start preparing things before people start arriving.

"Yes," I replied and started looking for disposable cups in the closets.

"I'm calling from Dr. Katzman's office, about the surgery." I suddenly froze and stood planted like a tree, waiting, "we have a date for your surgery."

"OK. When is it?" I looked for a pen and paper so I could write down the information.

"October 20th, it's about a week after the end of the holidays, does that work for you?"

"Yes, that's great." I found an old grocery list written in mom's hand. I turned it over and wrote down the date.

"Good, then I'll email you all the details. We'll be in touch before the surgery to make sure you have all the documents. In the meantime, don't forget contacting an anaesthesiologist and a surgeon, and have all your tests ready."

"Of course, thank you."

Things were moving forward. I had a date, and I had less than two months to finish all the procedures before it.

The first thing that crossed my mind was wanting to tell mom. It took me a second to remember she wasn't lying in her bed anymore, staring at a silly American sitcom. I texted Michael the date, so he could ask for time off.

***

"Gabi insists that we clear out mom's things," I told Jonathan when he and Maya came in. It seemed too soon to me, taking out all of her things during the Shiva, but Gabi said he just couldn't handle having it all in the house. "It's too painful," he said.

"Today?" Jonathan asked.

"We don't have to do it today, but he wants us to use the time we're here during the Shiva to go over her things. He said that after this we would each go back to our lives and won't have time to go over everything together."

"He's actually right," Jonathan said and poured himself some soda from the fridge.

"He's always right," I smiled. Gabi was always convinced he was right, even when he was wrong (which according to him, never was the case).

"So, just come in later and we'll start cleaning up."

While Jonathan went to speak with Gabi, I passed by Tommy's room. I was jealous of his ability to sleep so peacefully.

Then I went to mom's bedroom and opened the glass door to their large walk-in closet. Most shelves had mom's clothes, naturally, but what shocked me most, was the smell. It was her smell. When Jonathan and Maya walked in, they found me sitting on the floor and crying, surrounded by empty trash bags scattered around.

"Would you like us to come in later?" Maya asked gently as Jonathan started opening the draws to see how much work we had ahead of us.

"No, let's start." I picked myself off the floor and as I cried, I started filling up the bags. The entire day, as well as the following days, we used every moment in which there weren't any visitors, to go over her things. I didn't know mom had so much jewellery and scarves.

Every evening, I would come back home with a car filled with clothes and other items I just couldn't give to anyone else.

"I think we're going to need another closet," Michael said smilingly, as he helped me carry all the things into the house. But I didn't feel like talking or smiling. I just wanted this hard week to be over.

CHAPTER 68

On the last evening of the Shiva, I sat in the living room in front of a pile of albums and spoke with Julie. She told me stories about her and mom's childhood in Romania. Jonathan sat with Maya and a group of friends in the balcony so they could smoke. Tommy was in his room with Dan and some other guys I have never met. This week was exhausting, but obviously, things would be harder after the Shiva was over.

And then I saw Lisa walk in with a young woman I didn't know. She had long curly blond hair.

"I'm sorry for your loss," Lisa said and hugged me one long warm hug, one that only someone who understood and had been through it herself could give.

"Thank you," I replied as we hugged.

"This is Grace, who you've spoken with recently, remember?" Grace approached me and hugged me as if we had known each other for years.

"Nice to meet you. It's so sad that we're meeting under these circumstances. Come, let's sit outside." We made our way to the balcony, and they followed me. I found a spot outside in the corner where we could speak privately.

"I have a date for the surgery," I told them as we grabbed three chairs, "October 20th."

"That's great," Lisa sat down beside me and Grace sat on my other side. I felt surrounded by carriers. I was glad to be with women who understood me, I could see it in their eyes.

"How long ago did you have the surgery?" I turned to Grace. She really was a beautiful and confidant woman.

"Almost three months ago," she proudly answered.

"Are you still in pain?"

"Not anymore. I was in pain at the beginning but now I'm completely fine."

"That's very encouraging to hear. I'm very scared of this surgery."

Although the whole topic of being a carrier has been pushed aside this week, it still stressed me out. On the one hand, I wanted it to be over, and on the other, I was very scared of it. I didn't know how I would feel after, if I'd feel anything at all. I was afraid I wouldn't feel like a woman, that I wouldn't feel sensual ever again. I was scared I wouldn't be able lie on my belly and that the scars might not heal well. My head was filled with fears, but none was greater than the fear of the disease itself.

"Don't worry, you'll be back to normal in no time."

"I hope." Although Natalie promised to help me, I knew I would still have to take care of the kids on my own from time to time, and I wasn't sure how I was going to do it. Even the simplest things, such as tucking Romy in her bed, would be a serious challenge.

"Would you like to see them?" Grace surprised me.

"Are you serious?" I was shocked by her proposal.

"Sure, it would make you feel better. I went to see other women before I had the surgery. Everyone does it."

"OK," I was still shocked but I went with it.

"Do you have a quiet room?" Grace stood up and waited for me to take her inside.

"Come," I told her and we walked quietly among the people who gathered around the table and contemplated which pastry they would have next. We went into mom's bedroom and I shut the door.

"Look," Grace said and lifted her shirt, she also moved her bra a bit so I could see the results, "see? It's completely fine."

"Right," except for her nipples, or actually the lack there of, everything seemed fine. Where the nipples used to be there were two dark red lines. It gave me the shivers, but I tried to look past it.

"The scars will disappear in time," she explained as if reading my mind." It can take a year or so."

"That's reassuring, doesn't it hurt?" I asked again to make sure.

"Not at all. Except for breastfeeding, you can do everything. I started running again, and exercising, just like before." Grace put down her shirt and we went back to the busy Shiva.

"And how did you handle the children?" that was my second concern, after the pain.

"Look, it wasn't simple. My father and mother in-law helped a lot, they even slept over at the beginning." Grace pulled out her phone and showed me pictures of her children.

"Cute," I said, and thought how lucky I was to have Natalie.

"Don't worry, I'll give you plenty of tips before the surgery and you'll be done in no time." Grace sounded like a motivation personal trainer.

"Sure," said Lisa, who joined us by the pastry table.

"I hope, thank you for everything." Perhaps it had something to do with our intimate moment in the room before, but I felt close to Grace and knew that we would stay in touch. Now all I had to do was wait for the surgery and have it done. It was time that I saved myself.

CHAPTER 69

When the Shiva was over, so was the summer vacation, and Adam was very excited to start the first grade. Romy was very excited to start going to Tammy's daycare, and Ariel started preschool. It was a time of new beginnings, and mom had missed them all.

Michael and I took Adam on his first day, and attended the ceremony they had prepared for the new children. I cried throughout the entire thing, both with excitement, but also because I felt I had missed the chance to share this experience with my mom. Every incident such as this would end with me calling her and sending her photos. Now she wasn't here anymore, and I needed to adjust.

And I missed her. Oh, how I missed her. I missed our calls on my way home from the office. I would call her when I stepped out of the elevator, and sometimes, we would talk until I arrived home or to daycare. I was used to keeping her up to date about everything that happened. I still had Gabi, of course, but he had little patience for my stories. He was devastated, and tried to get back to some kind of routine, just as the rest of us did. But for him it was even harder since he was now living alone.

If I could, I would have told her that all the exams for the surgery came out fine. That I bought the special bras I heard about, and that I had prepared a detailed schedule for Michael and Natalie for each day I was supposed to be at the hospital. I made all the necessary preparations with the insurance company. I even booked a private room at the hospital. Everything was ready.

After the extra days off I had taken to help the children adjust to their new school and daycares, I went back to the office. It was weird. I felt as if I had taken a load off. I spent more time at home, and mostly didn't spend my time at any hospitals or in traffic on my way to one. But I was overwhelmed by sadness. I tried smiling to the children, and spending more time with them, but every second I was alone, a broken dam of tears uncontrollably rolled down my cheeks. I would cry in the shower, and while driving. Every song on the radio was about mom, as if written for me. I behaved like a teenage girl with a broken heart, and cried from every little thing.

With all these things I was going through, I did actually find some time for work. I went back to my cases and clients after having been away for almost one month. Everyone was very supportive and understanding. They even waited a few more days before gently sending emails, "how are you?" and "when can we see you?" The routine was stronger than sorrow.

And then came Rosh Hashanah. Our first holiday without mom. We have never been a family who devoutly celebrated the holidays, but meeting the family was an inseparable part. Eric and Ruth invited us over, and it was nice seeing everyone. However, mom not being there, made the whole event painful. I didn't really want to see grandmothers with their grandchildren, even if they were my relatives. It was just unfair, aggravating, but mostly painful. As if I had reopened a wound that had yet to fully heal.

Going back to the office wasn't simple either. It was hard hearing stories about mothers who would pick up their grandchildren from daycare, or cook, or in fact do anything that a mother would. The moment one of the girls started complaining about their mother, I would leave the kitchen under some silly excuse. But in Ali's case, I couldn't hold it in.

"Never mind all this nonsense about the candy. You have a mother?

She's healthy? Let her give them all the candy she wants." The girls immediately fell silent, and Anna stood behind me and placed her hands on my shoulders. Everyone quietly went back to their salad and pasta takeout boxes. No one looked at me.

"Sorry," I said, and left the kitchen, heading to my office. Anna followed me and closed the door.

"Are you OK?" she asked with caution.

"No, actually, not at all. I can't sleep and I keep thinking about my mom all the time. What would she say, what would she have thought? I can't let it go." I sat in my chair with despair.

"It takes time. It's called 'The Year-long Mourning' for a good reason. It doesn't end with the Shiva."

"I know. But I'm just so sad all the time. If it weren't for the children, I wouldn't have smiled at all. I keep trying just for them," I said through the tears.

"And it's good that you keep trying. You'll see, it'll get better," Anna stood next to me and hugged me. At that moment, I couldn't believe I would ever feel better. I couldn't believe I would ever feel truly happy. I couldn't believe things could be any worse. But I was wrong.

CHAPTER 70

The date of the surgery was approaching. A week before, Michael and I went over the instructions from Dr. Kaspi, the anaesthesiologist Dr. Katzman's recommended. Indeed, he seemed very professional and pleasant. During our meeting, he asked me a lot of questions in his South American accent and checked all the documents I brought with me.

"Any family illnesses?" he asked when he opened the red file that had a sticker with my name.

"Does cancer count?" I asked with a smile.

"Yes, but I'm referring to any heart conditions, heart attacks, etc."

"Not that I know of. Perhaps a heart condition on my father's side. I know that my grandfather had a heart attack, but he lived to be 90 years old, so it probably wasn't that bad."

"Good. I see that your blood clotting test results are good," he mumbled to himself, "good EKG. Good blood count. Good chest x-ray. So that's it. Don't forget to fast like I told you – from 9 A.M. and until after the surgery. In the morning you should only have a light breakfast. An omelet, some Greek yogurt, a snack pack." I was uncomfortable telling him that other than the omelet, there wasn't any chance I would eat any of the other things he had mentioned.

"OK, is that it?" I collected the documents into the folder I had received from Dr. Katzman.

"Yes, I'll see you right before the surgery." Dr. Kaspi looked up at me, but I kept sitting there. I felt as if I had other questions to ask, but couldn't think of any.

"What's the matter? Are you nervous about the surgery?" he asked as he put the documents back in the drawer and his stamp into his bag.

"A little. Yes, I think I am." This was my first surgery and I didn't know what to expect.

"I'll give you something to calm you down before the surgery," he opened the bag and scribbled something with his unclear doctor handwriting, "don't worry. You'll come to the surgery relaxed."

"Thank you very much. I'll see you next week." I stood up and left. I hoped that his 'something' would do the trick. It was too bad that a cocktail was out of the question. It could have been very relaxing.

On my way to the parking lot I had a sad-funny thought. During the surgery, I would sleep better than I had ever since mom had passed away.

CHAPTER 71

It was the day of the surgery. I settled for an omelet with shredded cheese and two slices of bread. I couldn't believe this tiny meal was supposed to keep me full the entire day. So far, having to fast was the hardest thing about this surgery.

I was so happy that the wait for the surgery was over. Aside from the constant phone calls, I also received plenty of "good luck" texts, there wasn't a single quiet moment. It felt like having a birthday, and perhaps, on some level, it really was. Even Tammy the daycare teacher called to wish me luck on behalf of the staff. It really moved me, but Michael wasn't too happy about it.

"You've told all these people that you're amputating your breasts?" he asked me after the umpteenth call.

"Why not? Is it a secret? Should I keep it to myself?"

"No, but don't go around telling everyone, either. Why don't you post a before and after on Facebook?"

"Let's not get carried away. I'll make the posts available for friends only." But Michael didn't smile back.

"Do whatever you want. It's your body. It seems pointless to me," he concluded and made himself another cup of coffee.

"I wanted to discuss something important with you," I told him as I followed him into the kitchen, "if something were to happen to me, I want you to remarry. Of course, only after having recovered from the pain and shock of my loss. I'm sure you'll be a very popular widower."

Michael gave me an infuriated look, "stop with that nonsense. You won't die and everything is going to be OK."

"Graveyards are full with people who thought everything was going to be OK."

"I don't care about other people. Only about you, and you're going to be just fine."

"OK, but if something were to happen, I want you to find someone who would take good care of the kids. If they stay just with you, they'll have pizza for dinner every day."

"That's what you're worried about? Pizzas for dinner?" Michael poured some milk and slowly stirred the coffee.

"Not just. Everything worries me. And something else, I had almost forgotten. Make sure that they have the genetic test only after they have a steady relationship. Not too early. But they can start having checkups before, around the time they graduate high school."

"Shirley," Michael looked at me with half-scornfully, half-smilingly, "do you also have instructions for the food we'll serve at your Shiva, or can I make that decision on my own?" he approached me and hugged me tightly.

"I don't care about the food as much; it's your call." We slowly kissed, and then Michael took his coffee and went back to the computer. He used this morning to work from home.

We left before daycare was over so I didn't see the kids again. That morning I said goodbye to them in the calmest way possible. They knew I was going to the hospital, but we were too scared to refer to it as a 'surgery'. A psychologist we had asked, said we should tell them that this is what the doctors told us to do. Surprisingly enough, the children were calm and the plan was for them to see me the day after the surgery. Assuming everything goes well, of course.

At 3 P.M. we grabbed my bag and left for the hospital.

***

"What a suite," Sarah said when she walked into my private hospital room on the fifth floor. Her curls grew out since I have last seen her, and they bouncingly followed her into the room.

"It's so great that you came!" I hugged her tightly, as long as I was still able to hug.

"How are you? Nervous?" Sarah hugged Michael, who was happy someone else would now keep me busy, since he wanted to go over his emails.

"The anaesthesiologist just gave me a sedative, so I'm cool." I sat smiling on the bed, wearing a ridiculous robe. Sarah sat beside me.

"This place looks beautiful. Not at all like a normal hospital."

"Right, the smell is different too. A normal hospital usually smells like cooked vegetables and disinfectants. There's a clean smell here. Right, Michael?"

Michael lifted his eyes from the screen for a second and shrugged. I think he couldn't wait until they put me out and he could get some quiet. I talked all day, non-stop, it was the stress, I guess.

"I'm contemplating what I should ask you to get me for dinner," I told Michael and tried looking out at the restaurants downstairs, "perhaps some pasta. Do they have pasta somewhere around?"

"Of course they do," Sarah said and started searching her phone for Italian restaurants nearby.

A nurse came in and looked at the file on my bed and said an orderly would soon come in to take me downstairs. When she left, Gabi walked in.

It was then that I was truly happy that I had no memories of mom from this hospital. This was an emotionally neutral place for me. Mom had never been here nor had any of her surgeries here. It was hard finding a hospital that answered these criteria in our area.

"This is Sarah, a friend of mine from the previous office. She was also at the funeral," I introduced the blunder of curls that jumped up to hug him.

"Nice to meet you. Forgive me for not remembering you. There were so many people and I wasn't all there."

"It's perfectly fine," Sarah said and sat back beside me. Gabi kept standing by the bed uncomfortably. Well, it isn't every day that your daughter amputates her breasts.

***

As I was taken on a bed and through the hallway to the surgery room, with the whole entourage behind me, I trembled with excitement. Or fear. It was hard to tell.

"Say goodbye, you'll see her again in the recovery room," the sparkly-blue-eyed orderly said, as he hit the elevator button, "your family can wait for you in the waiting area on the third floor." I kissed and hugged everyone goodbye.

The elevator doors closed and I took a few deep breaths to calm myself down.

"Breathe," I said to myself quietly, "just breathe."

During the surgery preparations I saw Dr. Katzman dressed like a character in *Grey's Anatomy*, with scrubs and a funny hat; completely different than what he looked like in his office a few months back. There were several beds in the room and it seemed like a shared hospital room. Different doctors and nurses calmly walked from one bed to the next and different instruments beeped around them. My surgeon, Dr. Shavit, was also waiting in the room, looking through my medical file. Grace also had her surgery with Shavit and Katzman. She said they were a winning team.

"Hello Shirley. Are you ready for the surgery?" Dr. Katzman sat in front of me and took a black marker out of his pocket.

"I hope," I said with a shaky voice.

"Could you please take off the top part of your robe so we could mark the area of the surgery." He closed the curtain around me and took the cap off the marker. Dr. Shavit stood next to him and looked at the area they'd be operating on; that is, on me.

I stood there exposed and looked for something to focus on to relieve my embarrassment. There were dots on the curtain and I tried counting them, but when I reached five, I gave up. I heard Dr. Katzman say, "Shirley Moshe, thirty-three years old, a double mastectomy candidate, and reconstruction. We'll make the incisions here," he drew black lines in different directions and everyone nodded.

Before I could put on my robe, a nurse came in. She took my file and asked me to follow her. No bed-rides anymore. I quickly closed the robe and walked behind her with the shoes I was given. Well, "shoes" is a bit of a stretch for what looked like two shower caps. Thanks to these, my feet stayed warm, but I was cold everywhere else. The hallway was freezing.

The nurse I followed was wearing a thick sweater, zipped all the way up. I wanted to tell her I was cold but kept quiet. She probably noticed I was trying to cover myself with the robe and said, "I know it's really cold here, but there's nothing much I can do about it. Soon you won't be cold, don't worry." I was still worried.

We passed by large surgery rooms with a lot of doctors and nurses running around inside. I felt like I was in one of those hospital TV shows. Until I reached my surgery room, it was small and crowded, almost about the size of our bedroom. Not at all like those TV series. It was filled with equipment and people who did all sorts of things. I noticed Dr. Kaspi standing there. I could barely recognize him with his blue scrubs and mask.

"Come, Shirley, lie down here," he said in his accent, and then I really knew it was him. "I'll insert an IV with anaesthesia."

After thirty seconds, the robe was taken off me and I was covered with a thin sheet. My entire body shivered. My hand was tied to a weird instrument and the needle inserted the IV tube in its place.

"Now you're going to sleep, and I will see you again in the recovery room. Good night."

CHAPTER 72

"There, she's awake," I heard a muffled voice and recognized Dr. Kaspi's accent. I tried opening my eyes. I couldn't remember where I was.

"Good morning, Shirley, can you hear me?" someone said and I tried opening my eyes again. This time I did a better job, and saw Michael's blurred figure. I nodded and tried moving my hand but fell asleep before I could do anything else.

Something squeezed my legs. I felt a balloon blow up around my calves and then release. I heard a lot of beeps but couldn't open my eyes. I fell asleep again.

Something squeezed my legs again. I woke up again. I opened my eyes. The white florescent light hurt me, so I shut my eyes and fell asleep.

I heard people speaking and then felt I was being moved.

"Is she waking up?" I heard Gabi, but couldn't see him. I couldn't speak.

"Perhaps you should go eat something?" I heard Sarah say, but it was more like a dream.

"I'm fine, thank you. You should go," Michael replied. I'm hungry too, I wanted to say, but fell asleep.

***

"She'll wake up soon," I heard someone say, "when she wakes up, she can gradually drink some tea and eat something light like a yogurt. You can make her tea down the hall. Just make sure it's not too hot."

When Michael came back to the room, I opened my eyes. He placed the disposable cup on the table stand and caressed my head, "how are you feeling?"

"I'm in pain," I whispered. My lips were dry and I felt I couldn't even muster the strength to move my head. I felt something heavy weighing down my chest, as if they had sown two rocks on it.

"Should I call a nurse?" he asked. I nodded, and he left the room. I fell asleep again.

They must have given me painkillers, because when I woke up again, it didn't hurt as much. But the weight made it harder for me to move. My breasts were heavy and felt like they did when I had a breastfeeding lump with Ariel.

The room was dark, but the door wasn't closed, a sliver of light shone in from the hallway. I moved my head to the other side and saw Sarah sleeping on the bed they had prepared for the person accompanying me.

"Sarah…" I called to her, and she immediately leaped out of her bed.

"How are you?" Sarah came closer and placed her hand on mine.

"Where's Michael? And Gabi?" I asked quietly.

"Michael went home, because it was getting late for the babysitter. Gabi was here up until recently. He said goodbye and you answered him. Don't you remember?"

"Not really," I shut my eyes again.

"Do you need anything?"

"I'm thirsty."

"I'll make you some tea. They said to make you tea." Sarah said as if she always did what she was told. It made me smile.

"OK," I closed my eyes again.

I drank the tea slowly with Sarah's help and felt I was really starting to wake up. Sarah lied on the bed again and fell asleep. I looked at my phone and found a lot of texts and unanswered calls. But all I cared about was the time. 2:30 A.M.

"Sarah, could you help me go to the bathroom?" I felt bad waking her up, but when she volunteered to stay with me, I had warned her there was a chance she wouldn't get much sleep on the first night. Grace told me that she spent the first night watching TV.

Sarah stood up and approached me. I tried sitting up, but was in so much pain that I screamed. It felt as if I was kicked in the chest. And then I saw them. I had tubes coming out of each armpit, and were connected to surgical drains. They were filled with a liquid that looked like blood. Looking at them made me sick. The drains were attached to my robe with safety pins.

"I can't lift myself up," I told her, and Sarah tried helping me stand up. After a few attempts and a lot of pain, I managed to sit on the bed. Sarah helped me put on my flip flops and we started our journey to the bathroom. I used my IV stand and leaned on it. Every movement of the tube caused me excruciating pain, but I didn't have much of a choice. I finally made it to the bathroom. At that very moment, I couldn't believe I would be back home in two days and back to normal. The thought of having to lie back again and then stand up, freaked me out so we called a nurse who helped me settle into the armchair.

Through the window, I could see a new hotel being built right in front of the hospital. I thought about the kids and how I would manage after the surgery. I thought about whether the surgery was successful and what would it look like the day they removed the bandages and I would see the results. I thought about a lot of things, but my thoughts kept going back to mom. She died and I had a surgery so I could live. If it weren't for her being sick, then we might not have found out I had the gene, unless I would have also gotten sick. My pain was mixed with guilt.

I sat on the armchair and watched the sky turn brighter, it changed from black to dark blue, and then light blue. At some point, I fell asleep.

CHAPTER 73

"You can go," I said to Sarah in the morning. "Michael will take the kids to daycare and school and come over."

"Are you sure?" Sarah pulled her curls back into a ponytail.

"Yes."

"OK, sweetie," Sarah leaned over and kissed me on the head, "I'll come again in the evening."

"I don't know what I would have done without you." I really didn't.

"If you want me to get you something, give me a call. I'm going." She took her purse and left.

Michael texted me he was on his way, but stuck in traffic. A nurse came in and checked my temperature and blood pressure, and said that the doctor would come soon for a checkup.

When Dr. Katzman came in he checked everything and confirmed everything looked well. "As far as I'm concerned, you can go home tomorrow," he said with satisfaction.

"When can we remove the drains?" They bothered me most in this absurd situation.

"It depends on the secretions. You need to check daily and see if they fill up. Keep me posted, and we can decide accordingly when to remove them. I'll see you next week at my clinic for a checkup."

When Michael came with the food I was already starved.

"You didn't pick up when I called so I brought you all kinds of things." He placed the bags on the bed and started taking out different baked pastries.

"Katzman was just here. He said I can go home tomorrow." I decided to take a mini-pizza roll. This was the only form of tomatoes I was willing to eat.

Michael spread a towel so I wouldn't get dirty and I ate the roll as quick as a flash.

"When do you think you'll bring the children over?"

"Probably around 5:30. There's traffic in the afternoon."

"OK, let me know when you leave the house so I can get ready. I don't want to look like a mess in front of the kids."

"No problem."

I finished my pizza roll and asked Michael to help me move to the bed.

It took fifteen minutes of pain, and by the time I was lying in bed I was already exhausted. When I woke up, Michael had already left to bring the children and I asked the nurse to give me something for the pain. I felt as if I had been run-over, but wanted to look my best for when the children came over, or at least as much as I could.

***

Ariel and Adam stood at the door and refused to come in. Michael walked in with Romy, who stretched out her hands for me to pick her up. But I couldn't even lift my hand to caress her. Michael brought her close to me so I kissed her. She smelled like daycare; a combination of sand, play-doe and sweat.

"Come say hello," I told them, but they clung on to each other and mostly to their snack bags.

"How was your day at school?" I tried encouraging Adam to speak, "did you get any homework?"

Adam just nodded and didn't say anything. He took another chip and placed it in his mouth. He dropped some crumbs to the floor.

Luckily, someone else had to clean up after them for a change.

I tried bringing Ariel closer to me again, but nothing helped.

After fifteen minutes, I gave up. Michael understood and took the children home. I sat in my bed with despair and cried. I felt so bad to have scared them like that. I couldn't tell them I did it for them. But that wasn't the only reason I cried. It's been exactly two months since mom passed away, and I missed her more than ever. I wanted to go home, to my room and my bed.

***

"You look much better than yesterday," Gabi said when he walked in with a large pizza, and after him Tommy following in reluctantly. The smell of the pizza overpowered the hospital smell and filled the room with pleasurable scents.

"I'm feeling a bit better but I'm still in pain."

"OK, the surgery was just yesterday. It will take some time." Gabi placed the pizza next to me and I immediately felt hungry again.

"Yes, I can barely lift up my arms," I showed him my new disability, "I can't even drink on my own. Can you give me a slice?"

"When are you going home?" Tommy asked, while separating one of the slices.

"Probably tomorrow, if everything goes well." I took a bite from the pizza that Gabi held up for me, as I tried eating in the cleanest way possible. I still wasn't allowed to take a shower and was actually afraid of the moment I would have to. I was happy to delay it as much as possible.

After an hour Sarah came, and Gabi and Tommy went home.

Even though the pain was bearable, the nurse offered me some painkillers before I went to sleep and I agreed. I was willing to take anything they offered me for a better sleep.

The painkillers helped a lot, because I woke up only when the nurse came in the morning to check my temperature and blood pressure.

"Everything looks great, you're going home today," she said in a cheerful tone.

"Good," I replied. I'm going home.

CHAPTER 74

A red and orange impressive bouquet, waited for me on the dining table, with a "get well soon" card from all the girls in the office.

Michael put my bag down by the front door. "Would you like to go to the bedroom or rest in the living room?"

"In the bedroom," I replied, and slowly started climbing up the stairs. The drains hurt with every movement I made. They would fill up every day and I had to overcome the disgust of having to empty them. I couldn't wait for when they'd remove them and I would be able to painlessly move.

Michael fixed the pillows for me, so I could sit in a comfortable position. When he got off the bed, the mattress shook and I screamed in pain, we agreed he would sleep in Romy's room so I could get some sleep at night.

I turned the TV on and looked for a way to kill some time. I flipped through the channels and found a rerun of one of those American sitcoms. I remembered how less than three months ago, I sat with mom and saw these ridiculous episodes, with the laughter track they added so that the viewer wouldn't laugh alone. I cried in bed and tried thinking what mom would have done if she were still alive. She probably would have come to help me with the kids, or just sit beside me to pass the time.

Michael walked in with the children, and I could hear their little steps approaching the room. The door opened and Ariel came running in.

"Don't jump on me!" I yelled at her just a second before she landed on top of me.

"Does it hurt, mommy?" she asked with a concerned look and sat on Michael's side of the bed.

"No, but you can't jump on me, OK?"

"When can I jump on you?" she asked, as if this were her one true aspiration.

"I don't know. For the meantime, you can't." She looked disappointed. "How was daycare?" I tried stirring the conversation towards a less scary direction.

"Good," she took the remote control and changed to the Disney Junior channel.

Adam walked into the room and sat quietly on the floor beside me.

"Maybe you should go watch TV downstairs and let mommy rest?" Michael asked when he walked into the room with a cup of tea.

"But we want to be with mommy," Ariel replied decisively for both of them.

"I want my mom, too," I thought to myself. And at that moment I realized something that I seem to have forgotten. I was so preoccupied with my own grief, I failed to notice it. I was too focused on myself, my loss, missing my mom, my fear of the disease. I took care of them, raised them with love, and tried being the best mother I could be. But this shadow that followed me, prevented me from seeing things as they were. It was a crazy rat-race of life and I didn't even stop to think. I felt as if I had discovered something new about myself. I am to them what my mom was to me. I don't know why, but I just didn't actually realize it until that moment.

"It's OK," I said to Michael, and placed my hand on Ariel's, "they can stay."

CHAPTER 75

Tommy, who was accepted to a film school in Melbourne, moved to Australia with great excitement and Gabi was left alone in their big apartment. I couldn't imagine how it must feel to find yourself alone like that. Though this wouldn't be Gabi's first time. When mom was sick, he spent a few months on his own in Australia. Still, this was different. It was a different kind of loneliness, one that I couldn't even imagine. There's something about the fact that your spouse is the one relative that you choose for yourself. The rest, are simply there. Gabi behaved as if he was fine, but we knew he was in pain. I hoped for him, that he could go back to having a better life and, despite it being difficult for me, find a new partner.

When it was time for my checkup with Dr. Katzman, Michael took me to the fancy clinic which we haven't visited in months.

"Everything looks great. How much have you had in each drain in the past 24 hours?" Dr. Katzman asked as he removed the bandages and checked the stitches. I couldn't bear to look at it.

"About 10 ml," I remembered emptying them yesterday and then rounded down the number a bit. I knew that if I wanted to get back to normal, I had to get rid of them and fast. I couldn't have them around the kids and had to stay away from them so they don't accidently touch the drains and make me scream with pain.

"So we can take them out. You'll feel a bit of a tug. Take a deep breath and exhale." I did as he told me and felt how the drain was being pulled out of my body. I was so stressed and scared, I wanted to throw up. The second time was even scarier because I knew what was about to happen. But after they were both out, I felt some relief.

"You can get dressed. Come back in a couple of days so we can see if everything is healing properly," Dr. Katzman said with a smile.

"Thank you," I replied. I hoped now, that the drains were out, I could lift my hands up easily. Before the surgery, I had scheduled with a special physiotherapist whom I received warm recommendations about from Grace, and there were still a few days left before my first appointment.

Gabi suggested that we all meet for dinner on Friday. I told him that if things continue to go on as well as they have, then I will come.

These meetings since mom had passed away, overwhelmed me with loss. Actually, everything that happened was divided into "before" and "after." Whenever I'd think of a certain event, I would stop to think if it was something that mom knew about. It's been a little over two months, and sometimes it seemed it was only yesterday that she called me to ask how were the children and how work was, and on the other hand, it felt like forever.

I tried going back to my routine at home as well. Natalie was with me, until Michael came back from work. With each day that passed I was able to do more and more things on my own. Romy quickly realized I couldn't pick her up and I would change her on the carpet in the living room. It was fun with Natalie, but I hoped that by removing the drains, I would quickly be independent again.

That day, I was able to grab a cup from the cabinet, all on my own.

CHAPTER 76

"I'm going to die." That was the first thought that crossed my mind when I first felt the pain in my back.

"No, it's impossible," I reassured myself out loud. "The surgery is exterior and doesn't affect interior organs." I repeated Grace's words to myself. Michael was still sleeping in Romy's room and I didn't bother anyone with my mumbling. I took a few deep breaths and tried alleviating the pain, but it didn't help. I barely succeeded picking myself up into a sitting position, which made things a bit better.

I took two aspirins, because I was told at the hospital it was good for the pain. They actually recommended a stronger version in drops, but it tasted so bitter that I preferred waiting 15 minutes instead of having to take it. So, I waited, and the pain really did pass.

I hardly slept sitting up, and woke up exhausted that Friday morning.

When the kids came back home, I took some of the Challah bread they made for Friday at Tammy's daycare, and went in to rest before our lunch with grandpa. Michael still hadn't finished something he needed to complete by Sunday, so we asked Natalie to come over. Now that she had a new boyfriend, she needed a lot of spending money.

I woke up ten minutes after I had fallen asleep. The pain was unbearable. Even going through labor didn't hurt as much, and I had two natural ones. Although one was unplanned (Ariel simply slipped out unannounced), still, I considered myself a true superwoman with a high pain threshold. But at that moment I realized this was a different kind of pain. I felt I couldn't breathe, I couldn't even cry out for Michael, so I called him on the phone and whispered, "come quick".

After a split second he stood at the door and hysterically asked, "what happened?"

"I can't breathe," I struggled to speak, "we need to go to the ER!"

Michael helped me go down the stairs, and on our way out he asked Natalie whether she could stay. She saw me and yelled as the door closed behind us, "of course, feel better, honey,".

At the ER, Michael placed me on one of the beds. No one refused us when they saw how much pain I was in.

A doctor approached me and I barely turned on my side and sighed with pain.

"Probably pulled your diaphragm muscle," he half-said half-inquired, "we'll give you a Voltairean shot for the pain and Etopan for the infection. In twenty-four hours, you'll feel like a different person."

Within minutes, a nurse came in and gave me a shot, and after fifteen minutes I felt some relief and could sit up in bed. Michael came back with a release form and we went back home. I was a bit humiliated for causing such a scene over a strained muscle. I felt so stupid at that moment.

When we got home, I texted Gabi that we wouldn't make it for lunch.

CHAPTER 77

That night passed by quietly and so did Saturday. I managed to clean the table from cereal leftovers all by myself, and even read a bedtime story to Adam, who insisted that I do it and not Michael. Poor Michael kept taking the kids out, over and over again so I could rest. I had a sneaking suspicion that he couldn't wait for Sunday so he could rest in his office.

"Do you need something before I leave?" he asked in the evening when the house was quiet and I was in bed (once again).

"Leave the aspirin close, in case it hurts again at night."

"Good night. Call me if you need anything." Michael placed the new aspirin pack he had bought for me, and gave me a good night kiss.

"Good night," I replied and he closed the door behind him.

I saw another *Grey's Anatomy* rerun (where everybody had their own private hospital room without having to book it first or pay extra). When I felt I was tired enough, I turned the TV off and tried to fall asleep.

Ten minutes later, it started again. Excruciating pain that almost made me weep. It was 1 A.M. and I didn't want to wake Michael up, because there really was nothing he could do to help. I took two aspirins and called Gabi. I knew that since mom had passed away, he wasn't sleeping too well. He couldn't fall asleep either. We didn't talk much about it, but I knew he was a wreck. I didn't know how he could even stay in their apartment surrounded by those memories. How could he sleep and see her empty side of the bed? If I were him, I would have definitely moved.

"What's going on?" he asked, and it didn't seem like I had woken him up.

"My back hurts again. The doctor said it would be over within twenty-four hours, but it's been almost thirty. I think the Etopen isn't working."

"Maybe you should go to the doctor again?"

"We'll see tomorrow," I said with complete despair. I just wanted to sleep well for one night.

"Call me tomorrow morning and let me know." Gabi sounded worried, but all I could think of was sleeping.

"OK, good night."

It was far from being a good night. It was in fact a very bad night. Every time I accidently lied on my back, I felt a sharp pain and I kept waking up over and over again. The hardest thing was, however, having time to think, think about what mom would have said about all of this. How she would have worried. Perhaps it was for the best that she wasn't here to see it. She would have probably felt even guiltier.

In the morning I got out of bed tired and aching, hoping things would get better as the day went by, and I could finally get back to normal. I was without the drains and could walk around and do different things. This pain made me feel sick again.

***

After yet another painful night, I realized I had to go back to the ER. I decided to call Anna and ask her to come with me. I didn't feel comfortable bothering Sarah again. Anna came after work and called me to come out.

"I'm going to have an X-ray at the ER and I'll be back," I said to

Natalie on my way out, "Michael will be here in about an hour, OK?"

"Sure, honey. No worries. Say bye bye to mommy." Only Romy cooperated and waved goodbye. Adam and Ariel were busy watching TV and couldn't care less about what was happening as long as they could keep watching.

"Number 13 to room 26," I heard over the P.A. and Anna stayed outside as I rushed into room 26.

It was Dr. Rubinstein, whose daughter was with Ariel in Tammy's daycare. Before this, we mostly met on daycare parties and the such. The thought of having to share with him the fact I had a surgery, embarrassed me, but I didn't have much of a choice.

"I thought I recognized your name," he said with a smile when he saw my name on the screen. "What brings you here?"

"I have a pain in my back since Thursday and also a little cough. They gave me Etopen and Arcoxia, but they don't really help. I haven't slept in a couple of nights because it hurts mostly when I'm lying down. So, I came for a chest X-ray because I was told it could be pneumonia."

"I see that you've had a surgery recently?" he looked at the computer. "A double mastectomy?"

"Yes," and I hoped the discussion about the matter was over.

"Look, I'll send you to have a chest X-ray like you wanted." He kept looking at the screen and kept typing different things, I smiled in victory, "but if it's turns out OK, then I'm sending you to the ER at the Tel Aviv Medical Center."

"What? Why?" I said and my smile faded away.

"Because if it's not pneumonia it can be a pulmonary embolism" images of mom at the hospital kept flashing in front of my eyes.

I tried pushing them aside and said, "but the oxygen levels in my blood are great, the nurse found 98%. I don't understand why you're sending me to the ER."

"I've already seen cases where people had 100%, and still they had a blood clot."

"And we can't check it here?" I was trying to negotiate so I wouldn't have to spend the night at the ER."

"No, because there are special blood tests they only have at that ER."

"OK, we'll talk after the X-Ray. Thank you." I took my file and left. I was sorry I got him and not the other doctor. The other one would have given me another shot of Voltairean after the X-ray, instead of sending me to the hospital. Michael told me he was staying late at work. Natalie's meter was ticking, and Anna had to go home at some point. I was so tired I felt as if I had a jet-lag.

How unfortunate.

***

"Number 13 to room 26."

I came back to him after the X-ray. Dr Rubinstein handed me the forms and asked whether someone could take me to the hospital ER.

"Are you serious?" I said, not even trying to conceal my disappointment, "I just want to have a good night's sleep."

"And I just want you to wake up from that sleep. Come on, go now. You have a letter from the hospital and a release form."

"Thank you."

"I wrote my phone number at the bottom, keep me posted." Yes, sure, I'll call you in the middle of the night to let you know you were wrong and I got another Voltairean shot.

"OK, thank you." I left the room depressed. Good thing Anna was with me.

***

When we were on our way to the hospital, I called Michael, "Michael,

I'm on my way to the Tel Aviv Medical Center."

"What? I thought you were going to the clinic."

"I was there and Dr. Rubinstein told me to go to the hospital. You know him. His daughter also goes to Tammy's daycare."

"I don't remember. Never mind. What did he say?" Michael sounded really worried.

"That it might be a blood clot in my lungs. Remember mom had one?"

"Yes. Strange."

"Right?! But I'm on my way to the hospital. Will you meet me there?" I wouldn't usually drag Michael along to every medical appointment I had these last years, but that night I really didn't want to be alone.

"Sure. Who's with the kids?" I heard him gathering his things and assumed I'd see him soon at the hospital.

"Natalie, I'll talk to her." She was almost always happy to work overtime.

"OK, see you there."

I texted Natalie and she promised to stay the night if necessary. I wasn't sure what I would have done if it weren't for her. My next phone call was to Dr. Kaspi, who had asked me to let him know if I didn't feel well after the surgery. I wasn't sure if he meant even 10 days after the surgery, but he was the only one who came to mind.

Dr. Kaspi said it was strange because I wasn't in any high-risk group, but that I would keep him posted (of course, he'd be my second call at 4 A.M., right after Dr. Rubinstein).

CHAPTER 78

After having waited for three hours at the ER, I became desperate. My entire chest hurt and I felt I couldn't take it any longer. As I went to the nurses' room and asked for some painkillers, I saw someone had taken my file. I signaled Michael to follow me and we followed the nurse who took us to an ER room with beds.

"Dr. Kaspi has called several times, and his intern has been here twice. He said it's not OK that no one has checked her yet," I heard the nurse telling the woman sitting at the reception with her Facebook open. In a different situation, I would have felt like a celebrity, but at that moment, I was in so much pain that all I wanted to do was lie down.

"Who is Shirley Moshe?" the nurse asked.

"Me," I said, and raised my hand like a schoolgirl.

"Come, the doctor will soon be here to examine you." She took me to the bed placed in the middle of the room, surrounded by blue worn-our curtains. Michael stood next to me.

"So, what brings you here?" a doctor asked when he walked through the curtain.

"My back hurts," I replied and before I could finish, he interrupted me.

"So, why aren't you at the orthopedic ER?"

"Because Dr. Rubinstein," I emphasized his name because I knew he worked at the same hospital", said he suspects it's a blood clot in my lungs."

"OK, if Dr. Rubinstein says so, we'll check for a PE, and then have some more tests." His tone became softer and he disappeared behind the curtain within a second.

A nurse came in and gave me something for the pain. After taking a blood sample she tried explaining to me what a pulmonary embolism was.

***

"Where is Shirley Moshe?"

"I'm here," I waved my hand at the doctor.

"You had a PE," he shook my hand ceremoniously, "frankly, you surprised me."

"I'm happy that you're pleased, but what does that mean exactly?"

"According to your blood tests you have a clot in your lungs, but we want to confirm, so you're going to have an angiogram CT to confirm." I remembered that was a procedure mom went through only a couple of months ago. Maybe it was the cold at the ER, but I suddenly felt my entire body tremble.

After a long night at the ER, they sent me to the ward and I got a private room. I was so exhausted and terrified that even that didn't make me happy. After being admitted into the ward, they gave me a painful shot in my belly to thin my blood. I got something else for the pain and then the nurse left. There was a strong smell of hospital disinfectants but the ward was quiet. Every now and then I could hear beeping at the nurse's desk. According to what I saw on my way to the room, I was significantly younger than the other patients in this ward.

Michael sat on the chair in front of me, completely wiped out "I think I'm going to take a taxi home."

"OK," although I wanted him to stay, I knew the children were about to wake up and it was best if they saw at least one of their parents.

He kissed me goodbye and left. I stayed alone in bed. A pigeon sat on the window. I looked at it walking back and forth until it flew away. And then I was really on my own.

I looked outside and the lights of the women's ward shone from afar. It was the same building my mom stayed at five years ago.

Everything started coming back to me. Mom also got these painful shots. How could she take it for such a long time? I couldn't believe I was there, at the hospital, with blood clots in both of my lungs. Like mom. How could this have happened? I stood up shortly after the surgery and kept walking around as much as I could. I was active. I have never smoked, nor was I overweight. I didn't meet any of the criteria. How did this happen to me?

And then I wanted mom. I felt like a little girl. I cried, and cried, and couldn't stop. The sun started coming up and I started realizing what had happened.

I tried going over the last few days. Did I take good care of myself? Perhaps I was too careless?

How could I have put myself in such a dangerous situation? I didn't even think something like that could happen in this type of surgery. I almost made my children motherless. That thought made me cry even harder. My chest hurt from the procedure. Everything was still swollen and I could barely turn over from one side to another. At home I slept on a pile of pillows, but at the hospital they could hardly find one, sad and flat pillow. There was no chance I could even nap in this terrible place. I had so many reasons to cry and I couldn't tell why I was crying so much; whether it was the pain, the longing, the guilt, or just my exhaustion from my previous, long sleepless nights.

I lied in bed and cried until I heard a soft knock on the door.

"Shirley?" I heard a familiar Argentinean accent.

"Dr. Kaspi, I can't believe you're here." I didn't think him coming over would move me so much. Now I was crying with excitement.

"I asked about you during the night, and wanted to see you before

I start my day."

"Thank you, only thanks to your phone calls did they even start treating me. If you wouldn't have insisted, I would have still been in the hallway."

"It's OK, no more crying. Everything is OK now."

"Yes," I said, and despite it being a little embarrassing crying in front of him, I couldn't help it.

"It's really rare what happened to you. It's unclear why it even happened in the first place."

"I know," I mumbled tearfully.

"As long as everything is OK now," he repeated and tried calming me down, "I have to go. Feel better and if something happens, call me."

"OK. Thank you so much again! You really saved my life!" I actually meant it.

"No need thanking me. Feel better," he said and left the room. I stayed there alone again.

The rumor spread, and Dr. Katzman also came to visit me in the morning in between his operations. He checked me there, instead of having me drive to his clinic. He removed my bandages and confirmed everything was healing as it should. At least my body was working properly in that regard.

"You, I won't forget," he said when he left. It was mutual, I thought to myself.

I was contemplating whether I should go to the mirror in the adjacent bathroom. I was scared to see my new breasts, and mostly the scar across them. I didn't know if I could handle it and decided to wait until I got back home.

***

"This is your release form, Shirley," the nurse said with indifference, "it is recommended that you have regular checkups with a hematologist."

"OK," I said and couldn't wait for her to give me the papers so I could go back home.

"Should I help you stand up?" Michael asked with caution because he had realized I was angry.

"No," I stood up quickly and sighed with pain. These twenty-four hours were excruciatingly long, and after so many sleepless nights, all I wanted was to get back home.

We left the ward quietly and went towards the main parking lot. This visit was short, but I had enough for a lifetime.

CHAPTER 79

It drizzled and felt like winter. It was as if I had been set free after years of being locked up. Everything seemed different. I was somewhat lucky they had found that complication on time, and on the other hand, I felt as if life had screwed me over again. Getting blood clots was a rare complication that would affect my future. One of the interns told me I would have to take blood thinners for a long time and that I would need injections before long flights. I would need blood thinners before my ovaries' removal, just to be on the safe side, he said, and that from now on I was in a high-risk group. Yet another high-risk group. That's about the last thing I needed.

"So, should I cancel the caterer?" Michael asked before he closed the car door for me.

"What caterer?" I was too busy with my thoughts and didn't understand what he was talking about. He got into the driver's seat and started the car.

"The catering for your Shiva. Everything's ready, should I cancel?" he smiled and looked satisfied with his joke.

"I think you should. You can let your admirers know that they need to wait a little longer," I smiled at him. The further we drove from the hospital the more I felt things were starting to get back to normal.

I came home exactly fifteen minutes before Natalie was supposed to come home with the kids, and I decided it was a good time to take a shower. Just the thought of all the hospital germs, freaked me out. I took off all my clothes and threw them straight to the laundry basket, then stepped into the shower.

It was the first time I took a shower without my bandages. I took a deep breath and unhooked the special bra I needed to wear for a few weeks. I tried recognizing myself in the mirror, but it was strange. I looked like a Barbie, at least when it came to my breasts. It didn't feel like they were mine. As if someone had photo shopped my face onto someone else's body. I approached the mirror and saw the scars. Two ugly red stripes replaced my nipples.

Dr. Katzman said that basically, we could recreate the nipples, but considering the blood clots, we should wait before we do something else. I wasn't actually too excited about it, and was happy I had to wait. I wanted to first get used to this new addition.

It was strange. I tried recognizing my body, but couldn't. My breasts were swollen and not at all what they would have looked like after three pregnancies and breastfeeding.

And then I saw them. All the stretch marks from my pregnancies and breastfeeding. Marks of the years that have passed. Only then did I recognize myself a bit and understood that even though there was silicone inside, they were still mine, and it was still me.

I took a quick shower and gently wore a buttoned shirt so I wouldn't have to lift up my arms. Everything was sore and painful. I looked at myself again before I left and for a second, I looked like myself again, like I would before leaving for work. I looked like a normal woman again. An outsider could have thought that nothing had happened to me. That I was just a lawyer, a mother of three small children, Michael's wife. But I felt like a survivor. I was now a true previvor.

I heard Ariel singing and Adam calling me. "Mom, where are you?"

"I'm in my bedroom," I replied, and the kids ran in. They weren't even aware that anything had happened, or to the fact that I hadn't slept at home.

"Mom, are you sad?" Ariel asked.

"No, sweetie, I'm very happy."

"Mom, can you watch Cathy's movie with me?" Ariel grabbed my hand and pulled me to the living room.

Natalie went home and we watched *Mamma Mia* together, for the millionth time. I looked at them dancing and having fun and I knew. I knew I had made the right decision. I would be here for my children. In a few years I will remove my ovaries and tubes, and anything else they might recommend that I remove. Just so I can stay healthy. Maybe I was lucky. I was given the right to save my own life.

And if I ever do get cancer, despite it all, I could look my kids in the eye and say: "Mom did everything she could," and this time, that 'mom' would be me.

Made in the
USA
Monee, IL